T0274401

Trinity

on track

Trinity
on track

Fiona Snyckers

Publication © Modjaji Books 2018
Text © Fiona Snyckers 2018
First published in 2018 by Modjaji Books Pty Ltd
www.modjajibooks.co.za

ISBN 978-1-928215-68-4 (Print)
ISBN 978-1-928215-69-1 (ePub)

Edited by Helen Moffett
Book and cover design by Monique Cleghorn
Cover artwork by Toni Olivier and Tammy Griffin
Printed and bound by Digital Action
Set in Palatino

To: Trinity Luhabe trinityluhabe@gmail.com
From: President of the Paranormal Association of South Africa
admin@paranormalSA.com
Re: Ghost of Sisulu House

Dear Ms Luhabe,

We were fascinated to hear about your close encounter of the eerie kind with a paranormal manifestation in your boarding house. How privileged you are to have had such an experience!

Yes, we can certainly help you out in your search for the truth behind this manifestation. As you so rightly point out, we *are* the experts. We strongly recommend that you make the following purchases from our website without delay:

1 x Full-spectrum POV Camcorder with FREE infra-red light –
R3,499.99
1 x Laser Grid Scope and Chromatograph – R15,699.99
with optional LED (highly recommended) – R599.00
1 x Oscillating Vibration-sensitive EMF-meter – R7,655.99

This is the absolute bare minimum in equipment you will need while ghost hunting. You will find our prices extremely competitive. And if your order comes to more than R15,000 we will deliver it FREE OF CHARGE to anywhere in South Africa.

So don't delay. Visit our website for 1-click ordering today!

Kind regards
Eufemia Batton
Paranormal Association of South Africa

To: Trinity Luhabe trinityluhabe@gmail.com
From: News Editor – Sandton Chronicle chronicle@caxton.co.za
Re: Ghost of Sisulu House

Dear Ms Luhabe,

Thanks for your email about the ghost living in the boarding house of your school. We were very interested to read about it. You have a lively and entertaining writing style, and your letter was a great hit in the newsroom!

Unfortunately, it won't be possible to "send a team of reporters" to your school in order to "investigate fully". I agree that this is a very touching story and quite mysterious too, but our reporters are fully committed to covering a story about pollution in the Braamfontein Spruit this week. I agree that this is a local issue and therefore of interest to Sandton residents, but I fear our managing editor would not see it in that light.

I will therefore be publishing your email in the letters column of our newspaper next Wednesday. Who knows? It might be read by someone who knows the history of your ghost and could shed light on it. I will forward you any replies we get. Good luck with the ghost-hunting!

Kind regards,
Sameera Aboobakar
Sandton Chronicle
Caxton House, Craighall Park

To: Trinity Luhabe trinityluhabe@gmail.com
From: Dean of Students – Sisulu House gcobani@sisuluhouse.
co.za
Re: Accommodation for Term 2

Hi Trinity,

We are, of course, delighted to hear how much you enjoyed your stay at Sisulu House during the first term while your parents were overseas. We can honestly say that it was a pleasure to have you, especially as Headmaster Dr Hussein decided to let bygones be bygones in the little matter of the Gumede Shield.

We are thrilled to hear that you wish you "could be a boarder forever and never go home again". Unfortunately, it would be against our policy to tell your parents that they have to let you board again this term. If your parents have made up their minds to keep you at home this term, not even the information that you are "a hundred times less spoiled" at Sisulu House than you are at home is likely to sway them.

I suggest you keep working on your parents if you really want to board again, but we definitely won't get involved.

Kind regards,
Grace Gcobani
Dean of Students
Sisulu House
Brentwood College

CHAPTER 1

My parents have the *worst* timing ever.

At the beginning of this year they shoved me into boarding school for a whole term totally against my will. I was like, "You can't make me go. I'll live in a cardboard box by the side of the road." And they were like, "Don't be silly, you'll get cold."

And now that they're back from opening a mine in Chile, they're, like, "We're back! You can move back home now. We'll all be together again."

Except, the thing is, I really want to stay in the boarding house this term. I don't want to move back home at all, but apparently that's "not an option".

"I'll live in a cardboard box by the side of the road!" I yell.

"I'll come and visit you and laugh," says my brother Caleb. My death stare warns him to stay out of this.

My father gives me an exhausted look. (Total ploy for sympathy and it is not going to work.) "Trinity, you were horrified when we told you that you were boarding last term. Now you want to stay there? What possible reason can you have for this change of heart?"

"I told you before – I can't tell you."

"Well, if you think we're going to pay to have you spend a term in Sisulu House for some secret reason that you won't even share with us..." My mother breaks off, shaking her head and standing up.

Now my dad is standing up too. My brothers are slithering towards the exits – their game consoles are calling to them. This family conference is over and I have lost.

"Okay, okay! It's because of the ghost," I say loudly.

That gets everyone's attention. My parents stop and turn around. They don't exactly sit down again, but at least they're listening. "What ghost?"

"The ghost of Jim Grey. He was this boy who died at Sisulu House in the 1960s, and his ghost still walks. I've met him. I've talked to him. Lael and I are going to find out who he is and how he died. And we seriously need to be at Sisulu House this term to do our research."

Gripping stuff, hey? I feel like if it was a movie, I could sell it to Hollywood.

But instead of sitting down and immediately sending off an EFT to Sisulu House so I can stay there for another term, my parents just sigh and shake their heads and LEAVE THE ROOM.

I know. I couldn't believe it either.

I fling myself on my bed and fire off a WhatsApp to my best friend Lael to let her know that my parents are being stubborn. She's online, so her reply comes back in seconds.

Lael: Bad luck, babe. But the good news is, my mom is totally cool with letting me carry on boarding this term.

Trinity: How is that good news??? Are you trying to make me jealous???

I look at the screen and see her furiously typing away.

Lael: Ha! Not at all. Think about it - if we were both living at home this term, we'd have no excuse to go into Sisulu House. Day girls aren't allowed

in unless they're visiting a boarder. This way,
      you can visit me all the time and we can go
      ghost-hunting.
Trinity: My parents won't let me visit you that much,
      especially if they know we're ghost-hunting.
Lael: Just pretend you want to join evening prep.
      Day girls are allowed. You can say you concentrate
      better during supervised prep. I bet your mom will
      practically force you to attend.

Hmm. My mom's not dumb. I think she'll be suspicious
of this sudden desire of mine to join evening prep. But
on the other hand, she tends to clutch at straws where
my schoolwork is concerned, so maybe she'll go along
with it.

♀

The day before school starts, I ask our driver, Lungile, to
drop me at Sisulu House in the afternoon so I can say hi
to all my friends in the Grade Ten dormitory. I'm really
excited to see them. Lael is the only one I've laid eyes on
this holiday. She spent a week with us in Cape Town at
the beginning of April.

Nosipho spent the last three weeks in New York with
her mom, who is a single parent who travels a lot. They
live in Joburg, but Nosipho has to board because her
mom doesn't have time to drive her around all afternoon
during term time. She boards during the week and goes
home or to her aunt on weekends.

Yasmin was in Durban, which is where her family
lives. And Priya went to the Seychelles with her family.

As soon as I walk into the dormitory and give hello hugs to everyone, I can see that Nosipho has a secret. Her eyes are huge and sparkling, and she looks twitchy.

Nosipho is the only one of us who has an actual boyfriend, so I'm guessing this has something to do with him. His name is Themba. I doubt they broke up because she doesn't look miserable enough for that. Maybe he told her he loved her. Whatever it is, she can't wait for one of us to ask her about it.

Lael is the first to crack.

"Babe. Stop bouncing up and down like that. You're making me nervous. Spit it out. What's happened?"

"Okay, listen. I've been dying for you all to arrive so I can tell you about this. Shut the door. I don't want Matron to overhear. You know how she sneaks up and down the corridors eavesdropping."

The matron of Sisulu House wears shoes with soft rubber soles, which turn her into a stealth missile of quietness. Also, she seems to know everything that goes on in here, so maybe she does eavesdrop. I'm not taking any chances, so I close the door, making sure it clicks shut.

"Spill," orders Lael.

"Well, you remember last term how we all went to the fireworks at St Mark's?"

Everyone nods except me. I missed the fireworks for the first time in three years. It's kind of a long story, but I was busy giving a statement to the police and evidence in a disciplinary hearing.

"Sorry, Trinity. I know you missed it." Nosipho gives my arm a comforting rub.

"No worries. I'll just picture you guys having fun without me. I've got a good imagination."

"Anyway, I was going to get a lift home with Themba. My mom was working late and couldn't fetch me, so she said it was fine for his mom to drop me home after the fireworks. But his mom must have misunderstood because she took me home to her place thinking that my mom would come and pick me up from there later in the evening. Of course, Themba and I didn't correct her because it meant more time for us to spend together."

"Of course," Lael agreed.

"Then … it got even better. His mom went straight out again for some PTA meeting at his sister's school. She thought my mom was coming to pick me up in a few minutes, otherwise she would never have left us alone."

"And I suppose you didn't exactly rush to ask your mom to come and pick you up?"

"Well, duh. In fact, my mom only came to pick me up after ten. So Themba and I were all alone for two whole hours. Two whole hours. All alone. In his house."

"No ways," says Yasmin. "You didn't. Don't lie to us."

We are leaning so far forward we're almost tipping off the bed. Priya flaps her hand in Yasmin's face to make her be quiet.

"Let her speak. You didn't, did you? You couldn't have. Or did you?"

Nosipho gives a slow, smug smile. "We did."

There's a chorus of gasps. This is big news.

Lael is the first to recover the power of speech. "What's it like?" she asks, almost shyly.

"Did you use a condom?" adds Priya, always the practical one.

"Of course we did."

"Was it sore?"

"It was a bit sore at first, but then it settled down."

"But what did it actually feel like?" I ask. "Did the earth move? Did you … you know…?" I mime earthquakes and fireworks, while making exploding noises. "Boom! Tish! Pew!"

"Um … I don't know. Maybe. I'm not really sure."

"My mom says if you're not sure, then it didn't happen," Yasmin says wisely. "She says you'll always know when it happens because it's unmistakable."

"Well then, maybe it didn't. The whole thing didn't last very long, to be honest."

"And was it worth it?"

"Oh, definitely. I felt incredibly close to him afterwards. And it meant such a lot to him. He was so grateful that I'd said yes."

"Why did you say yes?" Lael wants to know. "You've always said you wanted to wait and not rush into anything. I always thought you'd be one of the last of us to do it, not the first."

"He's the first boy I've felt that I could really trust, you know? I felt safe with him. I knew if I said stop at any time, then he would stop. He didn't try to pressure me into anything, and, like I said, we used a condom. But basically, if I'm going to tell you the absolute truth, I did it because I wanted to do it. It was almost like I couldn't help myself. This huge urge just took over my body and made me go through with it."

"Wow."

"Sjoe."

We sit back in awe. I don't know about anyone else, but I'm trying to imagine myself being swept up like that. It doesn't quite come into focus. I mean, it's not like

I've never had a boyfriend before. I was going out with this guy the whole of last term, and I certainly thought at the time that I was crazy about him. But when we kissed, I never felt as though I was losing control. It was more like I was hovering a few feet above myself, watching it happen.

I felt like if we were to go any further (which we didn't, just for the record), it would have been something I was doing for his sake – like an icky kind of necessity. I have no idea what Nosipho is talking about with her huge urges. And just between you and me, I feel kind of jealous now.

"I'm so jealous of you, Nos." Lael has no trouble admitting it. "I've never felt that way about a guy before. Not ever. What if I never do?"

"You'll feel differently when the right guy comes along." Nosipho is the wise elder now, initiating us into the mysteries of adulthood. "It's all about chemistry. And trust."

"So how many times have you done it altogether?" Priya asks.

"Just that one time. I left for New York with my mom soon afterwards, remember? And we only got back a couple of days ago. I'm still a bit jet-lagged."

"Do you think you'll do it again?"

Nosipho shrugs. "I don't know when we'll get another chance. It was a total fluke that his mom left us alone together for that long. I don't know when we'll get that lucky again. I mean, I'm stuck here all week, which is basically like being in Fort Knox. And on weekends we've both got sport and loads of homework, and moms who could qualify for the CIA the way they spy on us all the time."

"Ridiculous!" Yasmin shakes her head. "It's like they don't trust you or something."

"I know, right? How ridiculous is that?"

We disintegrate into cackles of laughter that only subside when Matron hammers on the door and tells us to find something useful to do with ourselves.

When all the excitement about Nosipho's revelation has died down, Lael and I find an excuse to sneak off alone. Without even talking about it, we head upstairs to the fourth floor where there's an old room that practically nobody ever uses. It is full of encyclopaedias that date from the pre-Google era. It has one tiny window and a kind of musty smell, so it's not a popular hangout spot for the girls of Sisulu House.

It's where I used to go last term when I wanted to be alone. It was the first time I'd ever boarded, and I wasn't used to having people on top of me all the time. I'd come up here sometimes for peace and quiet. But the main thing about it is that Jim Grey would come up here too.

Of course, I didn't know at the time that he was a ghost. He looked as real as you or me. I thought he was just a kid from the boys' boarding house. I still can't bring myself to believe he wasn't real. I know I told my parents about him, and Lael and I talk about him all the time, but it doesn't feel right. It feels like make-believe. Like when we were little and pretended to be part of the Time Riders or the Power Rangers.

Lael found an old school magazine from the sixties that shows Jim as a boy who died in Sisulu House fifty years ago. I've stared at those photos until my eyes ache. It's him. It's definitely him. I recognised him before Lael even pointed him out. But somehow, I still can't believe it. I keep thinking there must be another explanation. Like maybe the boy I used to speak to was someone who looked like Jim Grey. But if so, where is he?

Why did nobody ever see him except me?

And even if the boy I used to hang out with was a random student who's since left the school, what happened to Jim Grey? How did he die? The school magazine is vague about it. Sixteen-year-old boys don't just drop dead. Something must have happened to him, and we want to know what.

Nothing weird about that, is there? Nothing spooky or woo-woo. It's just natural curiosity.

"So, did you try that ghost-hunting website?"

I had managed to convince myself that this was nothing more than historical curiosity. Trust Lael to remind me about the supernatural angle.

"What?" she demands. "You said you'd look into it."

"Yes, okay, fine, I did. And, guess what? Ghost-hunting is big business – not to mention a total rip-off. There are hundreds of sites out there claiming to give advice on detecting ghosts, and they all want to sell you something. They lead you on with their descriptions of how you can get in touch with the 'other side', and before you know it, you've clicked on a link that takes you to the online store."

"So, what sort of stuff do they sell?"

"All kinds of junk. Machines that measure ghost waves

and ... what do you call it? ... protoplasm floating around."

"You mean ectoplasm."

"I don't know. Do I?"

Lael lifts a shoulder. This is new territory for her, too.

"They even sold sound recorders that supposedly pick up ghostly conversations and play them back to you. Load of nonsense, really. I didn't buy anything."

Lael shakes her head and jiggles a finger in her ear like she's got water in it. "Excuse me?" she says. "Did I hear correctly? You, Trinity Luhabe, visited an online store and walked away without buying anything?"

"I told you – it was just a lot of overpriced junk."

"Trinity."

"What?"

"Trinity."

"Stop looking at me like that. I didn't buy anything."

She crosses her arms and stares at me.

"Oh, all right! I might possibly have bought one or two teeny-weeny things."

"Now you're talking. Like what? Show me."

I pull out my phone to find the online catalogue I used. "Okay, but none of the stuff has arrived yet. I got an email that it was dispatched five days ago, so I'm expecting it quite soon."

I show her the full-spectrum camcorder I ordered, as well as the chromatograph, and the EMF-meter.

"What on earth is an EMF-meter?"

"Uh..."

"You paid over seven thousand rand for something, and you don't even know what it does?"

"It's an electro-magnetic field meter," I say, as my eye

lands on the fine-print description to the right of the photograph. "Essential for ghost-hunting. Look, it says so right here."

Lael shakes her head. "I still can't believe your parents gave you a credit card for online purchases. Even my mom is not that trusting, and she doesn't care what I do as long as I don't bother her."

"It's just the one credit card. And the Paypal account. And a few store cards. The limit isn't even that high."

"If it cleared all these purchases, it must be at Kardashian levels."

Honestly, Lael can exaggerate sometimes.

CHAPTER 2

To: Doctor Pulane advice@allaboutgirls.com
From: Nosipho Mamusa nosiphomamusa@gmail.com
Re: Menstrual irregularities

Dear Dr Pulane,

I am sixteen years old. My cycle has always been a bit irregular, but this month it is really late in starting. I'm not exactly sure when last I had a period, but it feels like it was maybe five weeks ago. Maybe even more than that. Should I be worried?

Regards,
Concerned Grade Ten learner

To: Nosipho Mamusa nosiphomamusa@gmail.com
From: Doctor Pulane advice@allaboutgirls.com
Re: Menstrual irregularities

Dear Concerned Grade Ten learner,

An irregular menstrual cycle at your age is fairly common and is normally no need for concern. You don't mention whether you are sexually active or not. If you are and your period is late in starting, then you should definitely take a home pregnancy test and organise an appointment at your nearest family planning clinic to explore your options.

All the best,
Dr Pulane Twala-Naidoo (MBCHB)

To: Trinity Luhabe trinityluhabe@gmail.com
From: Dean of Students – Sisulu House gcobani@sisuluhouse.
    co.za
Re: Permission to join Evening Prep

Dear Trinity,

Yes, of course you are welcome to join our evening prep sessions. A lot of day girls find that their marks improve when they do homework with the boarders. We provide a quiet and disciplined environment which many learners find more conducive to concentration than their home situations.

There is an extra termly fee that is charged for this. It will be debited to your school account. And yes, it does include the 7pm tea-break. You ask whether "the doughnuts and Chelsea buns will still be on the tea-break menu this term, especially the yummy ones with the white sprinkles" and I am happy to confirm that they will.

Looking forward to seeing you at evening prep, and even more to seeing an upswing in your term marks (especially Physical Science).

Kind regards,
Grace Gcobani
Dean of Students
Sisulu House
Brentwood College

I don't know if all matrons of boarding houses have naturally suspicious natures, but I think they do. It is probably one of the requirements of becoming a matron that you have to lack all faith in human nature.

Take our matron, for example. On the basis of no evidence whatsoever, she has decided that Lael and I are up to something. I know this because she cornered me before prep last night and said, "What are you and Lael Lieberman up to? I know you are up to something."

Except she said it in Xhosa because she thinks I need to practice speaking the language more. Apparently, my grasp of the idiom is 'inadequate' for someone who has a Xhosa-speaking father. So she keeps sneaking up on me and using ancient rural sayings that only about five people in the world understand. Life is very hard.

"We're not up to anything, Matron," I say, looking innocent. "What makes you say that?"

"I don't like the way you two are sneaking around Sisulu House at all hours. If I catch you up on the fourth floor again, I'll give you both a smack on the bottom."

"How can you not trust us? It is very hurtful to be suspected all the time."

Matron snorts. "I'd trust a starving dog with a lamb chop sooner than I'd trust the two of you. I've got my eye on you both. Just remember that."

See what I mean? No faith in human nature.

I report this conversation to Lael during the tea-break. She looks thoughtful.

"We'll have to be more careful. I thought nobody knew we were hanging out on the fourth floor. Trust Matron to have noticed."

She thinks for a while, chewing slowly on her doughnut. (It's called Mindful Eating and it's our latest diet. You can eat whatever you like as long as you are mentally present for every bite and chew really slowly and stop when you are full.)

"I've got it! Ask your driver to pick you up twenty minutes after prep. We can sneak around then. Matron always does a final inventory and sterilising of her instruments at about 8pm. She'll be too busy to wonder what we're up to."

"Good idea."

I send a WhatsApp to our driver, Lungile, and he agrees to pick me up a bit later than usual.

The last hour of prep seems to crawl by, but finally Lael and I make our escape. As we scoot up to the fourth floor, taking the stairs two at a time, we pass Matron's office. The light is on and the door is closed. She's doing inventory, just as Lael predicted. When we get to the top, there's no time to waste. We open the cupboard where we stashed the ghost-hunting equipment once it finally arrived.

"The camcorder and the EMF-meter both have long-life batteries," I whisper. "But the laser scope needs to be plugged into the wall."

Lael points silently to a plug that is half-hidden behind an old bookcase. I plug the laser scope into it and turn it to face the room.

"We need to cover the whole room." I check that all the devices are pointing inwards and giving us the best possible coverage.

"I'm more worried about hiding them properly. We

don't want to come back tomorrow and find them all gone."

"And we don't want *him* to spot them either."

"Exactly. The devices need to spot him, not the other way around."

I turn to face her. "Do you really think this will work?"

She grins. "Who knows? But we can have fun trying."

We stand at the door and look into the room, making sure none of the devices can be seen. They don't have to be completely invisible – just well hidden enough to pass a casual inspection. There is nothing in here except some out-of-date encyclopaedias and a few old desks. The only people who come up here are cleaning staff, and not all that often either.

When we are satisfied with our handiwork, we close the door and prepare to go back downstairs. I stand at the top of the stairs listening for a moment. Then I gesture for Lael to follow me. A couple of floors down, we pause at the Sisulu House display case.

"Remember last term?" Lael smiles at the trophies behind glass.

I tap the cabinet with my fingernail. "Hello, Gumede Shield! Nice to see you."

"Only a couple more months and it has to go back to Gumede House."

"I know. But at least we know it will be coming back in January. And now it will always be just as much ours as the boys'."

In the first term, some of us Grade Tens stole the Gumede Shield from the boys' boarding house. We were protesting the fact that it had always been considered their trophy, even though it celebrated women heroes as well as men. Somehow, we managed to convince the headmaster and governing body to see it our way, so now it spends half the year in Sisulu House and the other half in Gumede House.

"That's new," Lael comments, looking at something in the display case.

"What is?" I glance at what she's pointing at. "That old book? It's always been there."

"No, it's new," she insists. "Look. There's the book that's always been there. It's just a collection of old dining-hall menus from the 1930s. This one is different. It looks like a diary or something."

I try to peer at the writing through the glass, but there is too much reflection.

"Move your gigantic head," I say. "You're blocking out the light."

"Your head is more gigantic than mine. Hang on. Let me switch on my phone torch." Lael shines it onto the book.

"Wow, that's not easy to read. I can hardly make it out. I wonder when it's from?"

"There's a date in the corner," says Lael. "Looks like 1960-something."

We freeze when we hear a noise on the stairs.

"Come on!" I pluck at her sleeve.

"Wait! Hang on! Does that say Jim?"

"What?" I squint at the page, but the light is wobbling all over the place. "No, it says Tim, doesn't it?"

There's another noise, and this time I physically grab her by the arm and try to pull her away.

She tugs against me. "Just a second…"

The next second, the corridor is filled with a blinding flash. It's Lael taking a photograph.

I feel so confused. My mind is in a whirl. It is Jim's birthday today. He is sixteen years old. Apparently, his family is planning a big celebration for him when he gets back to the farm for the Easter holidays. It was his father's idea, which makes him so happy because he worships his dad. But today it was just the two of us. It is so unfair that his sixteenth birthday fell on a Thursday. We couldn't even get permission to go to town and see a film or anything. It was just a day like any other. He was miserable about this, the poor darling.

At least we managed to meet in our secret place after evening prep. I gave him my gift - a Zippo lighter engraved with his name. I could see he was pleased, but he just said he would have to hide it because his family doesn't know that he smokes yet. And of course, the housemaster at Jan Smuts House would skin him alive if he suspected.

Diary, it was awful to see him so downhearted on his birthday. I had to cheer him up. I snuggled into his chest and told him I loved him and drew him a picture in words of what our lives would be like when we were finished with school and could meet openly as often as we liked.

We started kissing. We always do. His kisses are so dreamy. They make me go limp in his arms. Soon he had his hand under my blouse. I felt a bit uncomfortable, but because I let him the last time, I felt I could hardly say no this time. Then his hand was wandering below the waist and that is where I drew the line.

Oh, Diary! You should have seen him! He was so upset and disappointed. I have never seen him so angry and distressed. He said this was the most disappointing birthday of his life and everything had gone wrong the whole day. He said if I really loved him, I would let him G.A.T.W. He said it would transform his birthday from the worst day of his life to the very best. But if I didn't feel like I could, then maybe we should break up because I obviously didn't love him the same way that he loved me.

Can you imagine my horror, Diary? I don't know what was worse - us breaking up or him thinking that I didn't really love him. I do love him! I do! With all my heart!

So, I said yes. And we did it. I let him G.A.T.W.

How can I describe it to you? It wasn't exactly what I expected. I knew it would hurt, and it did. But, somehow, I thought it would be more wonderful and romantic, and also that it would last longer. Afterwards, Jim said that his father told him there are some girls who are just cold and aren't capable of feeling anything during the Act. I suppose I must be one of those girls.

Anyway, it's a good thing that you can't get PG on your first time because I don't think Jim took any precautions.

Now it is the weekend and I won't see Jim for a whole two days. How will I survive, dear Diary? Every second I am parted from him feels like a month.

Love,
Amelia

♀

Lael looks up from the page two seconds before I do. She has always been the faster reader. It's the next morning at break-time, and we have finally been able to look at the photo she took together. She promised me she didn't take a look at it last night without me, and I believe her.

"What on earth does G.A.T.W. stand for?" I ask.

We look at each other for a moment and then say at the same time, "Go all the way."

"Yes, that must be it." I say. "And PG must stand for pregnant. How clueless was this girl, though, thinking you can't get pregnant on your first time? They must have had rubbish Life Orientation teachers in those days."

"I don't think LO was even a subject back then. Pity she never had Ms Bhamjee. That would have sorted her out."

We laugh. Our LO teacher is famous for leaving you with no misconceptions about the facts of life. She lays it all out for you. "No one who goes through my class can say they didn't know," she always says.

Among the many things Lael and I know is that you *can* get pregnant on your first time, and also that you can get pregnant at *any* time of the month.

"Shame, I wonder what happened to her," says Lael. "Looks like she was someone who went to school here in the 1960s."

"I'm still not sure if the boy's name is Jim or Tim."

"No, it's definitely Jim." She points at the last paragraph. "See that loop there at the top of the J? She writes her T completely differently. Look, there's a T. It's not the same at all."

I see that she's right, and feel a thrill ripple down my spine. "Do you think it's him? Jim Grey? Could he be the boyfriend she's talking about?" I wait for Lael to say no, that's too far-fetched, but she doesn't.

"It's possible. He was the only James in his grade – or in Standard Nine, as they used to call it."

"And look at that bit about the farm!" I stab at the letter with my finger. "He told me his family were mealie farmers near Brits, remember? It must be him."

"Hey, guys."

Lael is about to shove her phone back in her pocket, but relaxes when she sees it's just Nosipho.

"Hey."

"What are you doing?"

"Check it out," Lael shows her the screen. "We found this diary from the 1960s and—"

"That's nice."

Nosipho glances at the screen and slides down onto a nearby bench. Lael and I plant our butts on the bench on either side of her. There's a greyish tinge to her cheeks that I don't like the look of.

"Are you sick?" asks Lael.

"No, I'm fine."

"Dude, you're not fine." I touch her forehead with the back of my fingers like my mom always does. Her skin feels cold and clammy. "You look like a ghost."

"Gee, thanks."

"You know what I mean. Are you feeling sick? Like you're getting a cold or a tummy bug or something?"

"Or something." She sucks in air on a sob, and tears start to roll down her cheeks.

Lael scrambles up. "Nos! No. Don't do that. Don't cry." She fiddles in her lunchbox and brings out a doughnut. "Here, have this. It'll make you feel better."

Nosipho takes one look at the doughnut, glistening with white icing, leans over, and vomits onto the grass. She does it so neatly and quietly that no one notices except us.

"I'm sorry! I'm sorry!" Lael whisks the doughnut out of sight. "I thought it would help."

"I'm taking you to Matron." I stand up and tug her arm. "You've obviously got a tummy bug. Come on."

But Nosipho just pulls her arm out of my grasp and stays put, tears flowing even faster.

"Don't you understand?" she sobs. "I'm not sick, I'm pregnant!"

That shuts us both up. There's a long silence while we stand there gaping at her.

"Pregnant?" Lael says at last. "Are you sure?"

I hold my breath while Nosipho seems to consider the question. Then she shakes her head.

"No, I'm not sure. I just think I might be. I haven't done a test yet, but my period is two weeks late. Not to mention I'm feeling sick the whole time."

"Themba? I say. "That time you guys...?"

"Yes. Exactly. We used a condom, but it kind of broke."

"You need to be sure," Lael says. "You need to take a test and be a hundred per cent sure. You're probably worrying over nothing."

"I know, but where do I get a pregnancy test? I can't exactly go up to Matron and ask her for one. Our next outing isn't for another three weeks. I can't wait that long."

Lael has a lightbulb moment. "Trinity can buy one for you. Yes! Perfect."

I give her my best "you have got to be joking" face.

"Right. Absolutely," I say. "So, I'll just be like, 'Oh, Lungi! I need to stock up on pregnancy tests, do you mind pulling over at Clicks?'"

"No, dumbass! Tell him you need pads or tampons or something. He won't question it. And you'll come out holding a pharmacy bag. It's not like he's going to ask to search it."

"Okay, but what about this? Our pharmacist has known me since I was born. If I go in and buy a pregnancy test, he's going to be on the phone to my parents faster than you can say pee stick."

Lael and Nosipho look at each other. "She could say it's for someone else…"

"No, that won't work…"

"Or that it's for a class project."

"No way."

"She'll just have to go to a different pharmacy," Nosipho decides. "Somewhere far away from where she lives."

"Yes, good idea!"

"If you guys have finished talking about me like I'm not even here, let me explain why this is the worst idea ever."

They turn on me with huge smiles.

"Now, Trinity, don't be like that."

"An awesome person like you? You'd never let a friend down!"

"Trust Trinity. That's what I always say."

"Me too. Trust Trinity."

I sigh a deep, deep sigh.

And that's how I end up wandering around the Suresafe Pharmacy in Centurion two days later, trying my best not to look suspicious.

Centurion isn't my usual turf, but we had a basketball match against a school there and I asked Lungile to come and fetch me. Just before we got to the highway, I told him I needed to stop at a pharmacy. Lael was right. He was swinging the car around before I finished saying the word "tampon".

As we turned, I thought I saw a girl from my grade, Sophie Agincourt, following us in an Uber. She was also at the basketball match. But when I turned to look, she had disappeared.

Suresafe is one of those old-fashioned pharmacies where the aisles are really narrow, and the stock is all jumbled together. If you're picturing Clicks or Dis-Chem, you have the wrong idea. I keep seeing things I haven't laid eyes on since I last opened the medicine cabinet in my granny's house in Orlando East. Freshen laxatives. Tiger Balm. XXX-mints, Blue Magic hair conditioner.

But where are the pregnancy tests? Do they keep them in a section all on their own like the sanitary towels, or do they put them at the till? Oh, please tell me you don't need a prescription.

Okay, I've been up and down the aisles twice and I still haven't found them. Any minute now Lungi is going to come inside to check that I'm okay. As I pass the tills, I see a display of condoms. Normally I look away from those really quickly, although I wish I was brave enough to take a good look. I mean, they're intriguing, right?

Today, I might actually have to. It has occurred to me that they might keep the pregnancy tests next to the condoms. It makes sense, doesn't it? It's like Plan A and Plan B. If the condom doesn't work, you'll be buying a pregnancy test, right? Makes perfect sense.

I stand as close to the condoms as I dare and flick my

eyes over the display. Ribbed. Nibbed. Lubed. Premium. Sheer. Rough Rider.

Rough Rider?

If the manufacturers were here, I'd be giving them major side-eye right now. Anyway. No sign of a pregnancy test anywhere. I reach out my hand to move a random box of Panado out of the way.

"May I help you, Madam?"

I leap about a mile into the air and snatch my hand back from the display as though it's hot. A middle-aged white lady is standing behind me. She obviously works here – there's a badge that says Suresafe sewn onto the breast pocket of her shirt. Am I imagining it, or is she giving me a very suspicious look? As a black teenager, you get used to security guards following you around in shops and asking to search your bag on the way out. (And by "get used to" I mean, of course, "resent bitterly".) It doesn't matter how well-dressed and middle-class-looking you are. In fact, I think the fancier your clothes, the more they suspect you.

Anyway. Not the point.

This lady wants to know if she can help me, and I'm not at all sure what to say. I'm just about ready to admit that I can't find these things on my own. But the embarrassment factor in asking for a pregnancy test is huge.

I clear my throat a couple of times before my voice starts working.

"Um … hi. Good afternoon. I'd like to look at some pregnancy tests, please. Could you show me where they are?"

There is a flicker of something behind her eyes.

Disapproval? Pity? Satisfaction that I've lived up to her expectations? Who knows?

"Of course. Please follow me. They're right this way."

She takes me to the display and then – thank goodness – leaves me alone with them. And I see immediately why I had such a hard time spotting them. None of them actually say pregnancy test on the box. They're all like *Clear Blue* and *Answer* and *First Response* and stuff like that. I mean, am I supposed to use my psychic powers to figure out what they are?

I must have walked past this display three times already. I thought they were tests for diabetes or something.

I read the instructions on a few different brands. They're all pretty similar. Pee on the stick ... wait three minutes ... read what it says. One line means not pregnant. Two lines mean pregnant. Simple enough.

I grab three boxes of three different brands and take them to the till. The pharmacy is starting to fill up with people. I need to get out of here. I'm just reaching for my credit card to pay when it occurs to me that my dad might have something to say next month when a charge for three pregnancy tests appears on his Visa bill.

Back goes my card into my wallet, and out comes the cash. Thank goodness I have enough. Five minutes later, Lungile and I are back on the road to Joburg.

♀

"TRINITEEEEEEEEE!"

Aargh! I put my hands over my ears to block out the sound of my little brother Caleb yelling for me. His voice is just starting to break so he sounds like a squeaky toy.

A burst of insane laughter rolls through the house, followed by another "TRINITEEEE!"

Why can he not just come and look for me if he wants me? Why? He knows where my room is. Instead he yells from two floors away.

I stomp to my door, fling it open, and yell back, "Get lost, loser!"

More bursts of hysterical laughter. Then my other brother, Aaron, gets in on the act. "TRINITY! Come here! You have to see this." At fifteen, he is two years older than Caleb and his voice has basically finished breaking, except for this weird frog-like croak he still has.

I stomp back to the door and yell down the stairs again, "I'm not interested in watching Wrestling Bloopers or Epic Goals or whatever lame clip you weirdos are looking at. I'm busy!"

Five seconds later they burst through my door. (No, of course they don't knock first. Why would they do that? I've only asked them about a million times.)

"Trinity, you have to come and see this. It's totally rad." It's the squeaky toy, pulling on my arm and trying to get me to follow him.

"Seriously, dude," says the frog. "We're not even joking. You have to see this. It's about you."

"Me?"

Why didn't they say so before? I'm always down to watch video clips of myself. Maybe someone has picked up my Instagram video from the last Colour Fest we went to. I don't like to boast, but my dancing was on fleek that night.

"Show me on your phone," I say to Aaron.

"No way. Come down to Mom's study. This deserves the big screen."

I settle into my mother's ergonomic office chair with a grin on my face. Which slowly fades as the first seconds of the YouTube clip come to life.

It's the pharmacy. Suresafe Pharmacy. Where I was just a few hours ago. Was somebody filming me? Was it Sophie Agincourt? I *knew* she was following me! Oh, please let her just have caught me checking out the condoms. That's embarrassing enough, but at least it won't be a total disaster.

Sure enough, there I am standing in front of the display of condoms, squinting at them and shaking my head like I'm eighty years old or something. My brothers are sniggering their heads off. Thank goodness there's no sound on this track, and the quality is a bit grainy.

We watch as I almost leap out of my skin when the assistant sneaks up behind me. Then we follow me – oh, please no! – to the display of pregnancy tests, where I seem to take about ten years reading the instructions on the boxes. Then I go off to pay.

"Okay, this could be a lot worse," I babble. "I mean, you can barely see my face and at least there's no sound. And the clarity is awf—"

I haven't even finished when the clip suddenly comes into focus and blaring music blasts out of the speakers.

Tri-ni-teee!
Lu-ha-beee!
Coolest chick you'll ever see...

Oh, I don't actually believe this. Someone (Sophie!) has written a rap song about me and backed it onto this video. There I am again looking at the condoms, but this time in perfect focus and colour.

Tri-ni-tee!
Lu-ha-bee!
Went on down to the phar-ma-cee...

This time the video has audio. "May I see your pregnancy tests, please?" I hear myself asking in my cringey private-school accent. "Puh-puh-puh-please. Pregnancy tests, puh-puh-puh-please." She has remixed my voice to the music, making me sound like Nicki Minaj or someone. But not in a good way.

Tri-ni-tee!
Lu-ha-bee!
Thinks she might be puh-preg-gee...

This is like watching a car crash unfold in real time. I'm sitting there with my mouth hanging open, while my brothers are getting down to the beat.

"Tri-ni-tee!" sings Aaron, popping and locking.

"Puh-preggy!" Caleb joins in.

"Lu-ha-bee!"

"Phar-ma-cee!"

"What, may I ask, is going on in here?"

It's Mom. Caleb and Aaron snap to attention, while I hit pause on the clip.

"M-mom!" Caleb bleats. "We thought you were out until six o'clock."

"It *is* six o'clock."

"Oh."

We look at our phones, and sure enough – it's six.

"What, exactly, were you guys watching?"

"Uh … it's just this joke thing Caleb and I made on PowerPoint. We were … showing it to Trinity."

Mom sighs. "Try again, Aaron. I know a YouTube video when I see one."

"It's nothing, really!"

Mom turns her attention to Caleb. "Nothing, huh?"

Aaron and I look at each other. We know exactly what comes next. Caleb has not yet developed a shield to Mom's powers of persuasion. He is putty in her hands. It's basically Guantanomo Bay without the torture.

"Mom … I …." Caleb's face is a mask of agony.

"Caleb…?"

He cracks like an egg. Because, of course he does.

"Somebody made a YouTube video about Trinity buying a pregnancy test and Aaron and I were teasing her about it." It all comes out in a rush.

"Teasing her? Why would you tease your sister about something like that?"

Trust Mom to jump on that first. Pregnant daughter? No worries. But no one had better be bullying her about it.

"Mom, it's not real," says Aaron. "I mean, obviously Trinity's not pregnant. You're not pregnant are you, dude?"

"Um … *no*! But now everyone's going to think I am, thanks to this stupid video."

Mom is looking a little grim. Her lips have formed a hard line and her eyes have that crazed look that means it's a good idea to get out of her way.

"Why don't I take a look at this video for myself?"

♀

Gah! A family conference. Another one.

At least when I was still boarding, I couldn't be forced to attend these stupid family conferences all the time. The only upside is that my brothers have been banished from the room, so it's a family conference of three. Now if only Mom would banish my dad too, I feel like we could get somewhere.

I don't know if you've ever had to explain to your dad why you were buying pregnancy tests in the middle of the afternoon, but if you haven't, trust me – it's a little awkward. Especially when he's sitting there looking like someone hit him over the head with a knobkierie. I can practically feel the disappointment coming off him in waves.

"Dad … it's not what you think!" Even I can hear the desperation in my voice.

"Rrrrrrrr." He makes a kind of growling sound, and his jaw tightens. I can see why all his board members are terrified of him.

"Abel…" My mom puts a hand on his shoulder and turns to me. "We don't think anything yet, Trinity. Why don't you tell us about it from the beginning?"

"I wasn't buying them for me!" I blurt. "Honestly, I wasn't."

"Then who were you buying them for?"

"I … I … I can't say. I made a promise."

"Rrrrrrr."

I gulp. There's that noise again.

My dad lifts my mom's hand off his shoulder (first dropping a kiss on her wrist because they're gross like that). Then he stands up.

"Intombi yam," he says to me. "We respect your desire

to keep your friend's secret, but if we are to believe you fully, you need to tell us the whole story. You can trust us. We won't betray any confidences."

I look over at my mom. Surely, she will understand that I can't go around blabbing someone else's secret? But she is nodding in agreement.

"Your father's right, Trinity. We need you to tell us what's going on, otherwise we'll make our own enquiries. And believe me, we'll find out the truth. But we'd much rather you just tell us the truth from the start."

I swallow against the tightness in my throat. My dad has ways of finding things out. They're not leaving me with much choice here. Part of me wants to cry, but the other part knows I need to hold it together for Nosipho's sake.

"Okay," I say at last. "It's Nosipho who was in the dorm with me last term. There's a chance she might be pregnant. She obviously can't go around buying pregnancy tests for herself so she asked me to get one for her. I got three to be safe."

My mother clutches her hands to her chest. "O, my liewe aarde, Trinity! I know her mother. She's a friend of mine. I need to tell her."

"Mom, if you say one single word about this to anyone – especially her mother – I swear I'll never speak to you again for as long as I live!"

She turns to my dad. "Abel...?"

He shakes his head. "You can't, Sunet. We promised. This child has the right to make her own decisions. We can't interfere."

"But what is she going to do, Trinity?"

"We don't even know if there's anything to worry about yet, Mom. She hasn't done the test. This might all be one big false alarm."

"And if it's not?"

I swallow again. "If it's not, she has to decide what she wants to do. Lael and I will support her, but she needs to decide for herself."

Yes! Result.

My parents have backed off. They have promised to say nothing to Nosipho's mom, or anyone else. At first my mom was reluctant, but then my dad pulled out the A-word.

Autonomy.

My mom is all about autonomy – especially for girls and women. She believes we should all have the final say over our own bodies and what happens to them. So that took care of that.

But then my dad started freaking out about that stupid YouTube video and how everyone would think his daughter was pregnant. He was all fired up to call his lawyers and get them to take the video down and start suing whoever was responsible for it. Until Mom reminded him that this would only ensure that the story stayed on the front pages for longer.

So, we decided to do what we always do when the media carries stories about our family – starve them of oxygen. We give no comment and no interviews. We issue no statements. We don't tweet, Insta, Facebook,

Snapchat, blog or vlog. And eventually the story dies down because something juicier comes along. It works every time.

Right now, that YouTube video is the last thing on my mind. Today is the day Nosipho is going to take the test. It's Saturday afternoon and Lael and I are here to support her. Normally Nosipho goes home on weekends, but her mom is overseas on business this week, so she's boarding. Luckily, Sisulu House is virtually deserted. The rugby first team is playing a pre-season warm-up match at St Giles and practically everyone has gone along to support them. Even Matron is having an afternoon nap. We have the place to ourselves.

"So, you've decided then," Lael says. "You're going to do all three tests at the same time?"

Nosipho looks determined. "Might as well. That way we'll know for sure."

"How are you going to pee on three sticks at the same time? What if you miss, or your pee runs out?" This issue kept me awake last night.

"I thought of that. What I'm going to do is pee into a cup and then dip all three sticks into it. That way I can't go wrong."

"I swear if you use my tooth-mug for this," Lael warns her, "our friendship is officially over."

"As if! I'll use mine, of course."

"And you definitely need to go by now, right?" I ask.

"For sure. I've been needing the loo for, like, the last hour."

Lael and I give each other anxious looks as she disappears into the bathroom. The seconds tick past. I stare out the window at Sandton City in the distance. Normally that's where I'd be on a Saturday afternoon. Either with friends or alone. It's the only day of the week I have to devote to fashion.

I'm just losing myself in a fantasy about the perfect fake-fur *gilet* I've been looking for when the bathroom door opens.

"What does it say?"

"What does it say?"

Lael and I rush over to Nosipho.

"Chill, you guys. I've only just done the test. I've set the timer on my phone. I can look after three minutes."

"But you were in there for ages!" says Lael.

"Listen, it took me a while to unwrap all the tests. My hands were shaking so much I could hardly manage it. Plus they are all slightly different to each other. Then I couldn't relax enough to actually pee, so that took a while too. Then I had to dip them all in the pee and put them on a flat, dry surface to wait."

"Okay, so now we wait." I start pacing up and down.

Another three years seem to pass before Nosipho's phone finally buzzes. We look at each other with huge eyes.

"Okay, this is it," says Lael. "What do you want to do? Do you want to go in and look at them by yourself? Do you want us to come with you?"

Nosipho's face is pale. As she puts her phone back on the bed, her hand is trembling. "I want one of you to go and look for me and come out and tell me the verdict. I can't do it. I thought I could, but I can't. Trinity, you go."

"Sure, babes."

Now it's my legs that are shaking as I walk to the bathroom. The three pregnancy tests are lined up side by side next to one of the basins. I take my time looking at them. Then I gather them all up and go back to the dorm, where Nosipho and Lael are waiting for me.

"You're pregnant," I say, handing them to her.

CHAPTER 3

To: Themba Matlare thembamatlare@gmail.com
From: Nosipho Mamusa nosiphomamusa@gmail.com
Re: Lost your phone?

Hey,

Been texting and WhatsApping you all day but nothing's going through. Have you lost your phone? I need to talk to you, but not over the phone. Something has come up and I have to see you face to face. Please call me or email back or whatever. This needs to be soon.

N. x

To: Helen Momsen hmomsen@ubuntugold.com
From: Trinity Luhabe trinityluhabe@gmail.com
Re: Interview request from *Teen Dream* magazine

Dear Ms Momsen,

Please say no to this interview request as well. I don't care if they want me to make a statement in support of teen mums or whatever. No comment. No interviews. Nothing.

Yes, I saw the photo of me on their website. It must have been taken with a long-lens or something. I do find it a bit invasive, but this isn't the first time it's happened. We learned long ago that the only way to make them lose interest is to give them nothing to work with. My parents support me on this one.

No statements to the media. I know this is your job as media liaison but, believe me, it's what my dad wants.

Regards,
Trinity

To: Dean of Students – Sisulu House gcobani@sisuluhouse.co.za
From: Sunet Luhabe sunetluhabe@actionnow.co.za
Re: Trinity

Dear Ms Gcobani,

Thank you for your concern. I can assure you that my daughter is not pregnant. That YouTube video was a hoax. Unfortunately, our family is in the public eye so these things come up from time to time.

No, we don't want to release any statement to the press. We know from experience that it only fuels the fire. I don't agree that the school's reputation is at stake here. This is a private family matter that we are dealing with in our own way. I suggest you stick to a firm "no comment".

Kind regards,
Sunet Luhabe

Lael and I are trying to hold it together but it isn't easy. And we're not having nearly as tough a time as Nosipho. Themba won't return her messages, so she hasn't been able to talk to him since she found out she was pregnant. She seems to be feeling worse with every day. She is nauseous in the mornings, and dead tired the rest of the time.

The three of us are trying to keep up with our class work, but it's a bit of a nightmare. Lael and Nosipho get As most of the time, so they can afford a slight dip in their marks. I'm more of a straight-C student, so I really can't lose focus here. We use the rest of the weekend after the pregnancy tests for homework. It's Tuesday evening before I manage to get into the Grade Ten dormitory again.

I spend the evening doing prep with the boarders and then dash upstairs, hoping to have a chat with Lael and Nosipho before everyone else starts getting ready for bed. For the last two days, breaks have been taken up with meetings for extramurals, so we've hardly talked, except on WhatsApp.

I bound up the stairs two at a time, hoping to find the dormitory empty. No such luck.

"Sophie!"

She turns quickly, shoving something behind her back. I find myself staring into the innocent blue of her china-doll eyes and know at once she is up to something. As though that YouTube prank wasn't bad enough, she's coming after us again.

I should explain.

Sophie Agincourt is my nemesis. She is my Lex Luthor, my Dr Doom, and my Regina George. We were friends until we were about eleven, when we both entered the

Miss Sandton pageant for little girls. My mom was completely horrified that I'd put my name down and basically wanted to ban me from entering, but my dad talked her out of it because he thought it was cute and harmless. So she put me in a plain white dress, brushed my hair back, and banned me from putting on any makeup.

Sophie, on the other hand, spent weeks having manipedis, facials, haircuts, and a dress specially made for her. She was wearing so much makeup, it looked as though her face would fall off if she leaned forward. So of course I won because the judges liked my "natural" look – thanks, Mom! – and Sophie was my princess. She has never, ever forgiven me for that, and has been my mortal enemy ever since.

And by mortal enemy I mean that officially we are still friends, but she tries to ruin my life behind my back. I am constantly surprised that scary music doesn't start playing when she walks into a room.

"What are you doing here?" I take a casual step to the right to see what she's hiding behind her back.

She turns slightly to block me. "Just visiting the old home-away-from-home. I miss it sometimes, don't you?"

Classic diversionary tactics. But I should probably explain again.

Last term when my mom and dad moved to Chile for three months to set up Ubuntu Gold's latest mine, and my brothers and I were boarding – I told you that part already – Sophie immediately started boarding as well because she absolutely has to copy every single thing I do. Also, she likes to keep an eye on me so that she never misses an opportunity to launch an attack.

Do I sound dramatic? I probably sound dramatic. But

what would you say if I told you she set me up with a guy she knew had a history of abusive relationships? Nice, right? Very supportive and friendly. So, when I say I don't trust Sophie Agincourt, I have very good reasons.

"I can't say I miss it exactly," I say. "I like sleeping in my own bed and eating normal food."

"That reminds me…" She tosses back her pale golden hair and widens her baby-blue eyes at me. "How's that diet? The one you and Lael were on? 'A Brand New You', wasn't it called?"

See what I mean? Who does that? Who brings up some stupid diet that somebody used to be on?

I give her my best Zen / Namaste / Dalai Lama smile. "I realised I didn't need it after all, so I stopped."

She makes a funny noise in her throat that translates as, "Yeah, right!" Then she smooths her skirt complacently over her hips. The thing about Sophie is that she looks exactly like a doll – one of those perfect china dolls that little white girls used to play with. So not only does she look like the Bride of Chucky, but she has the personality to match. I think it was the doll thing that made it so impossible for her to accept that I had won the Miss Sandton competition and not her. How often does the black sidekick get to be the star of the show rather than Malibu Barbie? Exactly! Never.

A few years ago, I would have asked her to explain that funny noise she just made, but these days I know better.

"Is it just nostalgia that's got you creeping around up here while everyone's out?"

She smiles the smile of one who cannot be shamed. "Not exactly. I was poking around looking for evidence."

"Evidence?"

"Yes, evidence. You see, I saw a very interesting You-Tube video the other day. It was of you buying a handful of pregnancy tests at some random pharmacy. I came here to see if I could find out what was going on."

I fold my arms across my chest and lean against Yasmin's cupboard, grinning. "Oh, really? And what did you find, Sherlock?"

And then, I swear to you, she pulls her hand out from behind her back and holds up the three pregnancy tests – the exact three that Nosipho used last weekend. I am so completely gobsmacked, I am *this* close to yelling, "Witchcraft!" and running out of the room.

"How did you…?" My voice cracks and I have to start again. "Where did you…?"

"Get these? Oh, it was easy. They were lying right here in the bin, buried under a mound of toilet paper. It was almost as though someone were trying to hide them."

"But … but … the bins get cleared every day."

"I know! Weird, right? Someone has obviously got a bad case of pregnancy brain and forgot to throw them away earlier. I mean, look at this – three positive pregnancy tests."

My mind is boggling and I'm about to say something even more indiscreet when Lael and Nosipho come into the dormitory.

Their eyes widen when they see Sophie standing there with a bevy of pregnancy tests clutched in her French-manicured hand. I want to grab Nosipho by the shirt like they do in the movies, and yell, "HOW COULD YOU BE SO CARELESS AS TO LEAVE THEM LYING AROUND?"

But I don't. Obviously.

Luckily, Lael is a total star who rises to the occasion,

reminding me why I have been best friends with her since Grade One.

She smirks at Sophie and says, "I see congratulations are in order. When's the due date?"

Sophie drops the tests on Yasmin's bed. "Eeuw! They're not mine. Of course they're not mine."

"Don't be so modest," says Lael. "Munashe was saying to me just the other day that your tummy looks bigger than normal." Munashe is a friend of ours, and will back us up if she asks him.

"Don't talk rubbish. My tummy is perfect." But she shoots a sideways glance at herself in the mirror. I have to bite the inside of my cheek not to burst out laughing.

"Just as you say, but really, it's nothing to be ashamed of."

Sophie's big, round eyes narrow into slits. "Stop trying to put me off. This has nothing to do with me. It's one of you. Someone in this dorm is pregnant and I'm going to find out who."

"Haven't you heard?" Lael smiles sweetly. "It's Trinity. You must have seen the YouTube clip?"

"That's right." I pick up the story smoothly: "I am carrying the love child of DJ Rapp, that guy from *The Voice*, you know? Or, no, wait. It's actually the Pirates goalkeeper. *Sunday World* voted him Joburg's most eligible bachelor, remember?"

For a moment, Sophie stands there with her mouth hanging open, almost believing what I'm saying. Then she snaps out of it.

"Don't talk nonsense. If it's not you, it must be someone else."

She turns towards Nosipho when Lael flings herself on her knees at Sophie's feet and grabs her hand.

"Will you be my bridesmaid?" she demands. "I'm the one who's pregnant and I'm getting married to an Israeli arms dealer next week. But don't worry, it'll be perfectly safe. You can wear a Kevlar vest under your dress."

Sophie shakes her hand off with a look of extreme irritation. "You are so annoying. Someone in this dorm is pregnant. I'll find out who it is, don't you worry."

She glares at Nosipho who meets her eyes with a look of total innocence – even amusement. That girl is such a rock star, I want to give her a huge hug there and then. Under that bland smile she must be quaking in her boots. Sophie is the biggest troublemaker in school. She can create a drama out of anything. I hate to think what she'd do with a genuine crisis like this.

Sophie stands there for a moment, her eyes flicking from my face, to Lael's, to Nosipho's.

Then she changes tack. Her eyes soften and she smiles her perfect, pearly smile.

"The thing is, I just want to help. Whoever it is must be going through a really tough time right now, and I want to be there for her. She's probably feeling scared and lonely and needs someone to talk to. I'm a great listener. Everyone says so. I just want to offer my support."

Somehow – and I really don't know how – Lael manages to keep a straight face. "You're a regular Good Samaritan, Sophie. But here's the thing. We really don't know who those tests belong to. I don't think it's even someone from this dorm. It was probably a girl from another grade. I mean, who throws pregnancy tests into a bin in her own dorm? You'd have to be crazy, right?"

A sheepish grin flits across Nosipho's face.

"Well, whoever it is, I hope they know they can come to me in a crisis." Sophie presses a hand to her heart. "I just want to help."

She waits another moment to see if any of us will bite. We don't, so she pulls out her phone and checks the time. "Got to go, you guys. Later." Then she strolls out.

Nosipho sinks onto the bed and drops her head into her hands. At that exact moment, Sophie turns and looks back through the doorway. When she sees Nosipho's slumped posture, she smiles to herself and keeps walking.

We tuck Nosipho into bed with a mug of hot chocolate and an old episode of *Supernatural* on her iPad. On the nightstand next to her bed, I put a bottle of water and a couple of the ginger biscuits I managed to smuggle from home. According to the internet, ginger is supposed to help with nausea when you're pregnant, so I've been slipping her these biscuits for the last couple of days. She says it's helping a bit, but when the nausea strikes it's like trying to turn back a tidal wave with a sandcastle.

Themba has finally got back to her. Apparently, he had no data and had to wait until the beginning of the month for his new package to kick in. They are seeing each other this weekend, which is when she'll tell him she's pregnant. I know she's hectically nervous about how he'll react.

Right now, Lael and I are on our way upstairs to check on our ghost-hunting equipment. The video recorder sends a ping to my phone every time it records movement in the room. I've received quite a few pings over the last week, and we've been waiting for an opportunity to check them out.

"This is exciting, isn't it?" she says as we climb the last flight of stairs to the fourth floor. "It has definitely picked up something. We aren't going to watch a week's worth of nothing. We can skip ahead to the good parts."

"See? I knew I was right to invest in top-quality equipment."

"I still think you're crazy to have spent so much money on it, but it's nice that ghost-hunting has moved into the twenty-first century."

The room on the fourth-floor smells as musty and unused as ever. As we walk in, I'm convinced our equipment has been stolen because I can't see any of it. Then we go poking behind encyclopaedias and desks and lampshades, and find that it's all still there, thank goodness. We just hid it really well.

"Did you bring the thumb drive?" Lael asks.

I pull it out of my pocket. "Let's do this."

We plug it into all three devices in turn and download the information they recorded during the last week.

"Shall we watch it up here or downstairs?"

"Up here." I open my laptop and set it up on one of the desks. "There are too many nosy people downstairs."

There is a frustrating delay while the laptop downloads software for all three of the devices before it can display the recordings. And, of course, one of them fails to load after five minutes, so we have to start it all over again. Finally, we are all set. Lael pulls up a chair next to mine and we press play on the first recording – the camcorder.

We decided that would be the most interesting – the one we wanted to watch first.

"You see where all those blips are on the progress bar?" Lael points at the screen. "That's what pinged on your phone. Use the mouse to skip ahead to each one."

We watch with our noses practically pressed to the screen, as the first blip unfolds.

At exactly 11.05 on the first morning, a cleaner backs into the room, pulling a vacuum cleaner behind her. She pushes it over the carpet half-heartedly for a while, then switches it off and flicks a feather duster around the ceiling and over some of the old books. Then she leaves with her equipment.

I skip to the next blip and the same thing happens, except that she is wearing different shoes this time. I skip to the next day and she is back again with the first pair of shoes.

"It's a good thing she's not more conscientious," Lael says. "Or she might have found our equipment. I mean, imagine if she took every book off the shelf and dusted it. We would have been busted a long time ago."

"True. But is this really all we've got? Are we just going to watch her sliding the vacuum cleaner around every day?"

"No, look." Lael taps the screen. "See where those blips are clustered together at the end of the progress bar? Something else happened, for sure. And just a couple of days ago, by the looks of it."

"Should I skip ahead?"

"Better not," says the diligent ghost-hunter. "We might miss something important if you do that."

So we sit through a few more days of "Cleaners Gone

Wild" starring Ntombi (her nametag is clipped onto the pocket of her uniform in big letters). Then there is a blip that clearly belongs to the same day as her last visit, so we watch that eagerly.

"It's Matron!" I say, as a familiar figure walks into the room, glancing over her shoulder.

"What is she up to? She looks super guilty."

We watch as Matron crosses the room to where the windows are and pulls at one until it is open as wide as it will go. She is right at the edge of the camera's range and as she sits down, she moves out of our sight.

"Aargh! I knew I should have got the wide-angle lens."

"What is she doing?"

Something ghostly drifts across our screen.

"Ooh, is that ectoplasm?" I ask

"No … I'm pretty sure it's not."

"Then what is it?"

As we watch, more "ectoplasm" drifts across our screen and separates into wisps in a very familiar way. It hits us at the same time.

"She's smoking!" we say together.

"Matron! Smoking! I don't believe it."

"She's like the most anti-smoking person on earth." Lael shakes her head. "When I think of all the times she's lectured us about the dangers of tobacco! Remember that video she showed us last year about two characters called Healthy Lung and Smoker's Lung? How gross was that? It put me off my lunch for a week."

"There's no chance we're wrong, is there?" I stare at the screen, watching the smoke rise and sink. "We don't want to jump to conclusions."

"No, look there! Quick."

We see a hand move briefly into shot. It is wearing Matron's famous watch – the one with the metal strap that always slips around so that the face rests on her wrist and she has to twist her arm to see the time. And that is quite clearly a cigarette clutched between her fingers.

"Well, well, well." Lael shakes her head. "Talk about hypocritical."

"Oh, I don't know." I'm trying to be fair here. "I think it's often the smokers who are most fanatical about warning people against it. They know what it's like to be addicted, so they don't want kids to make the same mistake."

"I suppose."

We watch for another minute or two, until Matron stands up and walks out the room, carrying a little cardboard box she has obviously been using as an ashtray.

"Well, that's not our ghost, so let's keep looking." Lael encourages me to skip ahead to the next blip.

We watch the cleaner come in a few more times. Then, for a change of pace, one of the Grade Eights walks into the room and heads straight to the bookshelf. She seems to be looking for something in one of the encyclopaedias. Then she lays the book open on a desk, takes a photograph of the page she needs with her phone, and walks out.

Matron doesn't appear again.

Much to our disappointment, the last blip is completely blank.

"Oh, well." I lift my hand to close the laptop. "That was a waste of time."

"Wait." Lael touches my wrist. "Let's just watch that last one again."

"Why? Nothing happened."

"The camera must have picked up something or it wouldn't have recorded it as an event. We need to look more carefully."

I scroll to the beginning of the scene and we watch it again. "See? Nothing."

"Play it again."

I roll my eyes because it's getting late. I've already had a WhatsApp from Lungile saying that he's coming to fetch me right now whether I'm ready or not.

But it's only about thirty seconds long, so I rewind it again. And this time I see it.

"Hey!" I say it so loudly that Lael starts in her chair.

"What?"

"Didn't you see that?"

"What? I didn't see anything."

"I'm going to play it again at half-speed. No – quarter-speed." I rewind to the beginning and play it at twenty-five per cent of normal speed. This time, Lael sees it too.

"Oh. My. Goodness."

"Right? Can you see it now?"

As we watch, a very slight shimmer appears on the right side of the screen and moves slowly across to the left. Then it's gone. It lasts for exactly thirty seconds and is definitely the thing that activated the motion sensor on the camcorder. It's not ectoplasm or anything gloopy like that. It's just a slight distortion of what we are seeing – almost like our eyes have gone funny or the camera has.

"You don't think it's a fault on the camcorder?" asks Lael.

"I don't think so. Otherwise the camera wouldn't have recorded it as an event."

She brightens up. "That's true."

My phone buzzes and I groan when I look at it. "Lungi is waiting for me outside. I have to go now."

"We haven't even had a chance to listen to the EMF-meter or the chromatograph."

"We can listen at break tomorrow."

"Okay. I also wanted to have a look at the diary again while we're here."

"Why? It's behind glass. Nothing will have changed."

"I know. But there might be some detail we missed."

"Then we'd better hurry."

I pack up my laptop while Lael goes around the room making sure that the three devices are properly hidden. It was a shock to realise that people actually use this room for research now and again. The last thing we want is someone pulling out a book and discovering our ghost-busters equipment.

We trot down to the second floor to take a look at the trophy case. By this stage, Lungile has messaged me a second time so I'm feeling a bit stressed.

"There," I say. "The diary looks exactly the same as last time. And so does the rest of the cabinet. Let's go now or you're going to miss lights-out."

"Wait! Hang on." Lael peers at the diary with her nose practically pressed to the glass. "That's not the same page as before."

"What? Let me look." I nudge her out of the way so I can see. Once again, the faded writing makes it difficult to tell. "I can't see. You'd better take another picture, just in case."

"Fine," says Lael, and she does.

I saw Jim today and told him the truth. To be honest, I don't see how it could have gone any worse. First, he went white and said, "My dad will kill me." Then he went red and shouted, "How could you have been so stupid? I can't let you ruin my life like this."

Oh, Diary. It hurt to hear him say it, but everyone knows it is the girl's responsibility to ensure that the boy doesn't Go Too Far. We all know that boys can't control themselves the way we can. It is up to us to put the brakes on and to make sure that nothing gets out of hand.

I know I have been bad and that I deserve everything that is happening to me. I just wish I didn't feel so alone. It is exactly like they warned us in Sunday School. Bad Girls truly know what it is like to be excluded from God's grace.

To continue, Diary, I apologised to Jim for letting this happen, but then do you know what he said? He said the baby couldn't be his! He said I must have been "sleeping around" and that this must be another boy's baby! He said his father warned him that girls often try to trick boys in this way. Can you believe it?

I told him it wasn't true. I reminded him that it was my first time, and I told him that was the only time I've ever G.A.T.W. And he said, Aha! It couldn't have been my first time because everyone knows you can't get PG on your first time. I told him I'd looked it up in the reference section of the library and apparently that wasn't true. He told me I was lying.

And then, dear Diary, I am sorry to say I lost my temper a little bit. I really shouldn't have. I know it was wrong, but I was terribly upset. I said it didn't matter who was wrong or right. The baby was there now - or it would be in a few months - and we needed to decide what we were going to do.

He looked at me for a long moment, and, oh Diary, I really thought he was going to say he was sorry and of course we would have to get married. For a moment, I thought he was going to propose to me and all my dreams would come true. How happy we would have been together. I would have been a good wife to him.

But instead he said this baby had nothing to do with him and that I'd never be able to prove it was his.

Oh, Diary! It was so hurtful. But I said I was sorry and that I didn't mean to ruin his life. I said I knew he had a great future ahead of him. And then I'm sorry to say, I ran away crying. I thought he would come after me, but he didn't.

What am I going to do, dear Diary? I can't tell Mother and Father about this. I just can't. Maybe if Jim had agreed to marry me we could have gone to them together, but not now, not like this!

Oh, whatever am I going to do?

Love,
Amelia

"Can I just say one thing?" Lael asks as we finish reading the entry together in class the next day. We're supposed to be in Bio, but the teacher is absent so we're having a free.

"What?"

"Who on earth is turning these pages over for us? I mean, think about it, this diary is kept behind glass. It should be open on one page for display purposes and *stay* on that page. But every time we go and look, it's open on another page. And not just any page – the very next page."

"It's only happened twice," I point out. "I don't think we can start talking about 'every time' yet. Maybe it was the wind that blew the page over. Who knows?"

"Wind that just happened to get into a locked display cabinet? I don't think so."

"Then maybe it was one of the cleaners, or whoever keeps the key to that cabinet."

"Aha!" Lael lifts her finger like she's Sherlock Holmes. "The cleaners don't have the key. I asked them. That cabinet is supposed to be opened twice a year – once when the Gumede Shield gets taken out and moved to Gumede House, and again when it gets moved back to Sisulu House after six months. And that's it."

"Well, what do you think is happening then?"

Lael looks like someone who has a theory she can't wait to share. "I think it's Jim Grey!" she says excitedly.

"Babes…"

"No, listen. I think he's turning the pages over for us to read because that diary contains the secret of how he died."

"Oh, my word. You have officially lost it."

"Have I?" She flings her arms wide. (Why are all Drama students like this? Seriously, why?) "Think about what he did last term – warning you about Zach, helping us to steal the Gumede Shield. This is typical of his MO"

I crack up laughing. "MO! You actually think you're in an episode of *The Wire*, don't you?"

"You're the one who's seen him, not me. Wouldn't this be typical of him? To guide us toward the truth even when he's not showing himself to you anymore?"

"No," I say frankly. "It wouldn't."

"Why not?"

"Because he was the vainest guy you ever met. Totally full of himself. You could see he was one of those guys who thought a girl should count herself lucky if he even looked at her, never mind talked to her. That's just how he was – Mr Conceited. And this diary really doesn't show him in a good light at all. In fact, it makes him look like a total creep."

Lael drops the dramatic act and thinks about this for a while. "So, we've decided that the Jim in the diary is definitely Jim Grey? I thought you weren't too sure."

"I'm getting more and more convinced."

"Then maybe it's just our modern-day perspective that makes us think he was wrong. Maybe that was typical boy behaviour back in the 1960s. I mean, obviously we think it's despicable, but that's our opinion, not his."

I'm pretty sure there would have been people in the 1960s who would also consider his behaviour despicable, but I see what she means.

"The Jim I knew was nice to me in his own way," I say. "And he helped me see what an abusive situation I was getting into with Zach Morris. I didn't even realise how Zach was gaslighting me until Jim intervened. I'll always be grateful to him for that. But if this is the same Jim, I don't like the way he acted when he was alive. Maybe something happened to change him."

"I blame his father," says Lael. "From Amelia's diary, it sounds as though he really worshipped his dad. But that man seems to have been a toxic influence on him."

"What I want to know is how Amelia could have been such a doormat. Blaming herself for the whole thing.

Apologising to him. Letting him accuse her of sleeping with other guys. Why didn't she tell him to shove it?"

"It was a different time. Fifty-something years ago. That's like half a century. In fact, it's exactly half a century."

"Weren't they in the middle of a sexual revolution in the Sixties?"

"Not in South Africa. It was all apartheid and Christian National Education in those days." Lael flings her arms wide again. "This was mostly farmland around here. Brentwood was a small school in the middle of nowhere."

"I guess you're right." I lower my voice and look around to make sure no one is paying attention to our conversation. Most people are catching up on homework or scrolling through their phones. The teacher is marking some papers – probably our History essays, actually. "I just hope Nosipho is having a better time telling Themba than Amelia had telling Jim."

CHAPTER 4

Lael: Hi! How did it go? Did u see him?

Trinity: Girl! What happened? Lael and I have been thinking of u all day.

Lael: Don't blue-tick us! Trinity and I are dying here. How did it go???

Trinity: OK. We're really freaking out now thinking it went badly. Lael is beside herself. Give. Us. Some. News.

Lael: Going to bed now but I'm keeping my alerts on in case you want to send us an update.

To: Trinity Luhabe trinityluhabe@gmail.com; Lael Lieberman laelliebs78@gmail.com

From: Nosipho Mamusa nosiphomamusa@gmail.com

Re: Themba

Hi guys,

Sorry to swerve your WhatsApps yesterday. I was feeling a bit emotional. I'm chilling at my aunt's place this weekend. I'll be back at Sisulu House on Sunday night. My mom is still overseas and it looks like she won't be getting back any time soon. This deal she is project-managing is getting bigger than anyone expected, so she won't be back for weeks.

It's a good thing, I suppose. I can take care of this problem without her breathing down my neck on weekends.

Anyway. So, I saw Themba.

I guess it went okay. The part I'll never forget is the look on his face when I first told him. Think total and utter horror. But what was I expecting, right? Was there really some dumb part of me that was hoping he might be all like, "A baby? Really? Our baby? But that's wonderful! Let's get married straight away." And then I'd start picking out wedding dresses.

Lame, right?

That was NOT the way it went down. And to be honest, I really can't blame him. I'm pretty sure the look on his face was exactly the same as the look on mine when you came out of that bathroom and told me I was pregnant, Trinity. Not thrilled, in other words.

So, anyway, after the initial horror he was kind of a sweetie about it. He said he would support me whatever decision I made, and that we were in this together. I could tell he really wanted to push me to find out which way I was leaning, but he didn't. And it was obvious that he was hoping to hear I'd decided to get rid of it.

But again, I really can't blame him for that because that IS the way I'm leaning. I'm just a weirdo for feeling disappointed that he didn't ask me to keep it. So, *ja*, he gets full marks for being the supportive boyfriend. I don't know why I'm such an idiot that I started crying after he left. Must be pregnancy hormones.

I feel better now. I just need to decide what I'm going to do and how I'm going to do it.

Thanks for all your support, guys. I don't know what I would have done without you. Lael, I'll see you in the dorm on Sunday, and Trinity I'll probably only see you on Monday morning. Have a great weekend!

Love,
Nos

The three of us climb out of the Uber taxi and look up at the twin buildings in front of us.

"Which one do we want?" Lael asks.

I consult my phone and point to the one on the right. "That one. East Tower. Gynaecology and Obstetrics are on the second floor."

We trudge off in the right direction. It's a grey and gloomy day, exactly matching our moods. We're at the Raheeda Pelser General Hospital in the middle of town. It is Joburg's premier teaching hospital. It used to be called the St Mary & All the Saints General Hospital before they renamed it after this old guy who was on Robben Island with my dad. I still remember him coming to dinner a couple of times when I was a little kid. Uncle Raheeda. He passed away a few years ago.

Some people still call it All Saints, but the new signs are everywhere – RPGH. It looks scary and huge. My heart is hammering at the base of my throat. All I can think is that if I'm feeling like this, how must Nosipho be feeling? I give her hand a squeeze, and see that Lael is doing the same to her other hand.

We're here because none of us has enough money to afford to have this done privately. I mean, obviously, we could get our hands on the money if we were prepared to tell the adults in our lives what we were up to, but we're not. That was Nosipho's decision. She wants to handle this quickly and quietly without her mom knowing any- thing about it.

She spent a week thinking about it and decided she doesn't want to go through with the pregnancy. Which Lael and I support one hundred per cent, of course.

Okay, there might have been a *tiny* part of me that

wished she would have the baby just so I could be its auntie and help look after it, but that's just me. I love kids and I always have. Babies. Toddlers. Little school kids. I love them all.

When we visit our family in Soweto on the weekends, I'm the only one who never, ever moans about spending hours with our relatives because there are always baby cousins for me to play with.

So basically, it would have been awesome if Nosipho had decided to keep the baby, and I would have been the best auntie ever. And godmother. She would have totally made me godmother, right? I mean, who else?

But I'm not the one who would have to look after this baby for the next twenty-something years. My mom says it's the hardest job in the world, and I have no trouble believing that. Of course, I didn't say any of this to Nos. When it comes to babies, it's the mom's choice and nobody else's. End of story.

We've been told it can be a long wait, so we've come equipped with our phones, our tablets, and our e-readers. I even stuffed a few magazines into my backpack in case we got desperate. We've also got snacks coming out of our ears. Nosipho hasn't eaten since last night, though, and she won't until it's all over.

Like I said, we're not exactly jumping for joy here, but we are very determined. We're prepared to stick it out all day if necessary.

"You're sure you don't want us to call Themba?" Lael ask for the millionth time. And for the millionth time, Nosipho says no.

"This is what he wanted," she says. "He didn't come right out and say so, but I know this is what he was hoping

I'd decide. So it's not like I need to inform him of my decision before I go through with it. I can tell him afterwards. He'll be relieved."

"And you don't want him here to support you?" I ask.

"No, I'm fine with you guys. You won't leave me, will you?"

We squeeze her hands even harder. "Of course we won't."

Eight hours later – EIGHT HOURS! – the three of us are still sitting in the waiting room of the Day Procedures Clinic in the Gynaecology ward. We finished our snacks hours ago and the coffee shop on the ground floor is closed for renovations. There is a vending machine on the second floor that sells hot drinks, but it ran out of water at three o'clock. Lael found another machine on the fourth floor and has just brought me some hot chocolate.

We have read all the magazines twice, and our eyes are aching from staring at our screens. I don't know – I literally have no idea – how the patients are coping who don't have smart phones with them. They must be going out of their minds with boredom. We passed our magazines around the waiting room, and now everyone else has read them twice too.

We can't even take videos of ourselves horsing around and post them on Snapchat in case anyone figures out where we are, because that's something that Nosipho really doesn't want. We even turned off the location tagging on our phones, in case the words Raheeda Pelser General Hospital appeared in someone's feed.

"Miss Mamusa?"

We've been waiting for this moment so long we can't believe it's actually here.

"Miss Mamusa?" the nurse repeats.

Lael gives Nosipho a poke and she stands up. "That's me."

"Come through to the examination room, please."

Lael and I leap to our feet too, but the nurse glares at us. "Just the patient."

"Can't my friends come too? I want them to be with me."

"Are either of you family of the patient?" asks the nurse. We shake our heads. "Then you can't come in. Khawulezani, intombezana."

Nosipho and the nurse disappear behind a curtained-off area that serves as the examination room.

Lael stares at me. "Did that nurse just tell Nos to hurry up?"

"Yup."

"Isn't that a bit rude?"

"She's probably just overworked. I mean, we're exhausted after sitting here for eight hours. She's been working flat out."

"I guess." Lael gives the curtains a hard look. "I wonder if we'll be able to hear what they're saying."

Since we've been sitting here, we have heard a lot of things we could have done without. There is literally nothing more than a thin curtain between the waiting area and the examination room.

Before I can answer, we start hearing voices coming from behind the curtain. There aren't many people left in the waiting room. Most have already been attended to and left, including some who arrived after us. It was almost as if the nurses were deliberately ignoring us.

"What are they saying?" Lael asks.

"Dude, you know my Xhosa isn't great."

"It's still better than mine. Come on – translate for me. I know you can."

I close my eyes and listen to the rhythm of the words. I'm a child again, playing with my cousins at our village in the Idutywa area of the Transkei. That was the last time we all spoke isiXhosa together unselfconsciously. The older we got, the more they would insist on speaking English to me and my brothers because they wanted to practice. I used to beg them to speak isiXhosa to us, but they wouldn't. They thought it was more important for them to listen closely to our private school accents and try to imitate them.

Whenever I tried to initiate a conversation in isiXhosa, they would laugh at me because my accent sucked and I made so many mistakes. You try keeping up a language when you're ten years old and your cousins are mocking you. But still – they would talk to each other and to their parents in isiXhosa, and I would listen.

I'm listening now with my eyes closed. Trying to let the meaning of the words wash over me even while the grammar escapes my grasp. It doesn't help that their voices keep dropping and rising so that I'm missing practically every third word.

"Okay, the nurse is taking a history from Nosipho," I tell Lael. "You know – her general health. Whether she has ever been pregnant before. When was the first day of her last period. That kind of stuff."

"Fine. Fine. Keep listening."

I listen, but it's hard to ignore the way Nosipho's voice goes up and down. It wobbles and breaks. She is on the verge of tears, I can tell. She is explaining that she doesn't want to go through with the pregnancy – and talking about how overwhelmed she feels.

Suddenly the nurse's voice blasts out into the waiting room, full of blame and anger. My eyes pop open and I lose focus immediately. Now Lael is plucking at my arm demanding to know what's happening.

"Shh!" I hiss. "Let me concentrate."

I close my eyes again and try to get back into the moment. I'm six years old and my aunt is yelling at us because we found her big tin of condensed milk (hidden at the back of the kitchen under some boxes) and opened it and gobbled it all up, licking the sticky sweetness off our fingers as quickly as we could, knowing we'd get caught, but also knowing it was worth it. We'd trade a beating for these few moments of bliss any day.

Okay. It's coming back to me now.

"I know you bad girls," the nurse is shouting. "I know you with your legs that won't stay closed. You never learn. You come in here and expect us to sort out your problems for you, and then you come back a few months later with another one. The doctor is a busy man. How do you expect him to help a rubbish girl like you?"

Nosipho's voice breaks through the yelling, sounding wobblier than ever. "I'm sorry. I'm sorry. I never meant…"

"Yes, you never meant. Girls like you never mean it. It just happens, right? Or are you going to say he raped you, like all the other rubbish girls that come in here and lie?"

"No, no. I never said that. He didn't…"

"Of course he didn't. You girls always tell lies. Listen

to me! This is a hospital. We have sick people here. We don't have time to help rubbish like you."

Lael and I can hear Nosipho's harsh breathing through the curtain. She is crying now – sobbing. But as I listen, she gets herself under control. When she speaks again, there is steel in her voice.

"You have to help me. It's the law. I'm allowed to be here. I'm allowed to say I don't want to carry on with this pregnancy. I haven't done anything wrong."

"You haven't done anything wrong?" the nurse yells. By now, everyone in the waiting room is listening. We are sitting with our heads swivelled towards the examination area, our mouths hanging open.

"You haven't done anything wrong? You sleep around and get pregnant and then you come in here and expect us to sort it out for you? And you don't think you've done anything wrong? What about the taxpayers, girl? Don't you think it's wrong that they have to pay for you to sleep around all the time?"

"You have to help me," Nosipho repeats. Her voice isn't shaking anymore, but I know it is costing her everything she has to hold it together like this. "It's the law. I know my rights."

"It's the law!" scoffs the nurse. "Does the law say I have to help someone who comes in here after closing time? Hey? Does the law say that?"

Our heads turn to look at the clock on the wall. All except Lael, who has no idea what's going on. It is 16.59.

"It's not five o'clock yet," Nosipho says urgently. "Look! It's not."

There is a long pause while we all imagine the nurse watching the seconds count down on the clock. As the big hand reaches the twelve she gives a crow of triumph. "Five o'clock! We're closed. You'll have to come back tomorrow."

"But I've been here since seven o'clock this morning! An hour before you even opened. I've been sitting here the whole day, waiting. I haven't eaten or drunk anything."

"It's five o'clock. This clinic is closed. You can't expect the doctor to operate on you after closing time, can you? This isn't some kind of emergency. You come back on Monday and wait again."

Now Nosipho bursts into tears. "I can't come back on Monday. I have school."

"Monday, Tuesday, Wednesday. You come back on all the days. I'm working every day next week. You see if anyone will let you see the doctor."

The curtain starts shaking, and everyone in the waiting room stares at their phones as though they would never dream of listening to a private conversation.

At last the curtain gets ripped aside and Nosipho comes storming out. I'm pleased to see that she is looking more angry than sad.

"Come on, girls," she snaps. "We're going."

Lael and I jump to our feet and run to catch up with her as she marches out of the waiting room. Anger carries her into the lift, down to the reception area, and out into the parking lot. Anger has her stabbing at her phone to order us an Uber.

But once we're standing there waiting for it to arrive – eight minutes away – her anger evaporates and the tears start to roll down her cheeks.

Lael and I fold her into a group hug.

"Oh, babe. I'm so sorry." Now the tears are rolling down my own cheeks. I swipe them away, angry at myself. My job is to reassure her, not to make her feel even worse.

"That awful woman," Lael says. "How could she be like that? This is a government hospital. We should report her. Surely, she's not allowed to treat patients like that?" My hurried translation has given Lael an idea of what was said.

"What if she was right?" Nosipho sobs. "What if I'm a terrible person?"

"You're not!" Lael says fiercely. "You have done nothing wrong, do you hear me? Nothing!"

"I should never have got into this mess in the first place."

"No, listen to me, you did nothing wrong. You and Themba used a condom. You did everything right. Sometimes things go wrong even when you do everything right."

I make supportive noises.

"Okay." Nosipho shakes out her locs and ties them up in a ponytail again. "You're right. I'm going to stop blaming myself. I won't let that woman get inside my head."

Our Uber pulls up and we climb into the back seat. The driver is playing music, so we carry on our conversation in low voices.

"What am I going to do?" Nosipho says. Her voice has gone wobbly again. "We wasted our time. We spent the whole day here and have nothing to show for it."

Lael punches a fist into the palm of her hand.

"A social worker!" she says. "Yes. That's what we need. Someone sympathetic who knows the law. She will supervise your whole case and make sure you get the help you need. I'll take another day off school and we'll come back here on Monday. I'll demand to see a…" She trails off as she sees Nosipho shaking her head. "What's wrong?"

"I'm not coming back here."

"What do you mean? I'll be with you the whole time. Trinity will as well, won't you, Trinity?"

"I'm not coming back here." Nosipho's lips are tight and her eyes narrowed.

"But … you have to."

"Read my lips. I am not setting foot in that hospital ever again."

Lael sits back in her seat and blows out a breath. "Then what are we going to do?"

"I don't know. All I know is that I am never, ever…"

"You can go private."

They turn to look at me.

"You can go private," I say again. "A nice, private hospital where nobody tries to shame you like Nurse Ratched over there. And I know how to make it happen."

CHAPTER 5

To: Trinity Luhabe trinityluhabe@gmail.com
From: Dean of Students – Sisulu House gcobani@sisuluhouse.co.za

---

Dear Trinity,

Thank you for your email proposing a "Hot Girls in Bikinis" carwash in the school parking lot on Saturday morning. I agree that such a proposal would probably prove popular with the boys, and that your idea to "do a bubbly-sponge dance routine like Paris Hilton" would undoubtedly be "a hit".

Unfortunately, your refusal to tell us what exactly you are raising funds for means that we can't approve this proposal on school property. We also feel that the event is not completely appropriate as a sanctioned school activity.

I look forward to hearing "lots more ideas if you guys don't like this one". Your proposals are always entertaining.

Kind regards,
Grace Gcobani
Dean of Students
Sisulu House
Brentwood College

To: Trinity Luhabe trinityluhabe@gmail.com
From: Dean of Students – Sisulu House gcobani@sisuluhouse.
co.za

Dear Trinity,

Thank you for your email in which you set out your proposal for the "Take a Bite out of Bieber" celebrity cake sale.

I'm sure that cupcakes iced with the faces of popular celebrities would indeed sell like "hot cakes, ha ha!" as you remark in your email.

Unfortunately, we once again come up against the problem that you refuse to disclose what you are raising funds for. Until we know the exact nature of this enterprise, we won't be able to consent to any school involvement in it.

Kind regards,
Grace Gcobani
Dean of Students
Sisulu House
Brentwood College

Dear Trinity,

No, I'm afraid we can't "just take your word for it". Yes, we know you to be (mostly) a responsible young lady with a well-developed social conscience, but unfortunately that is not enough in this case.

I agree that the following are also "seriously sick ideas" – "The Lael Lieberman Totally Flourishing Tutorial Pack", the "Learn to Dance like J.Lo" hip-hop course, and the "Customise Your Jeans With Scissors and Glitter Glue" course.

But we are not in a position to agree to the use of school property for these or any other ideas as long as we don't know why the money is being raised. Your reassurance that "it's for a really good cause" sadly isn't enough.

Kind regards,
Grace Gcobani
Dean of Students
Sisulu House
Brentwood College

To: Nosipho Mamusa nosiphomamusa@gmail.com
From: Sindi Luhabe sindiswe34@heatmail.com

Dear Nosipho,

My name is Sindi and I am Trinity's cousin. Apparently, you said it was okay for me to contact you.

I am twenty-four now, but when I was seventeen I was in the same situation as you. I was pregnant, and the boy didn't want to know. I was so stressed and depressed.

I actually told Trinity's mom – my Auntie Sunet – and she helped me to end the pregnancy. She didn't tell anyone on my side of the family, although I have told some of them since then. I just want you to know that it was the best decision I ever made and that I have never regretted it. It gave me my life back.

I was able to follow my dream of going to hotel school and working overseas. I could never have done everything I've accomplished with my life if I'd had a baby in tow. I looked it up on the internet once and saw that 95% of women believe they made the right choice about having an abortion.

If you ever want to talk to me or ask me questions, I'll be happy to speak to you.

Yours in choice,
Sindi

It's half-past five and I am completely finished.

All I want to do is curl up on my bed and watch Netflix until drool runs down my chin. What I have to do instead is this:

- Collect all the cupcake trays
- Remove the cupcake liners, scrunch them up and throw them away
- Brush crumbs into the bin
- Stack the trays neatly
- Count the money in the cash box
- Take out the original cash float and separate it from the rest
- Work out how much profit we made
- Call Lungi and ask him to help me take all the stuff to the car

So basically, I won't see my bed for a looooong time. But it's okay, because I just counted it all up and we made nearly R1,800. I still need to check my calculations, but I think if we add that to my savings (including all my babysitting money), Lael's savings, and Nosipho's savings, plus the money we made from the tuition packs Lael has been selling at Sisulu House, plus the few pairs of jeans we customised, I reckon we've almost got enough.

Today's "Bite into Bieber" celebrity face cupcake sale was meant to be our biggest event. When the school refused to let us hold it on school property, we found a shopping centre that was willing to let us set up a table next to the car park on a Saturday morning.

Okay, it helped that my dad just happens to own the shopping centre. The name Luhabe was the magic password. Normally I hate using my surname to get favours, but this was different. It wasn't for me. And now we are almost there! We have almost enough money to get Nosipho a TOP (Termination of Pregnancy) procedure in a private clinic.

When I get home, I double-check the amount we've raised and send the total to the WhatsApp group Nosipho, Lael and I created.

Trinity: Guys, we are so close to our goal!

Lael: THIS IS SO EXCITING!!!!!

Nosipho: We're not just close, we've done it! I managed to convince my aunt to lend me R1,500. It took a bit of persuading, but I did it. She kept asking what it was for, but I finally convinced her it was private. She handed me the cash a minute ago and I've put it in my bag.

Trinity: Brilliant. Well done, girls. I knew we could do it. Now we just need to book you in for Friday afternoon and pay the Private Patient Admission deposit.

Nosipho: Friday afternoon?

Trinity: Sure. That way you'll have the whole weekend to recover.

Nosipho: This coming Friday?

Lael: We can't leave it much longer than that. You're ten weeks already. Nearly eleven.

Trinity: We'll come with you, of course.

Lael: Of course.

Trinity: And when your mom gets back it will all be over.

Nosipho: It just seems so soon.

Lael: The sooner the better. See you guys at school! Well done to all of us for getting the money together.

♀

Friday is a beautiful, sunny day. It literally could not be more different to that cold, gloomy day when we went to the Raheeda Pelser General Hospital. The sky is blue. The birds are tweeting. The money belt I'm wearing under my top is bulging with cash. And we managed to get ourselves excused from school without anyone –– teachers, parents, or relatives – catching on to the idea that we were up to something.

Nosipho's procedure is booked for eleven o'clock and she was told to check in by half-past seven. Lael is ordering us a ride with Uber. I'm checking Google Maps, and Nosipho is pacing up and down.

When we get to the clinic, it is the complete opposite of the RPGH.

"Look at that cute little garden," says Lael. "This place gives me a good feeling."

Nosipho stands and stares at the entrance as our driver pulls away behind us. She has a hand pressed to her stomach, as though she has a tummy ache.

"You're not feeling dizzy again, are you?" I take her arm just in case.

"No, not this time. Just getting my head together."

"We'd better go in." Lael holds her phone up for us to see. "It's nearly time."

The reception area is quiet and peaceful, with low lighting and indoor plants. Everything is designed to make you feel better. Under the aroma of furniture polish, I can just detect that horrible hospital smell that always makes my heart beat faster. But it's nothing like the cloud of ammonia that hangs over the RPGH.

There are two ladies at reception, both in nurse's uniforms. The one who steps forward to help Nosipho is wearing a kind smile and a badge that says "Sister Lumka Radipiwe".

That's all we wanted, I think. For someone to smile at Nos and welcome her and make her feel at ease during this difficult time. That's what we raised the money for. Not for the smell of polish, or the garden, or the indoor plants. Just this – this little bit of human kindness.

Sister Radipiwe talks in a low, soothing voice to Nosipho and hands her a clipboard and pen. "If you could fill in this form, please. All information is kept strictly confidential."

Nosipho sits down between us and starts writing her name. Lael and I smile at each other.

"Isn't this amazing?"

"So much better than that last place with Nurse Ratched."

"The sister is so kind!"

"Look how pretty the carpet is."

Nosipho keeps her head down and writes.

"Everything okay, babes?" Lael asks.

Nosipho doesn't answer, but a tear splashes onto the form in front of her.

We're quick to comfort her.

"Don't worry, it will all be over soon," Lael says.

"In a couple of hours, you'll be in recovery, sipping juice and eating cookies," I add.

Nosipho mumbles something.

We lean towards her. "What was that?"

"I said I don't want it to be over."

"You don't?" We have no idea where she is going with this.

"I don't want to be in recovery. I don't want cookies

and juice. I don't want any of this." Her voice starts out soft, but gets louder. She lifts her head and we can see tears running down her face.

Lael and I are opening and closing our mouths like goldfish.

Sister Radipiwe comes running towards us. Thank goodness, she seems to know exactly what to say, because we don't have a clue.

"Don't cry, my darling. Don't cry. Come and talk to Nurse. Come." She leads Nosipho away to a quiet corner of the room. Lael and I hesitate. I can see she is thinking the same thing I am – the last time a nurse talked privately to Nosipho, it didn't end well.

I start to babble. "Listen. I know this isn't strictly our business and we're supposed to respect privacy and everything, but don't you think…?"

"We should go bit closer?" Lael says. "Yes, I do. That nurse can't bully Nos if we're standing right there."

We do a sort of sideways shuffle that takes us across the lobby to where they're standing. Lael crosses her arms and tries to look intimidating, and I do the same. This time I don't have to translate because they are speaking English.

"I'm being silly, aren't I?" Nosipho sobs. "I'm being ridiculous. I've already made up my mind."

"Nothing you are feeling is ridiculous," says Sister Radipiwe. "It's your body. This is your decision and nobody else's. There is no right or wrong way to feel."

"I was so sure a couple of weeks ago. I knew I didn't want to go ahead with this pregnancy. I'd made up my mind. Why am I having doubts now?"

The nurse gives Nosipho's hand a squeeze. "Talk to me, darling. Tell me what you're feeling."

"I've been dreaming about it. The … the baby, you know? I dream about having a big tummy and about giving birth and then about having this little thing to care for. And … and I've been thinking about it in the daytime too, you know? Not just at night."

"Okay. That's all normal and natural. Everything you are feeling is very normal, including when you didn't want to go ahead with the pregnancy. But no one can make this decision for you, darling."

Nosipho sobs harder. "When … when my friend was talking about how I would feel when it was all over, I actually wanted to fight her. And when … when you guys were asking me to fill in the form, I just wanted to run away and protect my baby from all of you."

The nurse rubs her arm. "That is what choice means, my dear. It means paying attention to everything you are feeling. If you don't mind my asking, would you have any support if you decided to go ahead with this pregnancy?"

Nosipho glances up at us. We wipe the intimidating looks off our faces and aim for supportive instead. But Sister Radipiwe shakes her head.

"Not your friends, darling, important as they are right now. I'm talking about money, family, the father of the baby – people who will still be there in eighteen years' time when you're trying to send your child to university because you want nothing but the best for them. Do you understand what I'm saying?"

Nosipho is crying so hard now she can hardly speak. "I … I … don't … know!" she sobs. "My … my … mom. But I haven't … I haven't … I haven't even … told her!"

"Okay … okay. I understand. You must take all these factors into account when you make your decision."

There's a long pause while Nosipho sobs her eyes out, Sister Radipiwe rubs her back, and Lael and I stand around wringing our hands and feeling helpless. Eventually, her crying slows down. There are gaps between the sobs, and I can see she is trying to pull herself together. She takes slow, deep breaths. Then she takes the tissue the sister is offering her and blows her nose.

At last she looks up at all of us and presses her lips together to stop them from trembling.

"I don't care," she says. "I don't care that I don't know how my mom will react, or how Themba will react, or whether the school will kick me out. I'll make a plan. We'll be okay, my baby and I. I'll work for the rest of my life to make sure we're okay. And if I have to do it alone, that's also fine. And I just want to say that I appreciate how kind you've been to me, Sister." She looks over at Lael and me. "And I appreciate that you guys raised money for me so I could do this privately. And I really, really appreciate that I live in a country where this is my choice. But I've made up my mind. I'm keeping this baby."

We're standing outside the clinic waiting for the Uber to take us back to school. I'm bouncing up and down with excitement. I literally can't keep still, I'm so excited to meet the baby Nosipho is carrying.

"Babies are so cute," I gush. "They're so adorable. I can't wait for her to be born. Or him. Maybe it's a him.

I'm going to be the best auntie ever. You'll see. I just love babies! Don't you love babies?" I ask Lael.

She pulls a face. "Well…"

"Babies are the best. Just wait until you hold him. Or her."

Lael swallows visibly. "Hold him? Oh, I don't know about that."

"It'll be adorable. And wait until you change her nappy…"

Now she looks seriously green about the gills. "Listen, Trinity, just because you've been babysitting since you were twelve…"

"Oh, I've been looking after babies for longer than that. It's just since I turned twelve that I started charging for it. But I started looking after my little cousins when I was hardly bigger than a baby myself. Babies are the best!"

Nosipho rubs a hand over her tummy. She's been doing that a lot lately. I'm only now starting to realise what it meant. "I'm almost the youngest in my family," she says. "I was always the one the older cousins looked after. I only have two younger cousins. You'd better be on twenty-four-hour call after this one arrives, Trinity. I don't know the first thing about babies."

"Oh, I will, I will!" I give her yet another hug.

She pulls out the money belt she has been carrying in her bag. "Here. I must give you guys back the money you raised."

Lael and I glance at each other. When you've known someone a long time, you don't always need to speak to reach an agreement.

"Absolutely not," she says. "That money is your baby's college fund. Or nappy fund. Or whatever. We all raised it together, and we don't want it back. Trinity agrees with me."

I nod until my neck hurts.

"Yes, I do. It's a done deal. No more discussion. That money is yours. For the baby."

We watch in horror as Nosipho starts to cry again. Then we see that she is smiling too, and we relax. Happy tears are good. We can handle happy tears.

♀

It's only when we are back at school later that Lael comes to speak to me privately.

"Listen, babes. I know you love kids and everything, but I'm really worried about this decision Nosipho has made. She's sixteen years old. She still has two more years of school left, and then who knows how many years of varsity. I don't think she's thought it through. It's going to be much harder than she thinks."

Some of my baby euphoria has cleared away. I've been thinking about this myself. "I know. She has a tough road ahead of her. She's going to need a lot of support."

"She's a child herself. It's not right. Children shouldn't be having children."

Something about this phrase rubs me up the wrong way. I have to think carefully about how to answer her.

"Look," I say at last. "I hear what you're saying. But I don't think it's up to us to decide who should or shouldn't be having babies. I mean, who else shouldn't be having babies? The poor? The mentally ill? Do you hear how that sounds?"

90

"Sure. It sounds wrong, when you explain it like that. I didn't exactly mean it that way."

"I know you didn't. But think about it. Deciding whether to go ahead with a pregnancy is one hundred per cent the woman's choice. It's not up to us to wag fingers at her or second-guess her decision. Our only role is to support her as much as we can."

CHAPTER 6

To: Trinity Luhabe trinityluhabe@gmail.com
From: Secretary to the Headmaster katyaanderssen@
brentwoodcollege.co.za
Re: Spooky Creepo Diary

Dear Trinity,

Thanks for your email to Dr Hussein. The headmaster has authorised me to reply on his behalf. I'm sure you understand that he is a busy man and not able to respond to every student enquiry personally.

You asked about the diary in the display case on the third floor of Albertina Sisulu House. Dr Hussein wants you to know it is part of a display that represents the history of the boarding house – going back to the time when it was for boys only. The display is constantly being refreshed and updated by a curator, which would explain why you haven't seen it before this term. We have a lot of items of historical interest – too many to display at once – so we keep many items in storage and rotate them for display purposes.

I'm afraid I have no explanation for why "the pages seem to be turning themselves like in the movie *Haunted House of Horrors IV*".

I'm also afraid it won't be possible for you to "borrow the diary for a while" even if you do need it for a History project. Our display objects are quite rare and fragile, and aren't lent out to students.

Dr Hussein has instructed me to add the following: "Tell Trinity and her delinquent friends not even to think about trying to pinch the diary from the display case. I might have been lenient once, but I certainly won't be again."

Kind regards,
Katya Anderssen
Secretary to the Headmaster
Brentwood College

To: Secretary to the Headmaster katyaanderssen@brentwood-college.co.za
From: Trinity Luhabe trinityluhabe@gmail.com
Re: Spooky Creepo Diary

Thank you and message received! Please tell Dr Hussein we would never!

Can you possibly tell me who the curator of the display case is?

Yours sincerely,
Trinity

To: Trinity Luhabe trinityluhabe@gmail.com
From: Secretary to the Headmaster katyaanderssen@brent-woodcollege.co.za
Re: Spooky Creepo Diary

Dear Trinity,

The curator is your History teacher, Ms Waise. When she joined the school at the beginning of this year, she brought with her a great enthusiasm for artefacts and antiquities. And furthermore, as we told the Brentwood community in a recent email, she is amply qualified in this regard, having worked as a museum curator for nearly ten years.

So our display collection is in excellent hands and I'm sure Ms Waise would be happy to answer any further questions you might have. The keys to the display case are held by the deputy headmistress, Mrs Govender, who is on long leave in India this term, but Ms Waise will be able to give you more information about the display.

Kind regards,
Katya Anderssen
Secretary to the Headmaster
Brentwood College

So Lael and I are back on the trail of Jim Grey. I'm convinced that the secret of how he died lies in that diary. If only I could get my hands on it. I understand that it's old and fragile and everything, but I'd be really careful with it. Honestly, don't they trust me?

Anyway, it seems that's not an option. Mrs Anderssen made that crystal clear. We thought about pinching the diary for about half a second, but Dr Hussein's warning was just too scary. Neither of us wants to get expelled over this.

Meanwhile, Nosipho seems to be much better, physically and emotionally. She is over the three-month mark now, so she's feeling less vomity and horrible. She has an app on her phone that tells her exactly how big the baby is every day, and what new things are developing. Apparently, it's about the size of a lemon right now. Two weeks ago, it was a kiwi fruit, and in another two weeks it will be an apple. This app is all about the fruit, for some reason.

It's a special app for black moms, so it shows graphics of a black baby instead of a white one. Literally every single book and website we looked at showed pictures of little white babies. How are black moms supposed to imagine what their babies look like?

The only slightly odd thing is that Nosipho hasn't told anyone yet, except for Themba. She still needs to tell her mom and the school. I'm not sure which she is dreading more. She reckons she can put it off for a while because her mom is overseas, and she's not showing yet. But sooner or later she's going to have to face the music.

Meanwhile, Lael and I are in full ghost-hunting mode.

Last night after prep we went upstairs and found that

there was a new page of the diary on display. We took a picture of it on Lael's phone and now I'm waiting for her to get out of Drama and come to break so we can look at it together. I don't know why Drama class always runs late, but it does.

Lael comes rushing up to me. "Sorry I'm late! Sorry! We went over time. We were doing the theatre in the round and learning how to act to an audience that's sitting all around you. It was really interesting and…"

I put up my hand like a traffic cop. "Babes. There's twenty minutes left of break. Let's do this now, or we're going to run out of time."

I hand her the toasted cheese and tomato I got her from the tuckshop, and she takes out her phone.

DEAR DIARY | JUNE 1968

I think Mother is starting to suspect something. I keep noticing her looking at my middle, and yesterday she made a comment that my school skirt seemed tight. I think that if they saw me every day they wouldn't notice anything, but because they only see me at holidays and half-terms it's more obvious.

Anyway, I don't care. I'm not ready to talk about it yet. She'll have to ask me point-blank before I say anything.

The person I really want to speak to is Jim, but of course he's avoiding me. We don't have any classes together. I see him at assembly and we pass each other every morning as we line up and go into breakfast. He's another one who keeps sneaking glances at my tummy.

Last week, I heard he was seeing another girl. Oh, Diary! Can you imagine how that made me feel? I still love him despite everything. And he is the father of my baby, so I will always love him for that.

The girl he was seeing - Barbara - was seen crying her eyes out yesterday. They say he broke up with her because she bored him. I never bored him, Diary. He always said how much he enjoyed talking to me. Oh, why did I have to go and ruin everything like this? If only it could all go back to the way it was.

I'm trying not to think too far into the future, dear Diary. I know this life of mine is going to come crashing down soon. I won't be able to stay in school, and when I leave, I might not see Jim ever again. I should probably enjoy these last few weeks of gazing at him from afar. I just wish I had someone to talk to. There is no one I can trust with a secret this big, except perhaps Loretta. We went through a bad patch in our friendship earlier this year, but it seems to be better now. Maybe I should speak to her. After all, if you can't trust Loretta Mainwaring, who can you trust?

Love,
Amelia

It's weird to be reading this after everything we've gone through with Nosipho.

"It was so different back then," says Lael. "Thank goodness things have changed."

"I think things have changed for some people," I say. "But there are still girls who feel trapped and desperate, and have to put up with being shamed and having their choices taken away. Like when we were in the Raheeda Pelser with Nosipho. It was horrible. That awful nurse had all the power."

"True." Lael's eyes are straying to the screen. She is as fascinated by Amelia's letter as I am.

"In some ways, she's her own worst enemy," I say. "Amelia, I mean. She honestly believes it was all her fault. Like she went and got pregnant on her own. Meanwhile, it sounds like Jim really pressurised her into it."

Lael huffs and frowns. "Yes. Your Jim doesn't come out of this looking all that good."

"My Jim? Since when is he my Jim?"

"Since you were the only person ever to see him, remember?"

"That doesn't make him my Jim." To tell the truth, I've been thinking of him as my Jim ever since we found out that he died in Sisulu House in 1968. But now that I know how badly he treated poor Amelia, I feel like he can be someone else's Jim for a while. "I told you at the time how obnoxious he was. How he was sexist and racist and … and relgiousist."

"Anti-Semitic," Lael corrects.

"Right. I knew that. The thing is, we knew from the beginning what he was like."

"You know, we mustn't lose sight of our original mission," says Lael. "We started this to find out how Jim died. How does a healthy sixteen-year-old boy drop down dead in his own boarding-house during the holidays?"

"I also want to know what happened to Amelia. Did she make up with Jim? Did she have the baby? Imagine if she did. That kid could still be living in Joburg somewhere. How old would it be now?"

"Fifty," she says without even having to think about it. (And that, ladies and gentlemen, is why Lael is doing

AP Maths while I'm begging my parents to let me drop to Maths Lit.)

"That means Amelia would be sixty-six." (Yes, even I can add sixteen plus fifty.) "That's pretty ancient."

"If only we knew her surname, we could track her down."

"We still could!" I say, feeling a surge of excitement.

"What do you mean?"

"There must have been news reports when Jim died. It was the 1960s and he was a middle-class white boy on school property. It must have been in the newspapers."

Lael pulls a face. "I already checked, remember? I couldn't find a reference to it anywhere."

"Okay, but Google isn't the answer to everything. I bet there are plenty of old news stories that aren't online yet. The information could be out there somewhere just waiting for us to find it."

The next day at break, Lael and I stroll into the school library, trying to look as though this is something we do all the time. We avert our faces and slide past the reception desk, but a booming voice stops us.

"Good grief!" says the voice. "It's going to snow – definitely and for sure."

With a sigh, we turn to face Mrs Naidoo, the school librarian.

"Good morning, Mrs Naidoo," we say.

"Make that sleet and hail and hurricane too," she booms. For a librarian, she has the loudest voice you've ever heard. "I never thought I would see Trinity Luhabe darken the doors of my library unless someone were holding a gun to her head."

"What?" I'm insulted. "I read! I'm a reader. I read all the time."

"'Vampire Babes and the Demons Who Love Them'," she says. (Which is totally a made-up title.) " 'The Ghost Who Loves Me'. 'I Fell in Love with an Extra-terrestrial'. 'Betrayed by a Werewolf'." (More made-up titles. Mind you – I would defs read a book called "Betrayed by a Werewolf").

"Come on, Mrs Naidoo." Lael is trying not to grin. "You always told us that reading was reading. Whether it was Shakespeare or the back of a cereal box, you were happy as long as we were reading."

"Hmm." Mrs Naidoo won't concede a thing. "I'd prefer it if your friend didn't read everything on Amazon Kindle, Ms Lieberman. It's like she's trying to put us librarians out of business."

"How about if I promise to check out an actual paper book before break is over, Mrs N? Then will you help us?"

She beams. "Deal! Now what do you girls need help with?"

We explain that we are interested in finding out how a student died in Sisulu House in the 1960s. I'm half expecting Mrs Naidoo to turn all cold and silent on us. She'd be like, "WHY DO YOU WANT TO KNOW THAT?" And we'd be like, "We're just interested. It's a mystery, isn't it?" And she'd be like, "You girls shouldn't meddle in things that don't concern you." And we'd say, "We're not meddling. We just want to find out the truth. What harm could it do after fifty years?" And then she'd slam a stapler down on the desk. (No, a punch. A big, heavy one.) She'd order us to get out of the library immediately, and just as we were leaving, she'd yell, "Do you know what happens to nosy little girls? They get hurt, that's what. You stay away from the mystery of Jim Grey or you'll get hurt too."

Okay, it's possible that Lael is right, and I do watch too much TV.

Anyway, none of that actually happens. Mrs Naidoo gets swept up in the whole thing, so much so that we have to stop her from taking it all over herself.

"Fascinating!" she keeps saying. "How absolutely fascinating. It's a real-life mystery, isn't it? Ooh, I'd love to know what happened. Why don't I go and do a search on microfiche and you can come to me tomorrow for the..."

"Uh ... Mrs Naidoo..." Lael interrupts.

"Yes, dear?"

"We kind of want to do this ourselves. It's like our project for the term. In fact, we're thinking of incorporating it into our self-study assignment for History."

This is news to me, but it sounds like an excellent idea, so I nod along enthusiastically. This way we can spend actual school time on it, not just breaks and afternoons.

Mrs Naidoo pushes her disappointment aside. "Of course, Ms Lieberman, you're quite right. If you come to the reference room, I'll show you how to work the microfiche machine. Just promise me you'll let me read your project when you're finished? I'm dying to find out what happened to him."

"Of course!" says Lael.

Mrs Naidoo takes us into the back room where I haven't set foot since they gave us a tour of the library in, like,

Grade One or something. I mean, who needs a reference library when you've got Google, am I right? Well, apart from us, obviously, since we're here.

She dims the lights, and everything goes spooky and dark. Then she switches on a machine that looks like a photocopier, but without a cover. It glows into life. She shows us a cabinet of files with pull-out drawers. Each drawer has a year printed on it and is filled with alphabetical dividers. In each divider is a strip of what looks exactly like photograph negatives. I only know what they look like because I did Photography Club for a couple of terms. Mrs Naidoo explains that each negative contains an article from a newspaper and is filed alphabetically according to the title of the article.

We watch as she takes one of the negatives out and lies it flat on the glowing machine. She shows us how to look through the viewer to see the article. When it's my turn, I give a little squeak of amazement. There is the whole article in nice big letters, exactly as it would have appeared in the newspaper, pictures and all. I try moving it to the right to see the next column, but it moves to the left.

Mrs Naidoo laughs. "Everything is reversed on a microfiche machine. If you want to move it up, you have to move it down. If you want to move it right, you have to move it left, and so on. It takes a bit of getting used to."

"This is amazing!" says Lael. "Thanks so much, Mrs N."

"It's a pleasure. You girls have got until the end of break. Good luck finding what you're looking for. If you need any help, just come and ask."

As soon as she leaves, we rush over to the filing cabinet.

"Okay, what are we looking for?"

"There must have been a newspaper article about his death," I say. "What would it have been called?"

"Uh … Brentwood Boy Found Dead in Boarding House?"

We scrabble in the "B" divider for 1968 but find nothing.

"Dead Boy Identified as Son of Prominent Farmer?" I suggest.

Nothing under "D" either.

"Late Learner Loved Life."

Lael gives me a major side-eye, but checks in the "L" divider anyway. Nothing there either.

We eventually find it under "S" for school, as in "Schoolboy Found Murdered in Boarding House."

"Aha," says Lael. "My headline was the closest."

I stare at the headline, which has been handwritten in koki pen on a strip of paper on the side of the negative.

"Murdered?" I say. "He was murdered?"

It's stupid, but this makes it more real somehow. I feel almost as shocked as I did when I first found out he was dead. He seemed so alive when I knew him last term – so real and annoying and Jim-like. Why would anyone have wanted to murder him?

Lael puts her arm around my shoulders. She always knows when I'm upset – and why.

"I'm sorry, Trinity. I know this is hard for you. But we suspected this, didn't we? Sixteen-year-old boys don't drop dead for no reason. He hadn't fallen or had an accident, or anything like that. He was found sitting in a chair in the common-room. Someone must have done something to him."

"I know." I give myself a shake. "I'm all right now.

Let's read this article and find out what happened."

JOHANNESBURG The body of a schoolboy was found in
the boarding-house of a prominent private school early this
morning. The 16-year-old boy has been identified as Jim
Grey, a pupil at Brentwood College in Inanda.

A black cleaning girl found the body in the common room
of Jan Smuts boarding house at seven o'clock this morning.
It is not known what the boy was doing on school property as
school holidays commenced two
days ago.

According to Brentwood headmaster, Willem Labuschagne,
Grey was a popular boy who excelled at sport and academics,
and was expected to go far in life. He came from a farming
family in the Brits area.

Police are treating the death as suspicious and have
appealed to anyone with information to come forward.

"A black cleaning girl," I read out loud. "Charming. Like
her skin colour is somehow relevant to the story."

"Not to mention infantilising her with the word 'girl',"
Lael adds.

"I'm gladder than ever that we don't live in 1968."

"Remember what Mr Magaqa always says?" Lael says,
referring to our English teacher, who is really woke and
a cool guy. "There's just as much racism around today as
there was in the old days – it's just gone underground."

"I hear you. But I'm still glad I don't live in a time
when a cleaner gets referred to as 'a black cleaning girl'
in a national newspaper."

"This story doesn't tell us much more than we already
knew." Lael frowns at the strip of microfiche. "But at least

we know that it did make the news, and that the police investigated it."

She starts to slip the strip back into its divider when I stop her.

"Wait a minute. There's something else in there."

We pull open the divider and find another strip of microfiche half-hidden in the seam. It looks as though articles relating to the same story were filed together. This one says "Police launch manhunt for brother of murdered boy's girlfriend."

Lael and I stare at each other with eyes like saucers.

"Brother of murdered boy's girlfriend?" I say. "Amelia's brother? She hasn't mentioned any other family besides her parents."

"Quick, quick! Let's read it."

There is a brief tussle for possession of the strip. I win and plonk myself down at the machine. As a consolation prize, I read the article out loud to her.

JOHANNESBURG Police have launched a nationwide manhunt for Jack Lucite, a white male, who is wanted in connection with the murder of Brentwood scholar Jim Grey. Grey's body was found in the common room of Jan Smuts House at Brentwood College last week.

Jack Lucite is the brother of Amelia Lucite, formerly a Standard Eight pupil at Brentwood College. Headmaster Willem Labuschagne commented, "Yes, I can confirm that Amelia Lucite was until recently registered as a pupil at our school. She was removed by mutual agreement between her parents and the Governing Body. We believe she is now being educated privately at home."

Jack Lucite was last seen in Brits six days ago. A local

resident reports that he was talking wildly about going to Johannesburg to restore his sister's honour. "He said he was going to *sort out* that spoiled brat, Jim Grey," the resident told our reporter. "He was going to make him take responsibility or he wouldn't be answerable for his actions."

Anyone with information on the whereabouts of Jack Lucite should contact their nearest police station.

"You've got to love the euphemisms," Lael says when I finish reading.

"You mean like Amelia being removed from school 'by mutual agreement'? *Ja*, it's pretty clear that they kicked her out for being pregnant."

"This article makes it look like Amelia's brother did it. That he murdered Jim in a fit of rage and left him there for the cleaners to find."

Lael and I look at each other. It's a neat explanation, and one that the police were obviously pursuing, but for some reason I don't feel completely happy about it. And judging by her face, neither does Lael.

We dig around in the divider, looking for more strips of microfiche, but there's nothing.

"You know who would have more information about this story?" Lael says. "The local newspapers. I bet they have archives going back to when they first started."

Just then the bell rings, and we pack everything up in a hurry so we can head off to class. We both have Business Studies straight after break.

"Hey, your dad doesn't own any newspapers, does he?" Lael asks as we hurry along.

"Hmm." I try to think. My dad's company is called UbuntuGold and they own a lot of stuff. As in, a *lot*. But

I can't think of any newspapers at the moment. Not off hand.

"I don't think so," I say at last. "Why?"

"Because I don't think you can just waltz into a media building and demand access to their archives. Not when you're our age, anyway. We would need special permission."

As she says the word 'media', it jogs my memory into life. "Oh, hey. I've just remembered. He owns Tribune Media SA. Does that count?"

We come to a halt outside the Business Studies classroom and Lael gives me a patient stare. "Babes. That's only the biggest media corporation in the country. They own most of the newspapers in Joburg, including the one we were just looking at. And you're, like, 'Newspapers? Nah, fam. I don't think so.' I mean, seriously?"

"Okay, okay. I just forgot for a minute. It's hard to keep track."

CHAPTER 7

To: Trinity Luhabe trinityluhabe@gmail.com
From: Melinda Mmabatho melindammabatho@preggiebellies.
co.za
Re: Bulk Order of Preggie Belly™ Model No. 578/SM

Dear Ms Luhabe,

I hereby confirm that your order of fifteen (15) Preggie Belly™ velcro cushions, Model No. 578/SM, has been shipped this morning. You requested express delivery so we employed an overnight courier to handle the delivery. I trust there will be someone present at the Sandhurst address you gave me to sign for the delivery tomorrow morning.

As I mentioned on the phone, our Preggie Belly™ cushions are normally purchased by maternity shops so that expectant moms who aren't showing much yet can try their clothes on with a velcro cushion. They can then anticipate how the clothes will look and fit later on in their pregnancies.

We have occasionally sold our products to individuals, but never such a large order as this. We at Preggie Belly™ are all still wondering what you could possibly need fifteen of them for. You mentioned something about being a Social Justice Warrior, but that only made us more curious.

Still, the payment is all in order and the shipment has been dispatched. Many thanks for the business!

Kind regards,
Melinda Mmabatho
Head of Sales

To: Trinity Luhabe trinityluhabe@gmail.com
From: Xolela Parrish xolelaparrish@TribuneMediaSA.co.za
Re: Permission to access archives

Dear Ms Luhabe,

Your father mentioned to our Managing Editor that you would
be emailing us. You and your friend Lael Lieberman would
be very welcome to spend time in our archives room for your
school project.

Just announce yourselves at reception and you will be supplied
with ID lanyards. Someone will come down to lead you to the
basement where the archives are stored. Our records are
digitised as far back as 1970. If you need articles from before
then, they are available on microfiche. We do have hard copies
of every edition of the newspaper going back to 1919, but they
are fragile and handled only in exceptional circumstances.

We look forward to welcoming you to the *Gauteng Tribune.*

Kind regards,
Xolela Parrish
Staff Writer

We have a crisis on our hands.

Nosipho got called into a meeting with the head of the Life Orientation Department and some other teachers. The head of LO is called Mrs Oosthuizen, and she's an old bat with the most ridiculous ideas you ever heard. I wish they'd make Ms Bhamjee head of LO. She's been teaching us since Grade Eight and she's awesome.

Anyway, they told Nosipho that they had "received reports" that she might be pregnant, and was it true? So, she said it was, and that she was planning on keeping the baby. Then they threatened to tell her mom. And she said good luck tracking her down in Washington DC, and that she would tell her mom herself when she was ready. She also said that the aunt she is staying with knows all about the pregnancy and is supporting her decision. (Which is absolutely true.)

So then, if you can believe it, they said it was "problematic for the school's image" to have a pregnant learner in Grade Ten, and that she should either go to a private cram college for the rest of the year or do home-schooling. They told her they'd keep a place open for her to return to school next year if she wanted, which is something, I suppose. But they didn't seem to think that she would even want to return.

Apparently, Nosipho has thirty days' notice, at the end of which she must have "made other arrangements" and left the school.

Nosipho told us all this after school today. She was looking a bit pale and upset, but otherwise amazingly strong. If it were me, I'd be falling apart right now.

"That doesn't sound right to me," Lael says. "I can't

believe they're allowed to do this. We need to do something. We need to think of something."

"What I want to know is, who tipped them off?" says Nosipho. "I know it wasn't you guys, and I know it wasn't my aunt. Who else could it have been?"

"I can think of one candidate…" I say.

"Sophie Agincourt?" says Lael. "But how? I know she was suspicious, but she didn't have any proof."

"Think about it. Who was sneaking around going through our bins in the dorm? Who found the pregnancy tests? It has to be her. Who else could it be?"

"But why?" Nosipho says. "I don't even know her that well. Why would she do that to me?"

"Sophie doesn't need a reason," I say. "She just needs an opportunity. Telling on people and getting them into trouble has been her favourite thing since Grade One."

"I wish I could get back at her," Nosipho sighs.

I shake my head like the wise elder. "Don't even go there, young Padawan. Many have tried and many have failed. Believe me, I know."

Nosipho shrugs. "Okay. I suppose I won't have much opportunity anyway. You know … while I'm being home-schooled."

"That is not going to happen," I say. "We won't allow it. We're going to think of something."

Nosipho and Lael turn to me with hope in their faces. "Have you thought of a plan, Trinity?"

"Not yet. But let's sleep on it, and talk about it again tomorrow. We'll have thought of something by then, for sure."

♀

"Can I ask you something?" I say as my mom comes into my room to say goodnight to me that evening.

"Of course, my skattebol. Anything. Ask away."

"Okay … let' s just say … hypothetically speaking … that something was going on at school that wasn't right. And you had to decide whether to – *don't sit down!*" I yell as my mother plonks herself comfortably on the foot of my bed.

"Too late." She gives me a smug smile.

"Aargh!" I clutch my hair. "Mommmm! This is not a sit-down chat. It's nearly ten o'clock. I need to sleep. Stand up!"

"Nope."

I rock backwards and forwards in frustration. Once my mom sits down, there is no getting rid of her. She'll be here chatting half the night. She knows the rules – no sitting in my bedroom. But there she is, propping a cushion behind her back, getting comfortable.

"So … something at school, you say?"

I give in. The fastest way to get her out of here is to move the discussion along.

"Okay, let's say there was something happening at school that just wasn't right. And you wanted to make them change their minds about it. How would you go about it?"

My mom sits up like a soldier hearing the call to battle. She gives a power salute. "Protest action, of course."

I sigh hugely. "Mom … this isn't apartheid. We're not protesting the Group Areas Act. This is just a school thing."

"Doesn't matter. Injustice is injustice. This is a case of injustice, isn't it?"

I think about Nosipho being forced to move out of the boarding house, to leave school and try to get educated at home just because she happens to be pregnant. And I think about how nothing at all will happen to Themba, despite the fact that he is fifty per cent responsible for the situation. "Yes," I say. "This is about injustice."

"Mooi so!" She rubs her hands together.

I roll my eyes. "Really, Mom? I tell you there is injustice at my school, and your answer is mooi so? There's nothing mooi about it."

She clears her throat and looks a bit embarrassed. "What I meant was, we can work out a plan of action now that we know what we're dealing with. I will mobilise some protestors, and we can organise banners, and maybe get buses to bring in a crowd, and we'll get permission from the cops to hold a rally…"

"Hey, wait a minute!" I feel like one of those buses of hers is about to run over me. "It's not that kind of thing. My friends and I want to handle this our own way."

Her face falls. Then she perks up again. "Well, listen, I can still mobilise the NGO to raise awareness and conscientise the masses and…"

I drop my head into my hands. My mom runs this NGO that always seems to be fighting a different cause. One minute they are providing counselling for victims of domestic abuse, the next they are collecting clothes for the elderly, and the next they are putting together food parcels for children. They are always trying to raise funds, but they keep going bankrupt and having to be bailed out by my dad.

I know they mean well and everything, and they do really good work most of the time, but they are not exactly efficient. Basically, I don't want them anywhere near this problem. But how do I say that diplomatically?

"Mom ... the NGO is a total nightmare. They can't even organise blankets for Mandela Day without holding five committee meetings first. If you get them involved in this, I'm going to run away from home and go and live with Ouma and Oupa in Polokwane."

Okay, maybe that wasn't diplomatic, but at least it got my point across.

"Ag, okay my girlie. Point taken. So, what do you want from me if not my help?"

"Your advice," I say. "We really need your advice on how to go about this. How do we get an institution – like, hypothetically speaking, a school – to pay attention to our grievances?"

"That's easy. You make them uncomfortable. You make them so uncomfortable that they can't ignore you any-more. You hit them where it hurts. And if this hypothetical school happened to be a private school like Brentwood – you hit them with their public image. That's their Achilles heel. It's all about PR with these bourgeois places."

Needless to say, Mom wanted to send the three of us to the local government school, but Dad put his foot down.

"Hmm." An idea is starting to take shape in my mind. "PR ... public image ... hit them where it hurts. I can work with this. I can definitely work with this. Thanks, Mom!"

At this point, any other mother would be worrying about what kind of madness she had unleashed, but not my mom. Not the woman who got tear-gassed last year at a Fees Must Fall protest at Wits.

She just smiles and pats my leg. "It's a pleasure, skat. Now try to get some sleep."

Three days later when I get home from school, my parents' home manager comes to tell me that he signed for a parcel while I was out. The nice thing about him is that he doesn't run to my parents about every little package I might have ordered that gets delivered to the house. Or big package, for that matter. Because the box that has just arrived from the Preggie Belly people is not exactly small. Also, it has the Preggie Belly logo plastered all over it in huge letters.

He just hands the box over to me (or rather, gives it a hard shove across the floor in my direction) and tells me to have a nice day. I ask him nicely if someone could possibly bring it up to my room. They could even use the lift if necessary.

He gives me a patient smile and picks it up himself.

When I'm alone in my room with the box, I rip into it to see if the contents are as good as the website promised. And they totally are. This is so exciting! Now I just have to smuggle them slowly into the Grade Ten dorm at Sisulu House over the next few days, and then we can start hatching our plan.

It takes me five days to get them all into place, at a rate of three a day. They really are amazingly big and unsquishable. I put three into a backpack each day and take them in along with my usual school stuff, and it looks like I'm going hiking in the Himalayas. Thank goodness, they're not heavy if you only take three at a time.

On the last day, when I have hidden all fifteen of them in the spare cupboard at the back of the dorm, I call a meeting after prep with Lael and Nosipho. I haven't told them what I was up to, or shown them the Bellies, because I wanted it to be a surprise.

"Surprise!" I say, and pull the cupboard open with a flourish.

About six Preggie Bellies tumble out onto the floor. I stuff them back into place in case someone comes in.

"Babes," says Nosipho. "What on earth?"

"This is how we are going to get you to stay at school," I announce.

Lael and Nosipho stare at the Bellies with identical "Huh?" expressions.

"So … we're going to … pile cushions on top of them until they relent?" suggests Lael.

"Drop cushions on their heads when they walk past until they let me stay?" ventures Nosipho.

"You guys are hilarious," I say. "Now, if you will allow me to demonstrate…" I take one of the bellies and strap it onto my tummy, and drape my school shirt over it. Instantly I look about nine months pregnant. Not fat. Not plump. Not slightly pregnant. Full-on, about-to-give-birth, get-this-woman-to-a-hospital, nine months pregnant.

"Wow," Lael and Nosipho say together.

"So, here's the plan," I say. "I ordered fifteen of these. We get fifteen Brentwood girls to wear these to school every single day as a protest against Nosipho's exclusion. So instead of having to worry about one pregnant learner and what she might be doing to the school's image, they will have to worry about fifteen. Hopefully that will make them realise how ridiculous they are being."

"What if they decide to kick you guys out as well?" Nosipho asks.

"They can't expel fifteen of us. It will turn into a total PR nightmare. Plus, we'll wear the bellies to Sandton City and the Zone and Montecasino, and all over the place in full school uniform. If they don't want to be known as the pregnancy capital of Inanda, they will cave, and cave quickly."

A smile is spreading across Lael's face. "This is actually a genius plan, Luhabe. How did you come up with it?"

"No need to sound so surprised. I have genius ideas sometimes. But actually, it was something my mom said that gave me the idea. She said hit them where it hurts – their public image. I thought, what would give them more of a nightmare than fifteen pregnant schoolgirls?"

"Let me try one on." Nosipho takes one of the Bellies from the cupboard and starts to strap it on. As she lifts her shirt I can see for the first time that her tummy is changing shape. It is still completely invisible under clothes, but there is definitely a difference, especially if you look at it sideways.

I find it incredibly thrilling to think of the new life growing inside her. But I manage to restrain myself from rushing over and making squee noises and demanding to touch. Apparently pregnant women don't like it when you do that. I know! Totally unreasonable, right?

When I'm pregnant (sometime in the far distance future, I hope), I'm going to hang a sign around my neck that says FREE BELLY RUBS. Actually, no, I'm not. Eww. Now that I come to think of it, that's a totally gross idea. Hands off the belly. My belly, my choice.

Nosipho is swanning about in front of the mirror,

twisting and turning her head to look at herself from every direction.

"Look at this, guys! Look at me. This is what I'm going to look like in about five months' time. How awesome is this?"

We grin at her reflection in the mirror. "So awesome!"

"Now we just need to think of twelve more girls to do this with us," she says. "Who do you think? I thought maybe Amira and…"

"Hang on a sec," Lael stops her. "I don't think you should be part of it."

Nosipho's face drops. "Why not? I mean, it's my thing, after all."

"Do you agree with me, Trinity?" Lael asks.

"Yes, definitely. It must be like it has nothing to do with you whatsoever. As if it was just a bunch of us who spontaneously decided to start doing this."

"Which it was," Lael adds.

"Which it was," I agree. "It'll make it stronger if you aren't a part of it at all. Like, you're not their problem anymore – we are."

Nosipho thinks about this for a moment. Then she says, "Okay. Okay, I see what you're saying. I kind of wish I could be in on the fun, but I understand why you want me to sit this one out. Who are you going to get to do it with you?"

Lael starts counting on her fingers. "Definitely Yasmin and Amira. Definitely not Sophie."

"The snitch? Ja. No way."

"I think it would be stronger if it's not just a Grade Ten thing – if we got girls from other grades to take part too. Maybe even some matrics."

"They're stressing about Prelims now, but I'm sure we'll find some who are willing," I say. "And there's that Grade Nine girl that Aaron is dating. What's her name again?"

"Gugu. Yes, she's cool. She'll do it."

Slowly and carefully, we put together a list of girls we think will join us in our crusade. It can't be anyone who is going to chicken out or ditch us at the last minute. It also can't be anyone who will run to the teachers and tell them what we're up to.

Soon we have a list of twelve warriors that we all agree are a sure bet. But we are still one short. We kick around a few more names, but no one seems quite right.

"Hey, light-bulb moment!" says Nosipho. "What about Munashe?"

"A boy?" I ask.

"Yes, why not? Won't that make it stronger – that it's not just girls who care about this issue, but boys too?"

"They'll know he's just doing it because Trinity told him to," Lael says.

"True," I agree. "But that doesn't matter. We know we can trust him to go through with it. And let's face it, how many boys do we know who would agree to wear a pregnant tummy to assembly?"

Munashe has been in love with me since Grade Nought. His dad's family and my dad's family come from the same village in the Eastern Cape. He's okay because he doesn't mind that we're just friends. We've tried dating from time to time, but it never seems to last more than a few days. Eventually, he is going to accept what I have already realised – that we are destined to be buds and nothing more.

☥

It's half-term now and the Belly Protest, as it is officially known, has been postponed to next week when school starts again. We thought about maybe going around the shopping centres in our bellies over the long weekend, but let's face it, how often do you run into teachers outside of school? Not all that often, right? So it would be a waste of time.

In the meantime, Lael and I are making progress with the other pregnant girl in our lives – Amelia Lucite.

I asked my dad if he could get us permission to use the archives room at the *Gauteng Tribune* (formerly the *Johannesburg Tribune*), and he organised it in a flash. A lady called Xolela emailed me back and said we could come any time.

We planned to go on Friday, the first day of half-term, but it didn't work out. I woke up at noon and messaged Lael, but she was still asleep. Then we spent the afternoon alternating between watching Netflix and napping some more. That's basically what the start of every school holiday is like – we collapse in a heap to recover from all the homework the teachers give us and the pressure our parents put on us.

Anyway, by Saturday we're feeling much better. I wake up at 11am, which is basically dawn in school-holiday time. After lunch, I ask Lungile to swing past Sisulu House to pick up Lael, and then he drops us both at the office of the *Gauteng Tribune*.

It is right next to *Jozi Talks* radio, which is my favourite radio station of all time. We listen to it in the car every morning on the way to school. I'm a huge fan. Unfortunately, my dad doesn't own them too, because I would *love* to work there one day.

As Lungi drops us off at the entrance to the *Tribune* and drives off, we give each other a nervous look.

"You're sure your dad set this all up?"

"Of course!"

"They are definitely expecting us? It wasn't just some vague, 'call and make an appointment sometime' thing?"

"Give me some credit. It was an open invitation. Come any time. Bring your friend. It's all good."

Lael takes a deep breath. "Okay, then."

We walk inside and go up to the reception desk. For a horrible moment, it seems as if the receptionist has absolutely no idea what we are talking about. Then she asks us for the name of our contact person, and of course my mind goes completely blank.

"Uh…" I stare at her like a twit.

"Didn't you say it was Xolela?" Lael reminds me.

"Yes!" I say in relief. "Her name is Xolela."

"We have three Xolelas working here," the receptionist informs me. "Which one do you want?"

Three? Good grief.

"Just a moment, please." I take out my phone and scroll through my emails, hoping it hasn't been deleted. "Xolela Parrish!" I announce. "That's her name. It says here she's a staff writer."

"She's not in today." The receptionist sounds impatient by now. "She works every second Saturday. Can I have your name, please?"

"Trinity Luhabe."

There is a long pause as she sits there with her finger frozen over her touch screen. "Luhabe?" she repeats slowly. "Any relation of…?"

"Um, yes. He's my dad."

The attitude change is instant and complete. "I'm so sorry to keep you waiting, Ms Luhabe. My apologies. I had no idea. If you wait one more second, I'll get your lanyards ready and somebody will be down here to show you the way to the archive room."

In two minutes flat, we are in a lift going down to the basement.

Lael grins at me. "Listen, I know you hate it, but you have to admit it's very convenient to be able to flash your dad's name around like that and get five-star service."

"I didn't flash my dad's name around!" I say. "She asked me my name and I told her. And then she *asked* me if I was related to him and I told the truth. I would never…"

Lael touches my arm. "I know. I'm sorry. I didn't mean it like that. I know you never flash your family's name around. But, come on. You must admit it's useful."

"I wish we lived in a world where people treated you decently before they knew your surname," I grumble. "But I guess this is all in a good cause. We're going to find out what happened to poor Amelia, and hopefully also what happened to Jim. And then we can, you know, release him from his earthly torment."

This earns me a slight side-eye from our guide. I smile and explain nothing.

Lael and I came up with a theory last term that Jim was stuck in the human world because his death has never been solved. We reckon if we can find out what happened to him, he will be free to 'move on'.

Our guide is one of the junior reporters on the *Tribune*. He takes us down to the archive room and shows us how to do a search by theme, date, person or place. The

Tribune's records are much better organised than the ones in the school library. He tells us we can come and call him if we need more help, and then he leaves us to it.

I sit down at the computer. "What should we search for?"

"Search for Amelia's brother's name. What was it again?"

"Jack. Jack Lucite."

"That's right. If he was suspected of murder, he must be in there somewhere."

I enter his name into the search box and get an instant hit. "There are two articles tagged with that name. They both have the same file number."

"Okay, great. If you write it on a piece of paper, I'll go and look for it."

There are pencils and scraps of paper everywhere. I hand the reference to Lael and she disappears among the dusty stacks.

A creepy silence settles over the room as the sound of Lael's footsteps fades away. A beam of sunlight from the window hits the floor at a slight angle, highlighting a thin layer of dust. Little floating particles in the air turn golden and sparkly as they twist and dance in the sun.

I almost fall asleep watching them. Then I jerk awake and grab my phone to check the time. That's when I realise that Lael has been gone for a long time. A weirdly long time.

"Hey, are you still alive in there?" I call.

There's no answer.

"Lael! Where did you go?"

Silence.

I think about sending her a WhatsApp, but then I see

she left her phone on the desk next to me. So now what? What if she's gone forever? What if the archive monster got her?

I walk in the same direction she did, but stop when the high stacks on either side of me start shutting out the light. What if the monster gets me too?

I hurry back to the desk, where at least I'm within sight of an open door.

"Lael?" I yell. "Stop fooling around. If you don't come out now, I'm going home without you. They'll find your body in the morning, I'm warning you. And you're wearing your oldest jeans!"

Still nothing.

I open my mouth to shout again. Then I nearly have a heart attack when a hand lands on my shoulder. A scream rips from my throat before I can stop it.

It's Lael. Of course it is.

She's laughing so hard she is nearly bent double.

"You are so mean!"

"You are so gullible. *Lael!*" she imitates in a high, squeaky voice. "*Lael, where have you gone? Answer me, Lael!*"

I try to stop it, but I can't help the grin that spreads across my face. Maybe I was being a bit dramatic.

"What took you so long anyway? Did you get it?"

She puts a file on the desk. "Yes, I got it. It just took me forever to figure out their filing system."

"Great! Let's have a look." I take the file from her and remove the two strips of microfiche film from inside. "Okay, this is the one we've already seen about how they are looking for the brother in connection with Jim Grey's death. Now let's check the other one."

JOHANNESBURG Police confirm that they have questioned and released Brits resident, Jack Lucite, who was wanted for questioning in connection with the death of Jim Grey. Grey, 16, was a Standard Eight pupil at Brentwood College in the leafy suburb of Inanda.

A manhunt was launched for Mr Lucite five days ago when it was reported that he had been heard uttering threats against the person of Jim Grey prior to his death. He told acquaintances of his intention to
"restore his sister's honour".

Grey was subsequently found dead in the common room of Jan Smuts boarding house at Brentwood College.

Police uttered a terse "No comment" when asked by our reporter why Mr Lucite was released so soon after questioning. Sources say that Mr Lucite was able to prove that he was in the company of a female at a Hillbrow nightclub during the time of Jim Grey's death. This has not been confirmed by the police.

Captain 'Blikkies' Bezuidenhout of the Brixton Murder and Robbery Squad told the *Tribune* that Jack Lucite is no longer regarded as a person of interest in this matter. Other avenues of investigation are being diligently pursued.

I finish reading the article out loud to Lael. Then she takes my place at the microfiche machine to read it again herself.

"So that was a dead end?" She looks up when she's done.

"The deadest. What do you think they mean by 'other avenues of investigation'?"

"Not a clue."

We stare at each other in frustration. How can we have come this far only to hit a wall now?

"Let's see if there are any other articles about Jim's death. This can't be the end of it. What should I search for?"

Lael ticks off the search terms on her fingers. "Jim Grey. Brentwood College. Amelia Lucite. Jan Smuts House. Um … murder, death? No, that will get too many hits."

I search for everything she suggests and get just one more hit apart from the articles we've already read, both here and at the school library. This time I go and fetch it because I don't trust her not to pull another prank on me.

JOHANNESBURG As deceased schoolboy Jim Grey was laid to rest today, police have officially declared his death to have been due to natural causes.

The funeral took place at St Martin's in the Veld Anglican Church in Dunkeld, and was attended by family, friends, and local dignitaries.

Jim Grey, who passed away at the age of sixteen, was the son of James and Annamarie Grey, whose family has farmed maize in the Brits area for generations. The young lad was found by cleaning staff in the common room of Jan Smuts boarding-house at his school – Brentwood College.

Police pursued numerous avenues of investigation before declaring the apparently mysterious death to be due to natural causes. An anonymous source inside the Brixton Murder and Robbery Squad told the Johannesburg Tribune, "His heart just stopped beating. They can't find a reason for it, so it must have been a natural death."

Jim Grey is survived by his parents. "He was our only

child," James Grey said in his eulogy. "He was our hope to continue the honourable line of Grey farmers, but now that hope has been extinguished."

I frown. "I've said it before and I'll say it again – sixteen-year-old boys don't drop dead for no reason."

"No, they don't. Not just sitting in a chair like that. Not unless they have a serious medical condition, which the newspapers don't mention."

"And what was he doing there in the first place?" I say. "It was during the school holidays. Everyone else had gone home, even the teachers. Only the cleaning staff were still there."

"Exactly. He must have been there for a reason."

"Wait," I say. "What if there's someone alive today who still remembers what happened? There must be someone we can talk to about it."

Lael nods eagerly. "We should make a note of all the names we've come across so far. And maybe the diary will tell us more."

CHAPTER 8

To: Trinity Luhabe trinityluhabe@gmail.com
From: President of the Paranormal Association of South Africa
    admin@paranormalSA.com
Re: Ghost of Sisulu House

Dear Ms Luhabe,

I'm sorry to hear that your ghost-hunting has been unsuccessful so far. I must admit that I am very surprised because you are already in possession of our latest state-of-the-art equipment. If there were any paranormal activity to detect, the full-spectrum camcorder, chromatograph and EMF-meter would have detected it.

Perhaps your ghost is just shy! We get that sometimes. Beings of the spirit world are not always as willing to come forward as we would like them to be. I agree that the blip you detected some weeks ago sounds very promising, but unfortunately there is no way we can compel your spirit to repeat the performance.

I understand that you are not willing to hold a séance because, as you put it, "My mom would kill me and then we'd both be dead and what would be the point?" But I can strongly recommend our modern and fully digital Paranormal Automatic Writing Machine™ for the very reasonable sum of R1,950.99. This is a completely updated version of the old-fashioned planchettes which – while they had some success in the old days – were notoriously unreliable, and able to be interfered with by human agency.

The Paranormal Automatic Writing Machine™ is always on and always active, producing letters and words in a random sequence.

It is highly sensitive to manipulation by the spirit realm, so if your ghost wishes to communicate with you, he will cause it to spell out words that have significance to him. Best of all, the Paranormal Automatic Writing Machine™ is completely tamper-proof and cannot be influenced by humans in any way. Please don't hesitate to tap on the 1-click link above should you wish to order this superior product.

As always, we wish you all success in your ghost-hunting endeavours.

Kind regards
Eufemia Batton
Paranormal Association of South Africa

WHAT TO EXPECT AT 14 WEEKS (from www.whattoexpect.com)

BABY IS STANDING UP STRAIGHT
Growing by leaps and bounds, your baby is leaping and bounding. Now the size of your clenched fist, he's on the move almost constantly — and those movements are a far cry from those jerky twitches of last trimester (though you won't feel any of them for weeks to come). They are now ballet-like, smooth and fluid. Speaking of ballet, it'll be years before you'll start nagging your offspring to stand up straight — but unbelievably, he is doing it right now, without any prodding! No slouch anymore, your baby's neck is getting longer, helping his head stand more erect. This gives your foetus a more straightened-out appearance.

BABY IS SPROUTING HAIR AND LANUGO
By week 14 of pregnancy, your baby could be sprouting some hair and the eyebrows are filling in, too. Hair growth isn't limited

to the baby's head, though. He is also covered with a downy coating of hair called lanugo, largely there for warmth. Not to worry — he won't be like that at full-term: as fat accumulates later on in your pregnancy (the baby's fat, not yours, though that will accumulate too), it will take over the function of keeping your little bean toasty, so most of the lanugo sheds. Some babies, though — especially those born early — still have a fuzzy coating at delivery (it disappears soon afterwards).

Other developments this week include a roof of his own (inside your baby's mouth, that is) as well as some digestive system activity: his intestines are producing meconium, which is the waste that will make up his first bowel movement after birth.

"Hairy?" Nosipho squeaks. "My baby is hairy?"

I pull a face. How do you convince your friend that something is not gross when you all know that it *is* gross, and there's no point even pretending it isn't?

"Look!" I say, pointing at the screen. "It says downy. A downy coating of hair. That sounds like a little baby chick or something, doesn't it? It's cute."

"Yeah. Really cute."

Nosipho glares at us. "It's not cute. It's gruesome."

"It's normal," I say. "Your baby's fine."

"But what if it's not fine?" Nosipho nibbles on her thumbnail. "All this app does is tell me what my baby should be doing, not what it is doing. I want to know what is actually going on inside me."

Lael and I were talking about this just yesterday.

Lael pulls out a chair so Nosipho can sit down. "We think you need to go and see a doctor for a proper check-up."

Nosipho jerks back as if she's been slapped. "I'm not going back to the Raheeda Pelser!"

"Not the Raheeda Pelser," I say. "Never again. That was horrible. No, we think you should go to a private doctor."

"But I'm not ready to tell my mom yet. And if I see a doctor on the medical aid, she'll get a notification on her phone. I mean, I know I have to tell her eventually, but I'd rather wait until she gets back from America and I can speak to her face to face. That's why I didn't give the school her contact details in Washington DC."

We already thought of that.

"We think you should use some of that money we

collected," Lael says. "We'll even go with you for your first check-up, if that's what you want."

Nosipho leans forward and grabs one of our hands in each of hers. "I was hoping you'd say that."

The earliest appointment we can get is in ten days' time. There might be other obstetricians available sooner, but we decide to wait for this one. We went online and Googled stuff like "best obstetrician in Sandton" and "number-one obstetrician" and came across sites where people write about the experiences they've had with doctors – almost like restaurant reviews.

The one doctor who stood out was Dr Vaneesha Patel at the practice, Brown & Patel. They are based at the Morningside Fem-Clinic, which would be an awesome place for Nosipho to deliver her baby. They've got water-birthing suites and a top-class chef and a wine list, and stuff like that. It looks amazing. Not that Nosipho would need a wine list, but still.

But getting back to Dr Patel. So many people raved about her online that we were convinced. And one of the people who wrote a review was a teenager, just like Nosipho. She said that Dr Patel never once made her feel judged or stupid. That sealed the deal for us.

Unfortunately, it seems a lot of people had the same idea, which is why we had the ten-day wait.

But that's over now and we are sitting in our trusty Uber, on our way to the Morningside Fem-Clinic. It's really close – just a couple of blocks down Rivonia Road – which also makes it very convenient.

Lael and I are super-excited to see the baby on a screen at last, but Nosipho is twitching with nerves.

"What if there's something wrong with it?" she says, wringing her hands. "What if … what if it's not even alive anymore?"

"That's a bit morbid, babes," says Lael. "Don't think like that. I know bad stuff happens, but there's no point in worrying about it before we even know if we have something to worry about."

"Okay … okay, you're right. I'll stop." But she starts chewing on her thumbnail again.

"Listen, the one advantage of having a baby young is that you're fit and healthy," I point out.

"But what if I'm too young? What if the baby doesn't develop properly because my body isn't ready or something?"

"That is not going to happen. You're the size of an adult woman. You're taller than your own mom."

"Okay, that's true. Yes, I suppose that is true."

"Of course, it's true. Plus, your eggs are so young and healthy, you're probably going to give birth to a super-hero. Stop worrying!"

Nosipho subsides into silence. The Uber pulls into the parking lot of the Morningside Fem-Clinic and we all hop out.

Brown & Patel are on the second floor. They have a lovely, spacious waiting room with a reception desk at either end – one for Dr Brown and one for Dr Patel. We announce ourselves to Dr Patel's receptionist, and she gives Nosipho a form to fill in and a little plastic bottle with a screw-on lid.

Nosipho gives it a dubious look. "What is this for?"

"That's for your urine sample, dear. You will do one for Nurse every time you have an appointment. The ladies' bathroom is at the end of the corridor on the right."

Nos turns to us with a pitiful look on her face. "Please come with me, guys."

Lael and I hold up our hands.

"Nope."

"Uh-uh."

"You're on your own, sorry."

"You have to pee into a bottle. How hard can it be?"

We sit down on one of the soft, plushy sofas while Nosipho slouches off to the bathroom.

"Lots of reading matter here," Lael comments, looking at all the millions of pamphlets on offer. "Maybe we should grab a few for Nos."

We start flipping through them, looking for something useful.

I read through the titles in my handful. "Your Baby has Spina Bifida? Your Baby has Down Syndrome? Your Baby is Premature? Your Baby has Trisomy 18? Gosh, this is cheerful, I must say."

"Put them down, quick," Lael says, as Nosipho comes back clutching her pee bottle. "She's freaked out enough as it is."

Nosipho hands in her bottle and comes to sit with us. She is clearly still nervous, but looks happier now that she's here at last. Like me, she is looking around at the other women in the waiting room. Most of them have bumps, ranging from tiny to enormous. It's hard to imagine that Nosipho will be that big one day.

As we wait, we see women getting called in to see either Dr Brown or Dr Patel. Most of them come out wearing big smiles and holding CDs, flash-drives, or printouts of photographs.

Lael nudges Nosipho. "That's going to be you soon. We're going to see your baby. You'll get a photo and we can start an album."

Nosipho's frown lightens, and she starts to smile again.

♀

"What is that? What are you looking at? What's that weird little flashing light? It's a bad sign, isn't it?"

Nosipho is flopping around on the examination table like an eel. She keeps twisting herself around to look at the screen.

"Please keep still, Ms Mamusa," says Dr Patel. "The image goes blurry when you move like that."

"But the flashing light," Nosipho frets. "What is it?"

Dr Patel smiles as she concentrates on the screen. "That, Ms Mamusa, is your baby's heartbeat."

Nosipho goes completely still. "The heartbeat? Really? So ... so ... it's alive?"

"Alive and kicking, I'm happy to say. I'll turn the volume up so you can listen while I do some more checks and measurements."

She clicks on something with her mouse and the room is filled with the flub-dub, flub-dub sound of a heartbeat. I hold my breath. I've seen this scene in movies so many times, but it is incredible to experience it in real life. All my emotions are mirrored on Lael's face as we listen in wonder.

"But why is it so fast?" Nosipho asks. She has a point. The heartbeat sounds like it's galloping.

"That's completely normal," says the doctor. "A foetus of this age has a much faster heartbeat than you or I. Your baby's heart is currently beating at a rate of 144 beats per minute, which is spot-on for fifteen weeks. You, on the other hand, have a heart rate of 70 beats a minute, which is also perfect for a fit and active young woman of your age."

"I just wish I knew what I was looking at," Nosipho says. She is lying still now, but her head is still twisted around and she is staring at the screen with a deep crease between her brows. "It looks like someone is stirring a pot of soup on the stove. Every time I think I've spotted something, the soup gets stirred up again and it disappears. The only thing I can see for sure is the heart."

"No, look here." Lael points at the screen. "I've figured it out. This round thing over here is the head. And the thing that looks like a twisty little ladder is the spine. And look at the little arms – it's so cute! They're waving around."

There's a look of wonder on Nosipho's face as she suddenly sees it. It's like one of those optical illusions that comes into focus. I can also see it now – a perfect baby.

"Wow…!" she breathes. "That is so amazing. What's happening now? It almost … it almost looks like the baby is sucking its thumb."

Dr Patel turns around and smiles at her. "That's exactly what is happening. Thumb-sucking is also very common behaviour at this stage."

Tears spring to Nosipho's eyes, but that's fine because Lael and I have tears in our eyes too. This is the most amazing thing any of us has ever seen.

"Would you like to know the sex of the baby?" the doctor asks.

Nosipho stares at her. "The sex of the baby? You mean you can tell already? I thought it was too early."

"Fifteen weeks is a little early. Quite often we only know for sure at the twenty-week scan, but it just so happens that I got a very good look a few minutes ago, and now I'm a hundred per cent sure."

Nosipho chews her lip. "What should I do, guys? I can't decide."

"Totally up to you," says Lael.

"It's your call," I agree. "The fact that I'm desperate to know shouldn't influence you at all. Don't even think about me tossing and turning each night wondering if it's a boy or a girl. I mean, I'm only going to be the baby's favourite aunt, but don't let that influence you in the…"

"Oh, hush," says Lael with a laugh. "Don't listen to her, Nos. It's your decision."

"And you can change your mind at any stage," Dr Patel reminds her. "If you don't want to know now, but you do want to know at the next scan, that is also fine. You're in the driver's seat here."

"Okay, then I don't want to know yet. I still want to think about it a bit."

"That's perfect." Dr Patel tears off a few sheets of paper towel and hands them to Nosipho. "You can wipe the jelly off with this. Your baby is progressing beautifully, and so are you. Come through to my office when you're all cleaned up and we'll talk about your next appointment."

♀

The next few days are fairly quiet because Lael disappears on a tennis tour to Sun City.

I'm stuck at home feeling bored. The tennis kids left on Thursday afternoon and are only due to come back on Monday evening.

We have a ton of homework because the teachers seem to believe that the long winter term should be a time of misery and pain. They might call it "getting all the marks in before study week starts for exams", but I call it misery and pain. But with most of my friends away on tour, and Nosipho hibernating at her aunt's place, I actually get some work done for once.

Instead of going out on Friday and Saturday, I stay home and hit the books. I manage to write and practice a speech for English, build an anemometer out of straws and paper cups, prepare for a History test, and finish a case-study for Business Studies. Afterwards, I am burned out, but it feels good not to have anything hanging over my head for once.

Now it's Sunday and I have nothing left to do. We were supposed to go to church with my dad's family and then spend the day with them in Soweto, but three of my cousins have come down with 'flu, so it's been cancelled. You'd think my mom and dad would let us off church in that case, but you'd be wrong. We get dragged off to the half-past-seven service. Yes, half-past seven in the morning. They prefer that to the ten o'clock service because, apparently, "it leaves the rest of the day free to do things."

What things, though? Seeing as I have finished my homework and all my friends are somewhere else.

I go to my room and throw myself on the bed.

"What on earth…?" There is something lumpy under the mattress.

Then I sit bolt upright because I've just remembered what it is. On Thursday, a box was delivered while I was at school. I was hurrying to soccer practice and shoved it under my bed so Mom wouldn't spot it and start asking awkward questions.

I know exactly what it is – it's that Automatic Ghost Writing machine that I ordered from the paranormal website. Mom would have a fit if she knew what it was. She would probably send me to be exorcised – that's how scared she is of witchcraft and Satanism.

Anyway, this is not like playing glassy-glassy or anything stupid like that. You don't even have to be there. You just set it and forget it. If there's a ghost in the room, it can get in touch and leave you a message. Sounds perfect to me.

As I stare at the sealed cardboard box, I can't wait to open it. Getting stuff delivered from the internet is just the best thing in life. It's not reasonable to expect me to wait until Monday to play with my new toy.

I pick up my phone and send a message to Lungile.

"So, your parents are fine with you going to school on a Sunday?" asks Lungi as I strap myself into the back seat.

"Of course, they are. You can phone my mom and check if you like."

And that's exactly what he does, while starting the car at the same time. Lungile is not what you'd call the trusting type. Driving Aaron, Caleb and me around seems to have lessened his faith in human nature. Or in teenage nature, anyway. I can't say I exactly blame him – we've definitely taken some chances over the years.

Luckily my mom really has given me permission to go to school. She thinks I need to use the library in Sisulu House for a project, which is the same story I'm going to give Matron when she sees me. Perhaps I really will borrow a book for my Business Studies project, so it's not a complete lie. And the best part is that the Sisulu House library spreads over several floors, including the fourth, which is where our ghost-hunting equipment is set up. It's mostly dusty old encyclopaedias that no one ever bothers with, but at least I have an excuse for being in that room.

I've got the Automatic Ghost Writing thingy stuffed into my backpack. It's bulging a bit, but I don't think anyone will notice.

By the time Lungi drops me off at school, I'm in a much better mood than I've been in all day. It feels good to have a purpose. And when Lael comes back on Monday, I'll have something interesting to tell her.

I walk into Sisulu House with a smile on my face, ready to say hi to Matron if I see her. The smile is wiped off when I walk straight into Sophie Agincourt instead.

"*Sophie!*" I know I sound a little horrified, but I can't help it. She is absolutely the last person I want sneaking around while I'm setting up ghost-hunting equipment.

"Hello, Trinity." Her eyes go straight to my backpack. "What have you got in there?"

"Oh … er … nothing. Just some stuff for a project."

"A project, huh? Which subject?"

"History," I lie smoothly, picking the only subject of

mine that Sophie isn't also taking. "We … uh … have to make a 3-D model of the Titanic for next week. Ugh! Such a pain."

Her eyes flick past me to someone coming down the stairs. "It's lucky that Ms Waise is here to help you then, isn't it?"

I turn and watch with a sinking heart as my History teacher walks down the stairs. I mean, honestly. What are all these people doing at Sisulu House on a Sunday morning? Sophie doesn't live here anymore, and nor does Ms Waise. Don't they have homes to go to?

"Morning, girls," says Ms Waise. "Why is it lucky that I'm here?"

"Trinity was just saying that she has come here to work on her 3-D model of the Titanic for her History project. Apparently, she has everything she needs right there in her backpack."

Okay, I want to die. I want the earth to open up and swallow me whole. But there is no escape.

"Is that so?" Ms Waise looks from Sophie, to me, to my bulging backpack, and back to me again.

"It is, Ma'am." Sophie smirks. "Maybe Trinity should open her backpack and show us what's inside. Just so you can check that she's brought all the right stuff, you know."

That's it. I'm busted. Why did I have to say it was a History project? Why did I have to pick that subject? And why, oh why, did I have the horrible luck of running straight into Sophie?

My mind races around, looking for an excuse. Perhaps I can say that the Automatic Writing device is a mock-up of the radio system on the Titanic and I need it for the project.

(Except there is no project, Trinity. You made it up, remember? We're not even doing the Titanic this term. We last did it in, like, Grade Six, or something.)

"Oh, there's no need for that," says Ms Waise cheerfully. "I told the class exactly what they needed for their Titanic model. I'm sure Trinity has got it right."

I've been staring at the ground, but now I look up because I can't believe what I'm hearing.

"Good luck with the project, Trinity!" Ms Waise continues. "And don't forget it's due on Thursday. No excuses!"

Sophie's face is a genuine pleasure to watch. She looks as though she has just realised she's been walking around all day with smudged mascara (a fate worse than death for Sophie Agincourt.)

"We should get on now, Sophie, and leave Trinity to it. I can drop you at home on my way, if you like. Save your mom the extra trip."

I hold my breath as we wait for Sophie to answer. It would be so great if Ms Waise took her away. Then I wouldn't have to worry about her sneaking up on me while I'm busy on the fourth floor.

"Okay, Ms Waise," Sophie says at last. "Thank you."

Once they've left, I skip up the stairs, delighted that my luck has taken a turn for the better.

It's only when I get up to the fourth floor that I start thinking about how extremely strange that was. Why would a teacher support me in a lie like that? It doesn't make any sense. The only thing I can think of is that she didn't like the way Sophie was trying to get me into trouble, and decided to spoil her plan. Yes, that's probably it. There are some teachers who hate tattletales.

⚲

I can never go up to the fourth floor without remembering Jim Grey and all the talks we had last term. He used to drive me crazy with his sexist and racist attitudes, but I never once doubted his friendship. I always knew he was on my side.

I still can't get used to the idea that he was never really there at all. That I was talking to an illusion – something from the past. I remember how he warned me against Zach, the boyfriend I had at the time, and how right he was about him. I wasn't ready to hear it at the time. I had to find out for myself how awful Zach was. But even when I was fighting tooth and nail against his advice, I never doubted that Jim wanted the best for me.

How I wish I could talk to him again. I wish I could be sitting in here like I used to do, and look up to see Jim coming in through the door. He walked with such a swagger. His thumbs were always hooked into his belt loops, and he had these cool winklepicker shoes.

I'd ask him what happened to Amelia. Is she still alive today? Did she have her baby? Was it a girl or a boy? Where is it now? And I'd make him tell me what happened to him, too. I still don't believe that he just died in his chair. Something happened, and I want to know what it was.

I think my longing to talk to him is the reason I bought this Automatic Writing thing. I'm desperate for a message from Jim. I want him to get in touch with me. And maybe this machine will make it happen.

Before I start setting it up, I take out my USB cords and hook the other machines up to my laptop to check for recent activity. Lael and I haven't done this in weeks.

There are several blips on the timeline, but then there always are.

I scroll my way through the daily visit from the cleaners and the odd person who wanders in here because they seem to be lost. Matron appears twice – both times for a sneaky smoke. I've got so used to seeing her, it doesn't even make me giggle anymore.

There are a couple of anomalies, similar to the one we saw when we first checked the feed. These don't excite me half as much as they used to. When you play them back really slowly you can see a slight shimmer on the screen, but honestly, it could be anything. It could be a power surge or a blip on the screen, or who knows what. It could also – I suppose – be a ghost. But if that's all he's going to do – just cause a blip and nothing more – it's not particularly interesting.

No, I'm pinning my hopes on the Automatic Ghost Writer now. If Jim is ever going to get back in contact, it will be through that. I'm convinced of it.

I hide the machine inside a stack of old *Popular Mechanics* magazines. It's close enough to a plug that I don't even have to use the extension cord I brought. Then I switch it on.

There is a green LED display window at the front. As I watch, it leaps into life with a series of wiggly lines that snake across the tiny screen from left to right. Supposedly, these are the sounds of the "other" dimension that we can't hear with our ears, but that the machine can detect with its super-sensitive sensors. As soon as the machine detects a sound that resembles human speech, it will record it onto its hard drive. I'll give it a few weeks, and then download what it has recorded.

Hopefully there will be a clear message from Jim.

I pack up, feeling as though I've accomplished something at least. On my way back down to the ground floor, I decide to check on the display case. The diary has been stuck on one page for ages now. Lael and I have almost given up hope that it's going to change.

"Yes!"

There's a new page. The writing is as hard to read as ever, but I take a photo with my phone, knowing I can enlarge it at home and have a proper look. I can also forward it to Lael once she's on her way back from the tennis tournament. I don't want to bother her with it now while she's in the zone and trying to win matches.

It's a nice long entry too, stretching over two full diary pages. I can't wait to see what it says.

CHAPTER 9

So much has happened since I last wrote, I hardly know where to begin. First of all, mother confronted me, and I had to admit the Truth.

Oh, it was just awful, dear Diary. She called me a "slut" and a "whore" (pardon my language) and many other dreadful names. She tried to slap me across the face, but I ducked just in time. That seemed to make her even angrier. She chased me around the house with a wooden spoon, shouting at me to come back. I went and hid outside and waited for her to calm down.

Then my father came home and she told him the whole shameful story. I waited for them both to calm down and then tried to go back into the house. Would you believe it, Diary? They had locked me out! I had to spend the night in the shed. I cried my eyes out until our golden retriever Skippy came to keep me company. I wept into her fur and slept against her for warmth.

In the morning, the house was unlocked but Father wasn't speaking to me. I was given bread and water for breakfast and told to pack my bags. He took me back to school a day early. The drive was simply dreadful. Father didn't say a word the whole way. He drove me in angry silence. Then he dropped me at the school gates despite the fact that everything was locked up. The teachers weren't due to arrive until evening.

I got out of the car and he drove away as quickly as he could. I spent the whole day without food or water, standing in the hot sun. I tried to find shade against the wall. Cars kept stopping and people kept asking me if I was all right. And sometimes a car would stop and a man would make an indecent suggestion.

I felt so ashamed, dear Diary. For the first time, I really and truly understood the shame I had brought on myself and my family. How bitterly I regret that fateful day with Jim. If only I had done what my upbringing had taught me...

Anyway, eventually the first staff members started to arrive. I had to lie to them and pretend that I had only just got there. To tell them that my father had dropped me hours earlier would require an explanation.

I will have to keep all explanations to myself for as long as I still want to remain at school. The moment they suspect the truth, I will be out on my ear.

I just wish I knew what the future holds. I imagine Mother and Father are discussing it now and deciding what is to be done. I trust that they will know best. I thought we might talk about it together, but I suppose that was silly. They will make the decision and let me know in due course.

I had dinner at a table on my own in the dining hall that night. The teachers were all sitting at the High Table. I kept thinking they were talking about me because they seemed to glance in my direction all the time. But perhaps I was imagining things. After all, only someone who knows me really well would notice anything yet. I moved the button on my school skirt and now it fits perfectly again.

I told Loretta what had happened. She was very shocked, although she admitted she'd been worrying about me ever since I told her that I had G.A.T.W with Jim.

I was so pleased when she came into the dormitory after dinner that night. I'd thought I would be on my own until the morning. But Loretta is from Rhodesia, so she often arrives at odd hours. It is such a long way, after all. She'd had supper on the train, so we settled in for a chat.

Oh, Diary, guess what? She thinks my parents might agree

to adopt the baby and raise it as my brother or sister! That way I could be close to it. Apparently, Loretta has a cousin who became PG and that's what her family did.

That would be the most magical, wonderful thing that could possibly happen! That way I could even introduce the baby to Jim gradually, and soon he'd learn to love it as much as I do. Yes, that's right, Diary. I already love this baby! How could I not? It is my darling Jim's child, after all.

Love,
Amelia

I send the diary entry to Lael as soon as she messages me that she is on her way home in the bus. Then on Tuesday morning, we get together at first break to discuss it.

"Imagine how great it would be if Amelia's parents really did agree to adopt the baby," I say when we have finished reading over it together. "That would solve all her problems. I mean, I'm not saying it's ideal to be raised thinking that your mother is your sister, but at least they could be together."

Lael pulls a gloomy face. "I don't know, hey. Did those parents strike you as the soft and sentimental type? They shut her out of the house for the night. They dumped her at school hours early and left her to stand on her own in the sun. Their own pregnant daughter! I can't see them getting sentimental about her baby."

"I suppose," I say reluctantly. "And none of it tells us anything useful about Jim or how he might have died."

"The only thing her parents seem to have contributed to the situation was to make it worse."

"I wonder if they are still around today. And also that friend she mentions – Loretta. If we can't track Amelia down, we might be able to find her."

"Good idea."

"In the meantime, we need to think about what we can do to help our own pregnant friend," I say. "At least it's not too late for her."

"Yes! The belly campaign. Nosipho's tummy is getting more and more noticeable. It's just a matter of time until they ask her to leave the school."

"We'll start on Monday."

"I'm a bit nervous," Lael admits. "I've been trying to imagine walking around in public looking like I'm nine months pregnant. It's scary."

"I know, me too. But imagine being Nosipho and knowing that this is your life now. Shame, she wants me to take her along on my babysitting gig on Saturday night. I think she's hoping to pick up some tips on how to handle babies."

"If anyone can show her, you can, Trinity."

♀

This is true, even if I say so myself.

There is no one who is better at babies than me. I'm practically the baby whisperer. My mom tells me I've always been like that. When I was a toddler, I used to gravitate towards babies. Apparently, I would spend hours pulling faces at them and making them laugh. I even used to entertain my brothers back when they were still small and cute, instead of huge and annoying like they are now.

My mom and her friends say I was the best babysitter they could ever hope for. They would leave their babies on a blanket with me and some toys, while they sat on chairs next to us and had tea. I never got tired of playing with their babies. I still don't. I've been babysitting unofficially since I was tiny, and then when I turned twelve, I started doing it officially and charging by the hour.

I did a baby-and-child stimulation course and an advanced first-aid course in the school holidays, which meant I could push my rates up even more. I won't lie – I have expensive tastes. My allowance is generous, but I like earning my own money so I can spend it on random things like ghost-writing machines.

My booking on Saturday night is a good one for Nosipho to attend, because the family has a two-year-old and a six-week-old, which is practically a newborn. It will give her a good idea of what's involved. I just hope it doesn't freak her out completely.

On Saturday afternoon, we organise for Nosipho's aunt to drop her at my place at five o'clock. We are due at the Khumalos at half-past five – that's the family I'm babysitting for. I already cleared it with Mrs Khumalo that I'm bringing a friend. After six weeks at home with a toddler and a new baby, she is so keen to get out for a few hours she would probably have agreed to me throwing a wild party at her house. New parents, hey? Shame, they always act like they've been let out of jail when I arrive to babysit.

Nosipho looks a little nervous.

"Listen, Trinity. I don't know if this is a good idea. You're not going to leave me alone with them, right? I literally have no idea what to do with a baby."

I manage not to smile. "Don't worry. This is my thing, not yours. I'm going to do everything I normally do. You are just there to watch. If you want to try anything, you'll have to ask me first."

"What if I don't want to try anything?"

"That's fine. I won't judge you for being a giant scaredy-cat. Not at all."

Nosipho's giggle sounds a little cracked.

I tell my mom that we're leaving. She is under strict instructions not to say a word about Nosipho's condition. Until Nosipho's mom is back and knows about the baby, she doesn't want anyone talking about it.

My mom manages to keep her eyes on Nosipho's face, even though I know she is dying to look at her tummy and then go crazy about how cute her bump looks.

"You girls have fun now," she says. "Keep the security switched on at the Khumalos' house at all times and make sure you've got everyone's cell numbers. Trinity, please turn on the last-seen on your WhatsApp."

I roll my eyes. That is such a pain. How am I supposed to swerve people's messages when they can see exactly what time I was last on my phone?

"Now!"

I do it, reluctantly.

Lungile drops us off at the Khumalos. I'm quite looking forward to this evening. The thing is, Nosipho is better than me at nearly everything. She gets better marks, she is better at sport, and she can play the piano about a million times better. In fact, I gave up piano last year while she's still carrying on with it.

But today, just for one evening, I am going to be better than her at something. I know babies, and she is terrified of babies. Finally, there is something she can learn from me.

Mrs Khumalo welcomes us with open arms. It's my first time seeing the baby, a little girl. I hand over the baby gift I brought, and Mrs K coos over the soft leather Mary Jane shoes I found.

"These are adorable, thank you! Perfect for when she starts to walk, which I can't even imagine at the moment. And what's this one?" She holds up my other parcel.

"Oh, that's for you," I say. "My mom always says it's the mother who deserves gifts. The baby is just lying there chilling, while the mother does all the hard work."

Mrs Khumalo laughs and opens the bath salts and body scrub I've wrapped for her. She seems very pleased with them.

"So, I've just fed her, but I've left lots of expressed milk in the fridge. Sometimes she likes to cluster-feed before she will settle for the night. We normally bath her at half-past six and try to put her down at seven. And we have to fit in bathing Ntheko as well. Having two kids is way more work than one."

"I hear you, but don't worry. I've babysat two kids lots of times before. We'll be fine. You go out and enjoy yourselves. And don't hurry back – we've got this."

"You realise she's going to be messaging you every five minutes?" says Mr Khumalo.

"That's also fine. I'll answer every message and even send you pics."

The Khumalos finally leave in a flurry of goodbye kisses for the kids and reminders about dinnertime for me. It is six o'clock by the time we close the door behind them – time to give Ntheko his dinner. So, of course the baby, Bontle, immediately starts to cry.

I glance at Nosipho. She looks completely freaked out. There is no way I can ask her to hold the baby while I prepare dinner for Ntheko.

I pull out one of my many secret weapons – the baby pouch. I have no idea whether Mrs Khumalo is into baby-wearing or not, but it doesn't matter. All babies like it, even if they're not used to it. And I don't like using other people's slings or pouches because mine is more comfortable.

"This is going to be your best friend when you have the baby," I tell Nosipho. "A baby pouch. Our grand-mothers might have carried their babies on their backs, but I've never got the hang of it, so I do this instead. It frees up your hands so you can do stuff, and keeps the baby happy."

I tell her not to worry about trying to remember how to put it on because the one she ends up getting will probably be different to mine. I put my pouch on and pop Bontle into it. I have to walk up and down a few times before she stops crying and settles down. By this stage, Ntheko is pulling at my leg and saying, "Up! Up!" so I have to pick him up too.

"Hey, Ntheko," I say, pressing my nose against his in a way that always makes him laugh. "Are you hungry, my boy? You ready for some supper? Yum-yums?"

His little legs start kicking excitedly. "Yum-yum! Yum-yum!"

"I'll take that as a yes."

His mom left some sausages and mashed potatoes out for him, so I warm them up in the microwave.

"No vegetables?" Nosipho asks disapprovingly.

I laugh. "You're already turning into that mom who judges all the other moms for not feeding their kids right."

"No, I'm not! Am I? Okay, maybe I am. A kid should have some veggies with his supper. Isn't it, like, the law or something?"

"I wouldn't go that far, but watch this."

I get Ntheko into his high chair by distracting him with a toy. Then I cut his sausages into bite-size pieces and put them on a plastic plate with the mashed potatoes. Then I take some raw broccoli out of the fridge and put it on the plate as well.

Nosipho watches with an open mouth as Ntheko ignores the hot food and goes straight for the ice-cold broccoli. He starts gnawing on a floret like it's a lollipop.

"Wow!" she says. "That kid is a rock-star. You wouldn't catch me munching on raw broccoli like that."

"Me neither," I say with a small shudder. "I'll eat it if it's mixed with something else, but it's not my fave."

"How do you get a child to eat raw veggies like that?" Nosipho looks like she's ready to start taking notes.

"There literally is no formula for success. Some kids just like the taste. And the weird thing is, they often grow out of it. At some stage they wake up and decide all vegetables are yucky and will only eat food that's beige. That's when you have to start grating and mashing and hiding vegetables inside other things."

Nosipho looks at me like I'm Batman and Gandalf and a Jedi Master all rolled into one. "How do you know all this stuff?"

I try not to look smug. "Oh, you know. Just paying

attention over the years. And looking after babies and kids forever."

"You're amazing."

Ha! Respect at last! Now if only I could turn this knowledge into something useful, like better marks for History.

Ntheko munches away at his supper, trying a piece of this and a piece of that. I'm not sure how much is actually going in, but it doesn't really matter. Eating isn't a huge deal in their lives at this age, especially when they're still drinking milk. I decide to take advantage of the lull by feeding Bontle.

Mrs Khumalo has put three pre-sterilised bottles of expressed milk in the fridge for us. All we have to do is warm them up. I show Nosipho how to use the bottle-warmer, but she doesn't look very interested.

"I'm planning to breastfeed, not bottle-feed," she says. "Everything I've read says it's best for the baby."

"Oh, absolutely," I agree. "But are you also planning on never leaving the house for two years? What about finishing school? What about going out to have fun? You must be able to leave the baby sometimes, and the best way to do that is to have bottles of breastmilk handy. You need to know this stuff, girl."

"Hmm … okay."

She starts paying more attention to my bottle tutorial. She even holds Bontle's bottle for a while as I feed her. I notice that she's not exactly besotted with the baby, like I am. But that's fine. A lot of women aren't crazy about other people's babies, but love their own. Nosipho is already in love with her bump. She rubs it, cuddles it, and even talks to it when she thinks I'm not listening. It's kind of adorable, actually.

"So, what now?" she asks as Bontle finishes her bottle.

"Okay, well, did you notice how she was turning her head away towards the end? That tells me she's had enough milk, so I'm not going to warm up another bottle at this stage."

"Aren't you only supposed to give them a particular amount?"

"This is breastmilk, so she can have as much as she wants. If it were formula, I wouldn't go over the set amount."

Nosipho thinks about this, then she shakes her head. "Okay, I give up. Why not?"

"Because the calories in formula can makes babies obese, but the calories in breastmilk can't."

"Why not? Are they magic, or something?"

"They actually kind of are. Even if a baby gets hugely fat on breastmilk, it's not a problem. That fat will just melt away. But the weight they put on from formula can turn into a real issue later on, so the amount you give them has to be very carefully controlled for their age."

"Huh. I never knew that. So, now what?"

We look over at Ntheko who has now reached the throwing-food-on-the-floor stage of his meal.

"Well, this dude seems to be done. If he were still hungry, he'd still be eating. Now we take them both to Bontle's room so we can give her a bath."

Nosipho looks panicked again. "What are we going to do with the little boy while we bath the baby? Don't expect me to look after him. I never know what to say to kids."

"It's cool. He's not expecting conversation. I'll just do exactly what I would have done if you weren't here. Pass me my tog bag, please."

As she hands it to me, I unzip it and take out my secret weapons. These are toys that travel with me from job to job. They are guaranteed to keep kids happy while I'm bathing their little siblings. And then, while they're sleeping, I make them disappear again before they can beg to keep them forever and ever.

We traipse up the stairs with me carrying Bontle in one arm and holding Ntheko's hand with the other. While we are walking, she brings up about three winds, so I take the opportunity to explain the importance of winding to Nosipho.

I pop Bontle into her pram and wheel her into the bathroom with me while I fill up the little plastic bath. I've learned from experience not to leave toddlers alone with their baby siblings while I'm in another room. They do weird things like load stuffed animals onto them or poke a finger in their eyes.

The bath goes well. Ntheko plays peacefully on the floor with the shape-sorter and Mega Bloks truck I brought for him. I show Nosipho how to tell if the bath is the right temperature, and how to wash a baby's hair. She watches while I rub a mixture of aqueous cream and water onto Bontle's tiny body and then rinse it off in the bath. When I take her out and wrap her in a hooded towel, Nosipho surprises me by asking if she can dry her.

"Of course." I step back and let her take over. I'm happy to see that her technique is just right. She is gentle, but firm and not hesitant. Babies don't like to be handled by anyone who is nervous of them. It makes them scream.

Bontle stays calm and alert while Nosipho dries her and rubs more cream into her skin.

"Well done!" I say. "You're a natural. You're going to be a brilliant mom, Nos. Don't cry," I add as her eyes fill with tears. "Okay, you can cry for a little while, but then you have to stop. We're going to watch Netflix once these guys are in bed. I don't want you getting tears in the popcorn."

Nosipho wipes her face. "I've already stopped. It's just that when you said I was going to be a good mom, it was the first time – the very first time – that I thought I could actually do this. That I might actually cope."

"Of course you'll cope."

"Yes, but I didn't really know that. Not for sure. But when I was drying Bontle, I thought, 'Hey, I can do this.' It was a good feeling."

To build her confidence some more, I let her slip Bontle's vest on, and show her how to lay a Babygro down with all the poppers open, then place the baby on top of it, and clip her into it. By the end of the process, her face has lost its anxious expression, and her normal smile is back.

CHAPTER 10

To: Trinity Luhabe trinityluhabe@gmail.com
From: Dean of Students – Sisulu House gcobani@sisuluhouse.co.za
Re: Protest Action

Dear Ms Luhabe,

I have been asked to write to you in my capacity as Dean of Students to inform you that the senior management and Board of Trustees of Brentwood College disapprove of the protest action you and your friends are engaged in, and call upon you to stop it with immediate effect. They feel that it is lowering the reputation of the school in the eyes of the community.

I would also like to add in my personal capacity that peaceful protest is legally protected by our constitution and has been supported by Brentwood College in the past. The issue of teen pregnancy is very close to my heart. I was a teen mother who was forced to interrupt my education for many years. It was only through luck that I was able to finish my education and pursue a career.

But I must remind you officially that the school calls upon you to stop the protest, and warns that measures will be taken if you do not.

With all good wishes.
Kind regards,
Grace Gcobani
Dean of Students
Sisulu House
Brentwood College

To: Trinity Luhabe trinityluhabe@gmail.com
From: Head of Department – History jwaise@sisuluhouse.co.za
Re: Submission for School Newspaper

Dear Trinity,

Many thanks for the article you submitted to the school newspaper about the ongoing pregnancy protest you and your friends are engaged upon. I discussed it with the student editorial board and we would very much like to publish it. We feel it represents an important issue to our school community.

May I also compliment you on how well written it was. You have an accessible writing style that is a breath of fresh air for our paper. If you have any other burning issues you would like to write about, please don't hesitate to submit them.

Your protest is close to my heart as I was the child of a teenage mother. I have some inkling of how my mother struggled and how all the decks were stacked against her. I don't want to live in a world where this still happens to teen moms. I really believe that completing your education is the best chance you have of making a success in life. I would like to see all teen moms having that opportunity, and that's why I am 100% behind your campaign.

Good luck! I wish you all success and hope you get the ruling you are fighting for.

Kind regards,
Jenny Waise
Head of History
Brentwood College

"If I have to wear this belly for one more day, I am going to scream," says Yasmin.

"I know what you mean," says Lael. "I'm getting a rash on my tummy from where it rubs against my skin. It's so hot and itchy."

Amira unstraps hers and throws it onto her bed. "Ahhh…" she sighs. "That's better!"

Nosipho fiddles behind her back as though she also wants to unstrap a belly. "Oops, nope. Turns out this one doesn't come off. Apparently, I have to keep it on twenty-four / seven."

Lael laughs. "I bet yours doesn't make your skin look like this."

She lifts up her top to show us the blotchy rash that has developed around her belly button.

"Eew! Stop!" says Amira.

"Listen, if we're going to get into a battle over whether real pregnancy symptoms or fake pregnancy symptoms are the worst, I will win every time." Nosipho folds her arms and gives us a look. "Yes, I will. Do you guys want to hear about my discharge?"

"No!"

"Gross!"

"Enough!"

We throw our bellies at her until she begs for mercy.

Eventually we are all stretched out on various beds.

"Seriously though, you guys," says Yasmin. "How much longer are we going to have to keep this up? Is there any sign that the school is cracking?"

"They haven't said anything to me," Nosipho sighs. "As far as I know I've got two weeks left, and then I have to be out."

"That's not going to happen," Lael says. "We won't let it."

"All I know is that Ms Waise and Ms Gcobani are on our side." I explain about the emails I received from them. "Plus, there will be an article about the protest in the next edition of the school newspaper."

Lael checks the school calendar on her phone. "That's only coming out next week. I'm not sure we can wait that long. The more they get used to seeing us dressed like this, the less effective the protest becomes."

Nosipho is biting her thumb nail. I hate to see her stressing like this. I'm sure it's not good for her or for the baby. Aren't pregnant moms supposed to be all chilled, and, like, doing yoga all the time? It's not right that she has to worry about whether she will still be allowed to attend school in two weeks.

"We need to kick it up a notch, guys," I say. "We need to make a bigger impact."

"But how?" says Amira. "Are we going to buy more bellies? We hardly have enough people to wear the ones we've got. Every day there are spare bellies left in the cupboard."

"We need to make it more public. As long as it's on school grounds, they can hush it up. We should go somewhere like Sandton City and make a big thing of it."

"We boarders aren't getting an outing until next weekend," says Lael. "That's too far away."

"So, it will have to be the day-girls. And boy, including Munashe. Even five or six of us will make a difference. We can take lots of photos and post them to Instagram."

"My account is private."

"So's mine."

"And mine."

"Then we can make them public for a few days. And we can post pictures and videos to Snapchat as well."

"And Facebook and Twitter!" Lael sounds enthusiastic for the first time today. "We'll tag the school. We'll post our photos on the Brentwood College Facebook site. They'll get deleted, but not before a bunch of people have seen them."

I hold up a finger as an idea of total brilliance floods into my mind. "Wait, you guys, wait. I have an even better idea. Instead of protesting against Brentwood for refusing to allow a pregnant girl to continue her education, we should try to shame them by pretending that they have already agreed to let her stay."

Lael gets it at once. Our minds have always been in sync. "Yes! Genius. We could say something like, "I'm so proud of my school Brentwood College for not discriminating against pregnant learners."

"Yay for Brentwood College, the most progressive school in Sandton." Yasmin runs with the idea.

"I'm so glad I go to Brentwood College where young women are free to finish their education," adds Amira.

We grin at each other like lunatics.

"This could work, you guys," I say. "This could actually work."

Friday afternoon is D-day.

Sandton City is always crawling with Brentwood kids on a Friday because the school is so nearby. Nosipho has come along to be our official photographer. She won't appear in any of the photos, but she'll be the one behind the lens. She's really good at photography. Her Instagram account looks like it belongs to some professional influencer or something.

The other boarders had to stay behind, unfortunately, because they board on a termly basis, rather than going home every weekend like Nosipho.

We are quite a small group. It's just me, Munashe, Gugulethu (the one dating my brother Aaron) and a Grade Eleven white girl called Rebecca. I make a silent vow not to tease her about being the 'Becky' of the group, tempting as it is.

"Hey, you guys," she says. "Check it out. I'm the Becky of this group. I just noticed."

"Oh, man!" Munashe shakes his head. "I wanted to say that so badly, but I thought you'd get offended."

"It's cool," she says. "I own my Beckyness."

Lungile drops us at the Clicks entrance to Sandton City. I can tell he thinks we are all completely mad – especially Munashe – but he doesn't say anything because he knows my mom is fine with it.

We decided that we would mainly hang out at the food court and on the cinema level, because that's where we'd see the most people. We adjust our preggie bellies so they look as realistic as possible. Then we walk through the doors all in a line like we're the cast of *Ocean's 8*. Nosipho runs ahead of us to take pictures and videos as we walk.

"This is great," she says. "Hashtag squad goals."

To say that we turn heads as we walk past would be an understatement – three girls in full school uniform who all look at least nine months pregnant, plus one boy who looks about ten months pregnant because of how the preggie belly fits his skinny body.

At school, people were getting used to seeing us dressed like this, so they had stopped reacting, but this is the first time we've all been out in public together, and the reactions are extreme.

"Don't look now, guys, but those people over there are taking videos of us on their phones," says Rebecca.

Of course, we immediately turn to look, and she's right. People have stopped what they are doing and are standing still to gawk at us. Some are taking photos and some are taking videos. Gugu gives them a little wave, exactly like the queen riding past in her royal carriage. I have to slap a hand over my mouth to stop giggling.

"This is so going viral," Gugu says out the corner of her mouth. "We won't even have to help it along. This is going to be on everyone's feed in a couple of hours."

"Oh, man. Those guys over there used to play club soccer with me in primary school," says Munashe. "I am never going to live this down. As in, never ever."

I stand on tiptoes so I can sling an arm around his shoulder (when did he get so tall?)

"Never mind," I say. "You're doing it because you love us, right?"

He makes a humphing noise. "I'm doing it because I love Nosipho and I want her to stay in school. I'm not so sure about you, mntase."

"But I'm so lovable!" I give him a hug. "Seriously though, we are mega-grateful to you for doing this."

"Ja, ja."

We spend the afternoon, parading slowly around Sandton City, stopping now and then for Nosipho to take photos. And, of course, everyone else takes photos of us as well.

But it's in the evening that the real work begins.

At Brentwood College, Friday evening is the best time for posting anything on social media. Everyone who happens to be staying home is obsessively checking Instagram and Snapchat to see what other people are up to. And everyone who is out with friends or at a party is posting their own pics and also checking to see who might be having more fun than they are. It's what you might call rush hour on social media.

We adjourn to the common room of Sisulu House to launch our campaign. Normally we would go up to the dorm, but Munashe isn't allowed upstairs and he is a crucial part of our plan. We go through all the photos and videos that everyone took from the afternoon and pick out the best ones. Then we send them to each other. We don't all want to be posting the same images because that would get boring.

"Okay, troops," says Lael. "Ready, steady, post!"

"And don't forget to tag Brentwood in everything," I add.

"I'm posting the videos to my story, and the pics to my feed," says Rebecca.

"Good idea. Let's all do that."

We huddle over our phones and post photos, cropping and adding filters as we go for maximum effect. Each picture is captioned with a sentence praising Brentwood College for being such a great centre of enlightenment.

"My likes are piling up fast," says Gugu, not looking up from her phone.

"Me too." Munashe pumps his fist in the air. "This one

of the four of us walking in a row has got a hundred likes in a few minutes. I've never seen anything like it."

I click onto the Brentwood College Facebook site. "Some of the feminist moms have started commenting," I say. "Listen to this, 'Great to hear this news about my son's school. Hope other schools follow suit soon.' And, 'Teens moms should not be denied education. Well done, Brentwood for realising this.' This is totally catching fire."

"When do you think the school will realise what's going on?" asks Rebecca.

"Soon. Most of the teachers have social media accounts. They'll start seeing it in a couple of hours."

"I had such a weird dream last night," says Lael.

"Oh, yes?"

We are sitting in History, where we've both finished the work Ms Waise gave us. (Well, Lael has finished it. I have almost started.) Ms Waise normally lets us chat quietly in class when we've finished our work as long as we don't disturb anyone else.

"Aren't you going to ask me what it was about?" she whispers.

I roll my eyes. "Lieberman, we have five precious minutes until the end of the lesson and then it's double maths. Do you really want to spend it telling me about your dream?"

"Yes, I do. Ask me what it was about."

I sigh. "What was it about?'

"I was dreaming that I was actually lying in my bed and sleeping. You know how that happens sometimes?"

"Mm-hmm." Is there anything more boring than listening to other people's dreams? If there is, I can't think of it.

"And this voice started calling to me out of the darkness. It was like, 'Laellll …. Laelllll … hellllp me.' And I was like, 'Who are you?' Because the voice sounded sort of familiar, but not exactly, if you know what I mean."

"Uh huh." I'm listening more closely now because this is better than I expected.

"And, guess what, the voice said that she was Amelia. It was like, 'It's meeeee, Laellllll, it's Amelllllia. You need to hellllllp me.' "

"Gosh."

"Exactly. So, I was, like, 'What can I do? Tell me what I can do to help.' And she said, 'Lorrrrrrretta. Speeeeeak to Lorrrrrrretta. Finnnnnnd her. You neeeed to finnnnnd her.'"

"And then?"

"And then nothing. I woke up. But do you want to know what I think it means?"

"Sure."

"I think she was telling us to find her old school friend Loretta that she mentions in her diary."

This makes sense. We already discussed the possibility of doing this, but got distracted with the preggie belly campaign.

"Maybe Loretta still lives in Johannesburg and would be prepared to talk to us," says Lael. The only problem is, we can't go around Joburg looking for someone called Loretta. We need more than that to go on."

"One of the diary entries mentions her surname," I say. "I know it does. What was it again?"

"I have no idea."

"I still have all the diary entries saved on my phone. I'll go through them and find it."

"Cool. So that was better than the average dream story, right? Do you think it might actually have been her ghost speaking to me while I slept?"

Shame, I hate to burst her bubble.

"I guess it might have been," I say. "But we've got no reason to think that Amelia is actually dead. She would only be in her mid-sixties by now. She's probably alive and well. Besides, we were talking about this the other day, remember? About trying to track down Amelia's friend."

Lael's face falls. "Oh, ja. I guess the dream was just my way of reminding us that we still need to do it."

Ms Waise is looking at us, so I lower my voice. "It's our only option, until we get to see the next page of the diary."

"If we ever do."

"If we ever do," I agree. "We've got nothing to go on right now except the friend."

"So how do we find her?"

"Google?"

Lael slips her phone out of her pocket and hides it behind a file. Then she types, "How to find someone" into the Google search box and waits.

"Oh, man. I love Google. Look at all these brilliant hits."

"That's amazing," I say. I take out my own phone and start reading through Amelia's diary entries, looking for her friend's surname.

There is silence for a while as Lael reads articles on

how to track down missing people, and I struggle with Amelia's old-timey handwriting.

"Got it!" I say. "Loretta Mainwaring."

"I think it's pronounced 'Mannering'," says Lael. "But, good job! Now we can…"

"You know I don't allow phones in class, ladies."

We look up, startled. Ms Waise has appeared silently behind us. She scoops up our phones before either of us can move a muscle.

"Now, let's see what we have here."

Is there any feeling more horrifying than having to sit still while your teacher reads a message on your phone? Isn't it the absolute worst?

Okay, I've changed my mind. There is a worse feeling. It's when your teacher starts scrolling through your phone. And there's nothing you can do. You just have to sit there and take it.

Lael and I manage to restrain ourselves from grabbing our phones away from her. We turn purple in the face and make squeaky little noises of horror instead.

Ms Waise gives us a squinty-eyed stare. "I think you had both better come and see me in my classroom on Friday afternoon."

"Okay, Ms Waise."

"Sure, Ms Waise."

"And now…"

She holds up our phones as though she is thinking about what to do with them. Like, is she going to take them over to her desk and browse through our messages in peace? Or is she going to put them into the phone bucket, which means we'll only get them back at the end of the day? Or is she going to…

Give them back to us! Yes.

"Here you go. Put them away now and don't let me see them again until the end of the lesson."

We breathe sighs of relief. I don't know about you, but I don't feel completely at ease unless my phone is right in my pocket where it belongs.

"Well, that was stressful," says Lael, as the bell goes for the end of the lesson and we troop off to break.

"Tell me about it. At least she gave us our phones back."

"And a detention." Lael is determined to look on the gloomy side.

"True. But we can always use it to catch up on home-work."

☥

Normally, on days when I don't have extra-murals, I go straight home to chill.

But today, instead of stretching out on my bed scrolling through celebrities' Instagram stories, I am sitting in the Grade Ten dormitory at Sisulu House trying not to bite my nails from tension. Just as the last bell of the day rang, I got a message from Nosipho addressed to our whole friend group on WhatsApp.

Nosipho: You guys. I've been called into a meeting with the Dean, the headmaster, and Mrs Oosthuizen. I think this is it. They're going to tell me I have to leave. I'm trying to stay positive, but it's so hard. :(

We have congregated in the dorm, waiting for Nosipho to come back from her meeting, so we can give her moral support. It's a bad sign that Mrs Oosthuizen is attending the meeting. She's the one who wanted Nosipho to leave. She is a dinosaur from another age who should not be the head of any department, but especially not of Life Orientation.

Her attitudes are from the 1960s. I could imagine her fitting in all too well with the people who made poor Amelia's life a misery. It's not right that she still has the power to decide what happens to someone like Nosipho.

"What are we going to do if Nos comes back in here and says she's been kicked out?" asks Yasmin. "I mean, literally – what are we going to say to her?"

"We're going to talk about the next step," says Lael. "We're going to decide what we'll do next. There is no way we are taking that lying down."

"But what can we do?" I feel hopeless. "It's like we've used up all our options already. There's nothing left for us to do."

"We can leave the school in protest!" says Lael, walking around in circles. "We can all give notice and leave. They won't like that. That would cost them money in school fees."

I snort. "Brentwood has a waiting list of more than two hundred students. If we all left, they could replace us tomorrow. They wouldn't even notice we were gone. And then we'd have to go to some other ratchet school that would probably be worse."

Amira wrings her hands. "How can they do this to her? How? Don't they see that they are sabotaging her future? Have they got no feelings? Don't they care about their students at all?"

"We should march," says Lael feverishly. "We should organise a mass protest action to disrupt activities and…"

"Now you sound like my mom."

Yasmin writes down ideas on an exam pad. "We could start another social media campaign. Maybe get a teen-mom organisation on board."

"We will never surrender!" Now Lael is channelling some dead guy from history. "We will fight them on the beaches and on the … uh…"

"I'm staying."

"Huh?"

We were so worked up, none of us noticed Nosipho walk in.

"What did you say?"

"I said, I'm staying. They said I can stay until I've finished Matric."

We stare at her with our mouths hanging open. It's like we can't process the news after all our doom and gloom.

Nosipho looks puzzled. "Did you guys hear what I said? I'm not being kicked out of school. I'm staying. And it's all thanks to you."

Lael gives a high-pitched scream. I start ululating. And then the whole room descends into chaos as we cry, scream and hug each other at the same time.

CHAPTER 11

To: Trinity Luhabe trinityluhabe@gmail.com
From: Genealogy in Action FindPeople@GenealogyInAction.co.za
Re: Finding your person

Dear Mr Luhabe Trinity,

Thank you for your honoured inquiry to our website. We want to help you find your long-lost ancestor/relative/friend Loretta Mainwaring. Maybe Loretta Mainwaring was a pirate saling on the Spanish Main in the Days of Yore. Maybe Loretta Mainwaring was a knight of the roundtable of King Authur. We will help you find Loretta Mainwaring.

Our data bases are the Biggest in the World. If Loretta Mainwaring ever existed, we will Find him. Our fees are very reasonable, Luhabe. Sign up now for a monthly direct deposit payment of $400 for a QuikSearch service. Or $500 per month for a North American and Canada search. Or a $600 monthly payment to include Europe.

Luhabe, we will keep searching every month until we find Loretta Mainwaring. 75% of people who used our services found out that they were descended from Royalty. Perhaps you will too, Luhabe. You can claim that inheritance you have always wanted when we prove that you are descended from the Crouned Heads of Europe. A preliminary search for Loretta Mainwaring has suggested that he is Directly Descended from Charlemagne of Europe.

Whether you are looking for A Trace of Trinity or a Lure of Luhabe, we are sure to put you on the right track. Sign up today, to find your long-lost relative Loretta Mainwaring. Simply choose which option you want to select from the list below and then enter your credit card details. Don't forget to click on "Debit my account every month". And remember! Should you want to cancel your monthly debit order with us, it's as easy as clicking on this link: www.thelinkyouarelookingfordoesnotexist.com. We look forward to assisting your further in your search for Loretta Mainwaring.

Yours in kind regards,
The Team at Genealogy In Action

To: Trinity Luhabe trinityluhabe@gmail.com
From: Obert Nzingane – Proprietor onzingane@nzinganeinvesti-gations.co.za
Re: Your investigation

Dear Ms Luhabe,

Many thanks for your email. Yes, I used to be the in-house investigator for UbuntuGold back in the 1990s and early 2000s. I started my own private investigation firm more than ten years ago. It is good to hear that your father thinks highly enough of me to recommend me to his daughter.

I believe you are looking for a lady by the name of Loretta Mainwaring who was a pupil at your school, Brentwood College, in 1968. If you decide to engage my services, I could certainly help you with that. I would ask you to supply me with as much information as you have. A copy of the school magazine from any of the years that she attended, for example, would be a great start.

I charge by the hour. Please find my schedule of fees attached. As specified, I would be very happy to offer a 15% discount to the daughter of Abel and Sunet Luhabe.

If we get to the point where I have managed to find some definite contact details for this person, I would recommend a cautious approach in contacting her. I have often found that people are disconcerted at being "tracked down", especially by a stranger. They need a little time and space to get used to the idea. Having someone show up on their doorstep, for example, often evokes a bad reaction. Even a phone-call can be viewed as an invasion of privacy. I will try to get you a confirmed email address, and would suggest using that instead.

I look forward to hearing from you in due course once you have made a decision about whether or not to engage my services.

Kind regards,
Obert Nzingane
Proprietor

Lael rubs her chin thoughtfully. "Hmm … tough call. Which option to choose? I can hardly make up my mind."

I giggle. "I know. It's a challenge, isn't it? The dodgy website that will be debiting money from my account for the rest of my life, or the experienced private investigator who seems to know what he is doing and has reasonable rates."

"In defence of the dodgy website, they do promise to prove that you are directly descended from Charlemagne and can claim a huge inheritance as a result."

"They are such liars."

"Big, fat liars."

"So, I'll email this Mr Nzingane and tell him we want to use him. Will you find the right school magazines?"

"Yes, of course." Lael is the school magazine expert. She's the one who found a picture and a name for Jim Grey in the first place. "Leave it to me. I'll get onto it this afternoon."

"After our detention, you mean."

She clutches her head. "I forgot about that. Good thing you reminded me, or I would have gone straight to the library after school. There's no way we can get out of it, is there?"

"Not unless you feel like going to Ms Waise and explaining that it's not a hundred per cent convenient for us to attend her detention today and would she mind if we skipped it."

Lael shivers. "I wouldn't dare. She would roast us. I am so scared of her."

"I know. Me too. She's nice, though."

"She's nice, but there's something terrifying about her."

"She's someone you don't want to mess with."

I get through the rest of the day in a good mood, even though we have double maths, which is my absolute worst. Just knowing that Nosipho is being allowed to stay has cheered me up so much. She can stop worrying about hiding her bump now. Her aunt has a sewing machine and is going to convert her school uniform to fit better.

It's a bit of a downer that we have a detention on a Friday afternoon, but we can get some homework done, so it's not all bad.

I meet up with Lael outside the library and we walk to Ms Waise's class together.

"Hey, girls," she greets us. "You're right on time."

"Good afternoon, Ma'am."

"Afternoon, Ms Waise."

"Um … what are you doing?"

Lael and I look up. We are taking out our homework and spreading it on our desks. I feel like saying, *What does it look like we're doing*? But that would be cheeky.

"Uh … we're getting ready for our detention, Ma'am," says Lael. "Is that okay?"

"What detention?"

"The detention you gave us on Wednesday."

She looks puzzled for a moment, and then she starts laughing. "I didn't give you a detention. I never give detentions. I don't believe in them."

"But you said you would see us on Friday afternoon," I say. "That's teacher-speak for 'You've got a detention.'"

She laughs again. "Teacher-speak as a language – I like that. Unfortunately, I've never been fluent in it. I literally meant that I wanted to see you. I need to speak to both of you."

She sees the expressions on our faces and another cackle of laughter breaks from her.

"*I need to speak to you* is teacher-speak for *you're in trouble*, isn't it? Don't worry, you're not. I just wanted to ask why you are so interested in that old diary that's on display in Sisulu House. I set up that exhibition – Brentwood College in the 1960s. I saw on your phones that you were studying it, and I wondered why."

I glance at Lael, and see that she is thinking the same thing I am: proceed with caution.

"We were just interested in finding out what happened to the girl who wrote that diary," Lael explains. "And also to the boy she writes about. She was … she was…"

"Pregnant." Ms Waise says. "Yes, I know."

"They were both pupils at Brentwood, you see," I say. "The boy died. His name was Jim Grey. It's in the school magazine for that year, but it doesn't say how he died. We also don't know what happened to Amelia – that's the name of the girl. And we'd also like to know what happened to her baby."

"I see." Ms Waise gives us a thoughtful look. "And why are you so interested in all this? Is it for a school project?"

"It's not a project, exactly…" Lael stalls.

"It all happened so long ago – fifty years. I don't know many teenagers who are interested in that kind of ancient history."

"I met his ghost, you see," I blurt.

Ms Waise turns to look at me. Her expression suggests that I might have grown an extra head.

"*Trinity!*" Lael groans.

I don't know what to tell her. Sometimes I just blurt

things out. It's like my brain is not fully engaged when my mouth moves.

"You … what was that again?" Ms Waise is probably hoping she misheard.

I shrug. The secret's out now. There's no more point in pretending.

"Okay, see, this is what happened. Last term when I was boarding at Sisulu House, I met this boy. I thought he was one of the Grade Tens from Gumede House. So many new kids arrived this year that I still don't know all of them."

"Right…?"

"But here's the thing. I'm the only one who ever saw him. No one else was ever with me when I spoke to him. It turns out he wasn't a student at all. And when Lael showed me a group photo from the 1968 school magazine, I picked him out immediately as Jim Grey. Then she told me he had died that year and I couldn't believe it."

"What was he like?" asks Ms Waise.

"Um…" I wasn't prepared for this question. "He was a little bit sexist … and a little bit racist, I guess … but he was a good friend to me. He stood up for me."

"That's amazing."

"And ever since then we've been trying to find out what happened to him," Lael can't resist adding. "All the newspapers say is that he was found dead in the Sisulu House common room. We want to know why."

"I know it sounds crazy, but he was my friend," I say. "He helped me through a difficult time. I need to know the truth about what happened to him"

"I see." Ms Waise doesn't look quite so freaked out

any more. "And you think the diary could give you some clues?"

"Yes, we do." A brilliant idea suddenly occurs to me. "Oh, Ms Waise, please could you unlock the cabinet for us so we can take a proper look at the diary? I'm sure it holds the secret."

Lael looks eager, but Ms Waise shakes her head.

"I'm sorry, girls. I don't have the key. Once I finished setting up the exhibition, I handed the key back to Dr Hussein's secretary – Mrs Anderssen. You should ask her."

I pull a face. "I already tried that. She said no."

Lael is almost quivering with excitement. "But, Ma'am! I just thought of something. Did you read the diary before you put it into the cabinet?"

Yes. Genius. She could tell us what it says.

Ms Waise looks doubtful. "I started reading it, but the deputy headmistress, Ms Govender, took it back for the display before I could finish it."

"Oh," says Lael. "But maybe you can remember if there was anything in there that could tell us what happened to Jim?"

She shakes her head. "I don't think so. The diary seemed to end before his death. Amelia either left it here by mistake, or sent it here on purpose – maybe because she didn't want her parents reading it. Either way, it has been kept in storage at Sisulu House all this time."

"Hey, maybe she sent it to Loret…"

Lael coughs loudly, drowning out my voice. "I guess we'll never know!" she says. "Just one of those mysteries. Who knows why she did what she did? Trinity, we should get going now."

Ms Waise gives me a narrow-eyed look. "Just a minute. What were you going to say, Trinity?"

But I've learned my lesson. We're not giving away all our secrets to this teacher, nice as she is. The problem with teachers is that they're unpredictable. You never know how they'll react. And something tells me that if she finds out we've hired a private detective to track down Amelia's old school friend, she will freak out. She might even tell us not to pursue the matter, or threaten to tell our parents.

"I was just going to say that she might have given the diary to one of her friends for safekeeping," I say innocently.

"Yes, I suppose she might."

A thought strikes me.

"Ms Waise, if you don't have the key and we don't have the key, who keeps turning the pages?"

"That's a good question, actually. I noticed the other day that the diary was on a different page."

"It seems to change every few weeks," says Lael. "Maybe it's Mrs Anderssen."

"Or maybe it's Jim!" I say, only half-seriously.

I certainly don't expect Ms Waise to turn pale.

"What's wrong, Ma'am?"

"Nothing – I'm feeling a little woozy."

"Do you want us to call Matron for you?"

"No, thanks." She straightens. "I'm fine now. You girls can go on home. I wish you lots of luck in figuring out what happened to Jim Grey. Please let me know if you discover anything."

We promise that we will, but I for one have got my fingers crossed behind my back.

"Well, that was a bonus," says Lael as we walk down to the parking lot. "Now we've got a free afternoon instead of a detention."

"I know! It's awesome. And I'm really hoping that private detective guy, Obert, contacts me with good news on Monday. I want to get on with contacting Loretta."

"Yes. That'll be the next thing we do, definitely."

But it turns out that the next thing we do has nothing to do with Amelia or Jim or anything that happened in the 1960s.

On Sunday night, Lael and I get a panicked email from Nosipho.

Guys, my mom is coming back from overseas next weekend. She's landing on Saturday morning. My aunt swears she hasn't told her anything about the pregnancy, but I don't know whether to believe her.

I suppose if my mom slaps me across the face when I say hello, then I'll know.

I'm so scared, you guys. I'm more scared than when I was waiting for the test result to turn positive. My mom has always had this huge thing about pregnancy. Like, it was the worst thing that could happen to anyone, ever. She is going to freak out so badly.

I asked my aunt if she would stay with me while I told her, but she said she doesn't want to be on the same continent as my mom when she finds out. She's worried my mom is going to blame her for keeping it a secret.

I'm asking you guys if you will come and be with me while I tell her? Actually, I won't have to tell her. She will take one look at my tummy and she will know. I am quite big already. Basically, you guys will have to come with me to the airport to protect me.

No, wait. My aunt can fetch her from the airport and we can wait at home for her to arrive. So when she walks into the house and sees me, she can freak out in peace without strangers watching.

Please say you will, guys! Please, please, please.

I know it's a lot to ask but you have been there for me from the very beginning. You won't want to miss this part, will you? And it's not like she is going to be mad at you, right? I'm the one who will be the target.

Please say yes? Pleeeeeeeease.

Nos xxx

I'm not too surprised when my phone starts ringing the moment I finish reading the email.

It's Lael, of course.

These days we mostly WhatsApp or voicemail or Snapchat each other, but there are some things that are too long to type.

"Hi," I say gloomily.

"I presume you saw the email?"

"I did. We'll have to do it, I suppose, but I'm not looking forward to it."

"I know. Me neither. Did you see that thing about how Nosipho's aunt is too scared to be there when she tells her mom? That's her mom's own sister. But we're supposed to be cool with it?"

"Exactly. The thing about Nosipho's mom is that she's really nice and everything, but she's a bit intimidating."

"A bit?" Lael says. "Make that very intimidating. It's that whole no-nonsense, sharp-suited, corporate thing she's got going on. And I'm speaking as one who also has a scary mother."

"Your mom is fairly scary," I agree. "Do you remember when she put us on that diet last term? We didn't even think about saying, 'No, thanks'."

Lael groans. "Oh, my word. That diet. It nearly killed me. I'm still traumatised when I think of those stupid milkshakes and soups we were drinking. I swear I actually eat more these days just because I keep remembering what it felt like to feel so deprived of food."

"Me too. I don't know which mom I'd rather have the pregnancy conversation with – yours or Nosipho's."

"It's too close to call."

"I wish Nosipho's mom could be more like my mom. That would be easy."

"Your mom is a marshmallow," she agrees. "Your dad, on the other hand, is a bit terrifying."

"Sometimes when I want to scare myself, I imagine having to tell my dad I'm pregnant. It's like my worst nightmare. My mom would have to be there to calm him down."

"I don't think my dad would care. As long as his business associates didn't find out, he wouldn't mind."

Lael's dad lives in Pietermaritzburg with his second wife and new family. He only sees Lael twice a year on Rosh Hashanah and Hannukah, and even then, he sometimes cancels.

"Nonsense!" I say. "Of course he cares. He loves you.

He would freak out if something happened to you." I change the subject fast. "Speaking of dads – has Nosipho ever mentioned hers to you?"

"Nosipho's dad…?" Lael thinks for a moment. "I don't think so. It's just her and her mom, as far as I know."

"That's what I thought too. It's a bit strange, isn't it?"

There are plenty of kids in our grade who don't live with their dads, but we still have an idea of where they are. I can think of two kids whose dads have passed away, and a few who hardly ever see their dads, but Nosipho is the only one who has never mentioned her father at all.

"I suppose it is strange," Lael says. "We should ask her about it some time."

"How old do you think Nosipho's mom was when she had her?"

"She told me her mom is forty, so I guess she must have been twenty-four."

"Forty?" I say. "No way! She looks much younger."

"I'm really bad at telling how old adults are. They all look ancient to me."

On Saturday morning, we are a subdued threesome sitting around Nosipho's kitchen table and sipping hot chocolate.

Nosipho's aunt has gone to fetch her mom from the airport. Her plan is to drop her at home and then peel out of there in a spray of gravel. I kind of wish I could join her. Nosipho keeps obsessively checking the airport website, which is not updating quickly enough for her liking.

Lael and I are wearing our matching *Wife Life* T-shirts. In retrospect, this feels like an odd fashion choice for this occasion.

"It still says her plane hasn't landed," Nosipho grumbles. "What is wrong with this thing?" She gives her phone a shake, like that's going to help. Then she hits "refresh" again.

"Oh, my word!" she screams. "She landed more than an hour ago. How did that happen? She could be here any minute."

We sit up straight and clutch our mugs to our chests. Nosipho has dressed carefully for the day in a pair of skinny jeans and an oversized jersey. If you just glanced at her, you wouldn't notice her tummy.

"Quick, I have to tidy up."

"The place is already tidy," says Lael.

"I have to…"

"Too late," I say as we hear a car pulling up in the driveway.

"Guys, I feel sick. I want to run away."

I hug Nosipho from the left and Lael hugs her from the right.

"We're here," I say. "We're not going anywhere. Whatever happens, we'll stay right here."

Through the open door, we see Nosipho's mom get out of her aunt's car. She goes around to the boot and takes her luggage out. Then she grabs it by the handle and pulls it along behind her, waving goodbye to her sister as she walks up the driveway.

She looks like one of those celebrities that get photographed at airports showing off their immaculate style. From the top of her braided head to the tip of her suede boots, she is a model of elegance and sophistication. She pushes her Chanel sunglasses up onto her head as she enters the kitchen.

"Hi, Trinity. Hi, Lael. It's nice of you girls to wait with Nosipho."

"Hi, Thulani!" we chorus.

Then she drops her bag and holds out her arms to her daughter. "Come here, my baby. I've missed you so much."

Nosipho makes a kind of sobbing noise and flings herself into her mother's arms. "I've missed you too, Mommy."

Lael and I exchange glances. A hug that tight is going to tell Nosipho's mom everything she needs to know. And, sure enough, it happens right in front of us.

Thulani has her eyes squeezed shut, and her cheek pressed against her daughter's. Then her eyes pop open. You can almost see her thinking, "What on earth is that?"

She pulls away from the hug slowly, frowning. Her hands drop from Nosipho's shoulders to her waist and she feels her daughter's belly. Then her face crumples and tears start to roll down her cheeks.

Whatever Nosipho was expecting, it wasn't this. Anger and recriminations, yes. But not this silent sorrow.

"I'm sorry, Mommy. I'm so sorry." Nosipho's face is grey as her mom sinks onto one of the kitchen chairs and drops her head into her hands.

Lael and I are horrified.

"Come here," Thulani says between sobs.

Nosipho approaches her warily. Once again, her mom's hands come out to touch the swell of her belly. She runs her fingers gently over it from top to bottom. And all the while, tears are pouring down her cheeks.

"How far?" she asks.

"About five months. Twenty weeks."

"Have you been to a doctor?"

"Yes. Dr Patel at the Morningside Fem-Clinic. She's brilliant. I love her."

"Why did no one tell me?"

"I wanted to tell you face-to-face, Mommy. I made Auntie Mbaks promise not to tell you."

"And the boy?"

"You know him, Mom. Themba Matlare. It was just one time and we used protection, but it happened anyway. I'm so sorry."

Thulani shakes her head. "Just like your mom, my baby. Just like your mom."

We hold our breath. You could hear a pin drop. What is she saying? Are we going to find out the truth about Nosipho's dad at last?

"What do you mean, Mommy? You were much older than sixteen when you had me."

For a moment, it looks as though Thulani isn't going to answer her. She stares off into the distance as though she is weighing something up. Then she gives a deep sigh. It seems to come from the soles of her feet.

"Not me, my darling. I'm talking about your biological mom. My little sister."

This time the silence is so complete I can hear my heart beating in my ears. Nosipho looks as if an atom bomb has gone off in the kitchen.

"Wh-what do you mean? Your sister? My biological mother? Mommy, what are you saying?"

Thulani stands up slowly. She puts her arms around Nosipho's shoulders and presses her cheek against hers.

"I wanted to tell you, baby. I wanted to tell you from the beginning, but your grandmother overruled me. I had to bow to her seniority."

"Tell me what?" Nosipho's voice sounds high.

"Okay." Thulani pulls out a chair and sits down next to Nosipho, keeping a tight hold on her hand. "You know about Auntie Mbaks and Uncle Linda, but I've never told you that I had another sister when I was growing up. She was the last-born child of your granny. Her name was Nosiphiwo and she was five years younger than me. I loved her so much, my darling. She was my own special baby and I looked after her for her whole life. She was so beautiful. I used to rub oil into her skin and into her hair. We used to go everywhere holding hands. She called me her other mother."

"I … I've seen her in photographs," Nosipho says, wonderingly. "You have your arm around her in every photo. You told me she was a little cousin who died."

A single tear rolls down Thulani's cheek. "You always used to say, 'She looks like me, Mommy. She looks like me, that one.' And you were right. You look exactly like her. Every time I want to remember her, I just look at your beautiful face."

"But … but what happened?"

"She got pregnant when she was sixteen. In a way, I blamed myself because I had gone away to university – the first in our family to go. Nosiphiwo had nobody to talk to about such matters. Your granny was very old-school, as you know. But we were all so happy when the baby was born, when you were born. You were the most loved baby in the world. When you were just three days old, Uncle Linda took Nosiphiwo to the shops to buy some nappies and baby oil. They never made it. A taxi driver swerved onto the pavement and drove into them." The tears are falling fast now. "Uncle Linda had a few bumps and bruises, but your mother – my beloved Nosiphiwo – was killed instantly. I felt as though my life were over. The only bright side was that you weren't with them. Your mom had left you with me to look after."

Nosipho's eyes are wide and stunned looking. I think she is too shocked to cry. "How … I mean, why … I mean, why did nobody ever tell me this before?"

"Your granny thought she was going to raise you, but I wouldn't let you out of my arms. I hardly put you down for a week. I wouldn't let anyone near you. They tried to argue with me. After all, I was just twenty years old and a student. But I didn't listen to them. You were mine and that was the end of it. So the elders all got together to discuss it, and eventually they let me have my way. But they decided that you would be brought up believing I was your birth mother. I didn't agree, but it wasn't my decision. You know how these things work. Then when your granny died two years ago, she said I could tell you the truth, but only when it became important in your life. I think this qualifies."

"You … you wouldn't put me down? For a whole week?"

Thulani strokes a finger down Nosipho's cheek. "Not even for a second. I was so scared somebody was going to try to take you away from me. I loved you for your own sake, you see, and for the sake of my sister. You were my blood and my bone, and you still are."

Now Nosipho is crying. Tears are flowing faster than she can wipe them away. She presses her face against Thulani's beautiful linen shirt.

"I love you, Mommy."

"I love you too, my baby." Thulani kneels and hugs her daughter.

I glance at Lael and see that tears are trickling down her face, too. She's such a softie. Then I touch my own cheeks and feel the wetness there. Turns out I'm a softie too.

Eventually we all blow our noses. Thulani makes us all some more hot chocolate, and apologises to Lael and me for making us sit through all the family drama.

"They don't mind," says Nosipho. "Do you, guys?"

We shake our heads.

"I asked them to be here for support while I told you about this." Nosipho touches the gentle swell of her stomach.

"Do you know if it's a boy or a girl?" Thulani asks.

"No, I want it to be a surprise."

As we sip our drinks, Nosipho asks her mother some of the questions that are bubbling away inside of her. Like whether she was ever formally adopted.

"Of course," says Thulani. "It's all signed and sealed. I got the final adoption papers when you were just four months old. You are my daughter under South African law. I told you I was twenty-four when I had you, but I was actually twenty when you became mine. I am thirty-six, not forty."

"I knew it!" I say. Everyone turns to stare at me. "Sorry, it's just that I knew you weren't forty. You look much too young."

Thulani smiles at me.

"And what about my father?" says Nosipho. "Do you know who he is? Does he know about me?"

"That was another thing your grandmother and her brothers decided about. They didn't want to know who your father was, or for him to know about you. But I remember who my sister was close to in those days. I can easily find out for you, if you want. I can find out who your father is, and who his family are, because they are your family too."

"I do want that. I want to know everything."

Lael and I are in the Uber heading back to school when she turns to me with a troubled look on her face.

"Babes?"

"What's up, sister wife?"

"It bothers me that Nosipho made this decision without consulting her mom and her aunt."

"What do you mean? It was no one's decision to make except hers."

"Sure. In a way. But it's going to affect them too. She's landing them with a baby that they are going to have to take care of for years and years."

"You saw how Thulani was stroking Nosipho's tummy." I can't help smiling at the memory. "She is going to love the baby. They both will."

Lael rolls her eyes. "Of course they will love the baby, but that is totally not the point. The point is that they were given no choice. This is going to derail their lives big time and they weren't given a say in the matter."

She sees the doubtful look on my face and doubles down.

"Obviously I'm not saying it should have been anyone else's choice, but it doesn't only affect Nosipho. It is actually a feminist issue."

"How do you figure that?"

"What if Thulani is ready to live her own life now that Nosipho is nearly grown up? What if she doesn't want to be saddled with a newborn baby? She's had her agency taken away."

I hold up my hand. "Okay, babes. Slow down a minute. Do you remember you once said that I should tell you if you were ever being a white feminist?"

"Yes, but..."

"You're being a white feminist."

Lael is close to losing her temper. Anger flashes into her eyes. Anger and hurt. She makes an effort to push them away.

"What do you mean?"

"Everything you say is true, but there is cultural stuff happening here that you don't understand."

"So tell me."

"In our culture, a baby doesn't just belong to the mother like it does in the white community. A baby is raised by the extended family, and the whole community. There isn't that same sense of *your* baby or *my* baby. It's more like *our* baby."

"Okay, but..."

"And women don't stop raising babies when their own children are grown. If you are doing well financially, you invite other family members to come and live with you, so they can also get a good education. You must have heard Nosipho talk about her little twin cousins who are going to live with them when they are ready to start nursery school?"

"Yes, I think she mentioned…"

"When she is speaking Xhosa, she doesn't even call them her cousins. She calls them her sisters."

"But still, the burden on Thulani…"

"First of all, Nosipho is going to raise that baby herself. That's why she's reading every baby book ever written. And second of all, it won't all fall on Thulani. She will hire a woman – probably a family member – to come and live with them and look after whatever babies happen to be in the house at the time. It might even be the same person who helped to raise Nosipho. Nothing will get in the way of Thulani's career, I can promise you."

Lael's face is flushed. I have hardly let her get a word in, but she is listening carefully.

"Sometimes you just have to accept that you don't have all the answers, babes, especially when it comes to someone else's culture."

She swallows. This isn't easy for her to hear. Lael is used to being right.

"I'm not saying every African family is like this," I say. "Or that it's going to be an easy road for any of them. But I am the child of a teen mother, and Nosipho is the child of a teen mother, and you know what? The world didn't come to an end for any of us."

Lael nods, accepting what I am saying. Tears glisten in her eyes. To her credit, she doesn't let them fall.

CHAPTER 12

To: Trinity Luhabe trinityluhabe@gmail.com
From: Obert Nzingane – Proprietor onzingane@nzinganeinvesti-
gations.co.za
Re: Your investigation

Dear Ms Luhabe,

I am happy to report that I have found Loretta Mainwaring.
She is sixty-six years old and lives in a little town called Kroondal
near Sun City. Her married name is Loretta Backeberg.
Her husband passed away seven years ago and she has one
child – a son who lives in Canada.

It seems she has no access to email and no mobile phone that
I could track down. All I managed to get was a physical address
and a landline number. Please find them both attached to this
message. I know I told you to email first before phoning, but
unfortunately that won't be possible in this case. She is only
contactable by telephone. If you want some tips on how to
approach her, I would be happy to help.

In answer to your more recent question, your friend and her
mother are very welcome to contact me for assistance in tracing
her biological father. I will help in any way I can.

Kind regards,
Obert Nzingane
Proprietor

To: Trinity Luhabe trinityluhabe@gmail.com
From: Jeanette Harms SleepHollowGuestHouse@gmail.co.za
Re: Sleepy Hollow B&B Kroondal – your reservation

Dear Ms Luhabe,

Many thanks for your enquiry. Unfortunately, we are fully booked for the weekend you are asking about. Our accommodation is usually booked up a year in advance so guests need to make their plans well ahead of time.

I doubt you will find any other accommodation in Kroondal at such short notice. May I suggest central Rustenburg as a place to look for suitable accommodation for you and your friend.

Kind regards,
Jeanette Harms
Sleepy Hollow B&B

To: Lael Lieberman laellieberman@gmail.com
From: Jeanette Harms SleepyHollowGuestHouse@gmail.co.za
Re: Sleepy Hollow B&B Kroondal – your reservation

Dear Ms Lieberman,

We would be delighted to welcome you and your friend to stay at Sleepy Hollow Guest House for the weekend you are enquiring about.

This is a very quiet time of year for us, so you will have your choice of accommodation. You can stay in our Harmony suite, which features a king-size bed and a view of the sunflower fields. Or you can stay in our Tranquillity suite, which offers two twin beds and a stand-alone shower. Or you can choose our deluxe Honeymoon suite, which offers a rose-petal turn-down and a complimentary bottle of sparkling wine. I am attaching a schedule of rates for these three options. I think you will find them very reasonable.

There are many attractions in the area for weekend visitors to enjoy. I will supply you with a full complement of brochures when you check in. To secure your accommodation, please pay the deposit by EFT into our bank account and fax me the proof of payment. We look forward to welcoming you, and giving you a taste of Kroondal hospitality.

Kind regards,
Jeanette Harms
Sleepy Hollow B&B

Lael is so angry she is practically foaming at the mouth.

"This is ridiculous. It's against the law. Surely it's against the law? How can we find out if it is?"

"I don't know." I can't seem to find my anger. Yet. All I feel is depressed.

"She took one look at your surname and realised you were black. This is racism, pure and simple. We need to report it to someone."

I shrug.

"Why aren't you madder? You can't take this lying down, Trinity. We need to do something."

"It's not the first time it has happened to me. And I doubt it'll be the last."

Lael's mouth drops open. "Still? In this day and age?"

"Yup. This one time my mom and I wanted to go to Polokwane to help look after my ouma when she had an operation. We didn't want to stay at the house and make extra work for her, so we tried to book into a B&B. Every single place was fully booked until my mom actually phoned them, and they heard her Afrikaans accent. Then all of a sudden they had plenty of space. And there was another time we were going to Port Elizabeth to watch Aaron play rugby. Mom didn't want to do the whole private jet and fancy hotel thing, so she tried to make a booking on AirB&B. The whole of Port Elizabeth was full until she attached a profile picture to her application and then, surprise, they had place for us."

"That's disgusting. That is just absolutely … I feel sick to my stomach."

"I know. Me too. But literally the only people who don't know that this still happens on a regular basis are white people."

"Gah!" She grabs me in a hard hug. "I'm sorry white people suck so much."

I relax into her hug and start to feel a little better. It helps to have a friend who doesn't try to explain that "not all white people" are like this.

"So what are we going to do?" Lael asks once she lets me go. "I presume you don't actually want to stay at this place even though I can get us a booking?"

"Urrgh, no." I pull a face. "Spend the night at a place that doesn't want me – that was prepared to lie to avoid having me to stay? I don't think so."

"That's what I thought. What should we do? Do we keep looking?"

I think about it for a moment. "You know, it's only a two-hour drive. We could do it in a day. We could drive there in the morning, have a chat with Loretta, and drive back in the afternoon. I know we were planning a week-end road-trip, but maybe we should keep it to one day."

"I suppose. It's a bit disappointing, though."

"The main thing is that we're going to talk to Loretta. She'll be able to clear up so many mysteries for us. She might even know how Jim died."

"That's true," Lael says, brightening. She glances down at her phone as it buzzes in her hand. Then she holds it up for me to see a text. "Look. It's from Ms Waise."

Jenny Waise: New page of diary visible today. Quite interesting. You and T should check it out. Wish I knew who was turning the pages!

Lael and I were starting to think we would never get to see a new page of the diary. I check the time on Lael's phone, but there are only two minutes left of break. We'll have to contain our excitement until there is enough time for us to go back to Sisulu House.

DEAR DIARY | OCTOBER 1968

Today is the day I leave school forever. I knew this day was coming, but somehow, I don't feel quite prepared for it. The only bright side is that Jim agreed to see me when I told him I was going away. We met behind the bicycle sheds at the bottom of Botha field.

At first his manner was strange and reserved. He wouldn't look me in the eye. His gaze was continually drawn to my midriff with a kind of fascinated repulsion.

I asked him if he wanted to touch my stomach, to feel his baby moving around. He refused. And, oh Diary! The look on his face when he said no was awful to behold. He looked horrified at the thought. It was as though it would burn him to touch me.

Of course, I said nothing. My duty was to enable us to part on good terms, and let him know we would welcome him back in our lives with open arms at any time in the future. Besides, there is nothing as unattractive as a nagging girl.

He asked me what I was going to do and I told him I would live at the farm with my parents. Then he said he meant what would I do about the baby. I told him my parents hadn't decided yet. He reminded me that the baby had nothing to do with him, and that his father wouldn't be blackmailed into contributing anything to its upkeep. He said I could never prove it was his, and even if I did a blood test it had a twenty per cent chance of being wrong.

Oh, Diary! How cruelly he misunderstands me.

Does he not know I have no desire to trap him or force him into anything? I love him. I want him to be happy. Of course, I don't want to ruin his life. This is my fault, and my problem to deal with on my own.

I just wanted a kind or loving word from him to sustain me for the journey that lies ahead.

But it was not to be, Diary. His heart is too full of anger and resentment towards me. He blames me for this situation, and isn't able to think of anything beyond that.

I asked him to give me his blessing before we parted, and perhaps one last kiss. He said he would give me his blessing but not a kiss because he no longer found me attractive in that way.

And so we parted, dear Diary, quite possibly never to see each other again. Although I still have hopes that when the baby is here, he will love it for its own sake and perhaps we can become a family at last. I have heard of many cases like that, and Loretta has told me of many more. Apparently, it is quite common for a boy to reject the concept of his own child, only to embrace it when that child is placed into his arms. Oh, how I pray that may happen later this year when this sweet angel is finally born!

I thought my parents would be the ones to fetch me from school later that day, but it was my brother Jack who came for me in the bakkie. He has been working in Rustenburg for the past few months, so I was quite surprised to see him.

I rushed up to him for a hug, but he held me at arm's length. There was disgust in his eyes when he looked at my swollen belly, but something told me that his feelings weren't quite as hostile as those of my parents.

At first, he wouldn't speak to me. He just threw my trunk into the back of the bakkie and told me to climb in next to him. We drove in silence for miles. Only after an hour had passed did he respond when I addressed him. I asked him about his job and about the farm, and he replied quite civilly.

I know I don't deserve it, but it was such a comfort to have a member of my family speak to me calmly. It was as though the clock had been turned back and life was normal again.

That ended when we got to the farm, of course.

My father still won't talk to me, and my mother barks orders as though I am one of the servants. Jack began to withdraw again as soon as we drove up to the house.

So, here I am, dear Diary, in my childhood bedroom. And I wonder what will happen to my baby and me now?

Love
Amelia

Lael and I take turns reading over the latest diary entry in the car. It is Saturday morning and Lungile is driving us to Kroondal. Luckily, it's a long weekend, so we aren't missing any school sport. The roads are busy, with lots of people are heading to Sun City for the three-day weekend. I wouldn't mind popping into the Valley of the Waves for a quick swim myself, but a) I didn't bring a swimming costume, and b) we have more important things to think about.

"Every time I read one of these diary entries, I kind of want to burst into tears," Lael admits, handing my phone back to me.

"Me too. She had such a hard time, the poor girl. I mean, in a middle-class sort of way."

"That's true. At least she had a roof over her head and food on the table. Lots of girls in South Africa don't even have that while they're pregnant. But I still feel sorry for her."

"It must have been so weird not knowing what was going to happen to you," I say. "Just waiting for your parents to decide your fate and not having any say in the matter."

"That's kind of what being a kid is like though, isn't it? Your parents are always the ones who get to decide stuff."

"I don't know. I think kids these days have more say than they used to. Most parents at least take our wishes into consideration."

We sit in silence and watch the countryside go by. Thinking about all the bad stuff that happens to people is making me depressed. I remind myself that being depressed is not going to help me find the truth about Jim and Amelia. I need to stay focused.

Why does it even matter so much? asks a little voice in my head. *It all happened so long ago. What possible relevance can it have now?*

Which is true, but somehow it does feel relevant. Not just for Jim's ghost, because it's been so long since I last saw him that I almost don't believe in him anymore. There is something else pushing me on to discover the truth behind this mystery. Something is telling me that it does still matter. It matters a lot.

"This is Kroondal up ahead," says Lungi, pulling me out of my thoughts. "It's one of those blink-and-you'll-miss-it places."

Lael and I sit up and press our noses against the windows.

"Look at that gorgeous little church," she says, pointing.

"It's so cute. I want to pick it up and put it in my pocket."

"You'll have to fight me for it."

"Look, there's another church," I say. It's not nearly as cute as the first one. It's all sort of gloomy and austere.

We pass a couple of shops, a school, and a general store, and the next thing we know, we are heading out of town again. This place really is tiny.

"Are you sure we haven't passed it?" I ask Lungi.

"No, it's up ahead on the left. Look, there are a couple of houses there."

Sure enough, there is a gravel road off to the left that leads to some higgledy-piggledy cottages. We turn down the road slowly because of the ruts.

"There it is," says Lungi. "Number three, with the rose bushes at the front."

Lael and I climb out the car, yawning and stretching. Lungi parks in some shade and takes out his iPad and the lunch our cook packed for him this morning. He will wait for as long as it takes. I really hope this will turn out to be longer than five minutes, considering how far we've driven to visit this lady.

"Now that we're actually here, it feels weird to pitch up at someone's door like this," says Lael.

"I know. And then to say, 'Hi. We've just driven two hours on the off-chance you might be in.' It makes me feel like a stalker."

"There's no way we came all this way for nothing. We need to make this happen."

"Agreed. So, knock on the door."

"You knock on the door."

"No, you knock. I'm shy."

Lael laughs. "Nice try, Trinity. You're the one who's been taught to speak to strangers since you were tiny. Cabinet ministers, CEOs, ambassadors – you're used to talking to all of them. And besides, this is your show."

"What makes it my show?"

"Your ghost, your show. I'm pretty sure that's an actual saying. Jim appeared to you. He wants you to find out the secret of his death."

"Aargh!" I clutch my head. "Okay. All right. But what do I do if there's no answer?"

"We'll cross that bridge when we come to it. Now knock."

I step up to the front door and grab the brass lion's-head knocker. I give three medium-firm taps with the knocker, and then we wait.

Within a few seconds we can hear rustling on the other side of the door, so someone is home, thank goodness. An oldish white lady opens the door and looks at us enquiringly.

"Hello?"

I put on my best speaking-to-cabinet-ministers voice.

"Good morning, Ma'am. We're sorry to trouble you. We would have phoned ahead if we could, but your number isn't listed. May I ask if you are Loretta Backeberg?"

"Who wants to know?" She is suspicious, but not actively hostile. I think she thinks we're trying to sell her something.

"My name is Trinity Luhabe and this is Lael Lieberman. We are Grade Ten learners at Brentwood College – your old school. We're doing some research into something that happened in the 1960s and we think you might be able to fill in some details for us. I can give you the name and number of our History teacher, Ms Waise, if you would like to confirm with her."

The lady peers at us for a long moment, possibly trying to figure out if we are axe-murderers. She seems to decide we're okay.

"No, that's all right. You'd better come inside. I'll put the kettle on."

As soon as we walk into the little house, I am reminded of the time my parents took us skiing in the Black Forest in Germany. It's the smell mainly – pine needles and wood-smoke and something spicy baking in the oven. The rooms are cluttered with furniture – lots of high-backed chairs, with those things that look like white doilies on the arm-rests and head-rests. Antimacassars. That's what they're called.

"Backeberg is a German name, isn't it?" asks Lael, thinking along the same lines as me.

"That's right. My late husband was German. His family has lived here for generations. This cottage was part of the original farmhouse from 1897."

"My mother's family are Ashkenazic, and my dad's family came from Germany," says Lael. "Your house reminds me of my bobba's place in Durban."

"Then this should remind you even more," says Mrs Backeberg, putting some freshly baked cookies on a plate, three-cornered pockets of pastry stuffed with Nutella.

"Hamantaschen!" Lael says. "We have them every year at Purim. I love that you've put chocolate paste in them instead of poppy seeds."

"I have a sweet tooth."

We settle in the sitting room as Mrs Backeberg pours

out some milky looking tea. I decide to concentrate on the hamantaschen instead.

"Well, young ladies, tell me about this project you're researching," she says.

I glance at Lael, who signals me to go ahead.

"Okay, well, first of all, can we confirm that you are in fact Loretta Mainwaring? The one who attended Brentwood in the sixties?"

"I am."

"And you were friendly with a girl called Amelia Lucite?"

Mrs Backeberg freezes with a pastry halfway to her mouth. A look of terrible sadness crosses her face, and I know that however this story ended, it was not happy. Nothing good ever brought such sorrow into someone's eyes.

"Amelia," she says slowly, lowering the pastry to her plate. "My poor Amelia. We were friends from Sub A, you know."

I'm puzzled for a second, and then remember that Sub A was what some schools used to call Grade One.

"Then we have definitely come to the right person," says Lael. "We're trying to find out what happened to Amelia, and also what happened to her boyfriend, Jim Grey."

Mrs Backeberg has a faraway look in her eyes. It is as though she is staring into the past, looking at a time and place we can't possibly understand.

"I haven't heard that name in fifty years," she says. "Jim Grey. I was so angry with him at the time. So angry and resentful. And then he died. Snuffed out at sixteen years old. Well, you can't stay angry at the dead, can you?

Poor boy. Poor, poor boy. It was a dreadful situation all round."

I swallow a lump in my throat. That is exactly how I feel about Jim. When I read how he treated Amelia – how he reacted to her pregnancy – I get so mad at him. I want to grab him and say, "Hey! How can you do that? How can you not accept that you're at least fifty per cent responsible for this situation?" Then I remember that he's been dead for five decades – that he never had the chance to become a better man, or to become a man at all. And then I just want to weep for him.

"Do you have any idea of how he died?" Lael asks.

"No, none. It was a mystery. He was found dead in a chair in the common room by one of the cleaners during the school holidays. No one could understand why he was even there. The school had broken up and everyone had gone home a few days earlier."

"Yes, we read that in the news reports," I say. "We were hoping that someone who knew him personally might know more."

Mrs Backeberg sips her tea and shakes her head with a sigh. "No one knew what had happened. Not even his closest friends. It was all anyone talked about for the rest of that year. There were crazy rumours, of course. He'd been murdered. He'd been poisoned. He'd suffered a heart attack, or an aneurysm. An evil spirit had captured his soul. The theories got wilder and wilder as term went on. Then final exams started, and we all settled down to study. And then somehow, we forgot about it and moved on to other concerns, as teenagers do. But the mystery was never solved."

I can see that Lael is as disappointed as I am. We are no closer to finding out what happened to Jim, which was our original goal. But I find I am as curious to know what happened to Amelia – and that, surely, is something her best friend can tell us.

"We've been reading excerpts from Amelia's diary," I tell her. "It's locked up in a display cabinet, so we haven't finished it yet. We've got up to the part where she leaves school for the last time. Do you remember that?"

Mrs Backeberg smiles. "That diary! I haven't thought of it in years. She was always scribbling away in it. I remember when we were fourteen, a few of us tried to pinch it. We wanted to see what she said about us, but she hid it too well. We never did manage to find it. Of course I remember the day she left. I was devastated. We'd been friends for so long and now she was moving on to a phase of her life that I couldn't even imagine. She was going to be a mother. It seemed an incredibly grown-up thing."

"Did she keep in touch after she left?" Lael asks.

"She wasn't allowed to. Her parents had decided that Brentwood College was to blame for the situation their daughter was in, and they wouldn't let her keep in contact with anyone from the school. I sent a few letters, but they were all returned to me unopened by her mother."

"But surely you heard when the baby was born? There must have been a notice in the newspaper at least?"

"You'd think so, but there wasn't. I checked the *Joburg Tribune* in the library every single day, but it never appeared. I don't even know if the baby was a boy or a girl. All I know for sure is that it was born."

Mrs Backeberg's hand shakes slightly as she reaches

for the teapot to top up our cups. She makes a clucking noise when she finds it empty.

"Oh, dear! I'm so sorry. I didn't make enough. Let me brew up a fresh pot."

"Not to worry," Lael says quickly. "We don't want to put you to any trouble."

"It's no trouble at all, dear. It will only take a moment."

Lael opens her mouth to protest again, but stops when I catch her eye and give a tiny shake of my head. If there's one thing I've learned, it's that some people like to fuss. They enjoy going to a lot of trouble for their guests.

Mrs Backeberg comes back into the sitting room with a fresh pot of tea. She looks steadier now.

"It must have been really hard to lose touch with Amelia after she left Brentwood College," I say, sympathetically. "Did you ever try to get in contact with her later?"

Mrs Backeberg pauses in the act of lifting her teacup to her mouth. She looks stricken as she lowers the cup carefully back to the saucer.

"Oh, my dear," she says. "You mean you don't know?"

Lael's face reflects the dismay I'm feeling. "Know what?" she asks.

"Amelia died many years ago. She came down with meningitis about two years after she left Brentwood. It was very quick."

"Are ... are you sure?" I know how silly that sounds. Of course she's sure.

"Positive. I was at the funeral. My mother saw the death notice in the newspaper and encouraged me to go to the funeral because Amelia and I were such good friends."

I am stunned. Somehow, I always believed we would find Amelia and speak to her – that we would be able to ask her about her baby and about Jim. I thought she would be able to answer all our questions and put our doubts to rest. The knowledge that she has been dead all this time is shocking. She outlived Jim by only two years.

"I'm so sorry for the loss of your friend," Lael says, and she adds the traditional Jewish blessing when someone has died: "I wish you a long life."

"Thank you."

"The funeral must have been hard," I say. "You were still a teenager yourself."

Mrs Backeberg has that faraway look on her face again.

"It was very hard. I was hoping to hear news of how Amelia had been during those two years. I thought I might even see the baby. Amelia and Jim's baby. It would have been wonderful. I didn't even know whether she'd had a girl or a boy. But it wasn't there."

"In my father's culture, small children don't usually attend funerals," I say. "In my mother's culture, it's also quite unusual."

"For us, it's more flexible," says Lael. "Some families choose to include children in funerals and some don't."

"You don't understand," says Mrs Backeburg. "It wasn't just that the baby wasn't there. It was as though it had never existed."

Lael and I stare at her.

"None of them would admit that there had ever been a baby. Not her brother, and especially not her parents. I went up to them to express my condolences and to talk about how close Amelia and I had been. They were wary right from the beginning. As soon as I said that I'd known

Amelia from boarding school, they were on their guard. Then I said something about how hard it must be for the little one to be motherless now, and they gave me blank stares. It was as though I had started speaking Greek."

"What did you do?" Lael asks.

"It was clear that they were going to stonewall any oblique references I might make to the baby. They were going to pretend not to understand me. So I decided to ask them directly."

"What did you say?" I ask, sitting forward.

"Well, her father was like a stone. There was not a hint of weakness anywhere. I knew there was no point in speaking to him. But her mother was more emotional. She seemed more fragile, and I'm afraid I took advantage of that. I asked her: 'What about the baby? Where is Amelia's baby?'"

"And then?" we prompt.

"Her eyes filled with tears and she started to speak, but her husband cut her off. He turned his body so that he was between her and me and he said, 'You are mistaken. There is no baby.' Then he led her away from me, and I didn't have the courage to approach them again."

"What does that mean?" I say. "Is it possible … that the baby was never born? That Amelia had a miscarriage?"

"No," says Lael. "Mrs Backeberg told us a moment ago that she knew for a fact the baby had been born. How did you know that, Ma'am?"

"Something arrived in the post for me a few months after Amelia left school. There was no note with it, or any explanation at all. I still have it somewhere. Wait a little while I see if I can find it."

She heaves herself to her feet and disappears into the back of the house.

"I knew I still had it somewhere." She comes back holding a small black-and-white photograph. She hands it to me. It shows a tiny baby in the arms of someone whose head is cut off. I know babies, and this one looks very young to me. Like, just-been-born kind of young.

"Wow! Is this the baby?" asks Lael.

"I think so. As I say, there was no note with the photograph, but the letter was posted in Brits, which was where Amelia was from. Jim too, come to think of it. Their family farms were not far from each other. But Jim was at school at the time, so it definitely wasn't from him."

"What's this written on the back?" I ask, trying to decipher the faded blue ink. "Is it a date?"

"The 29th of November 1968," says Mrs Backeberg. "I think it was the day Amelia's baby was born."

Lael does sums in her head. "Yes. That date works. That's almost exactly when her baby would have been due. Who is this holding her? Do you think it was Amelia?"

"Oh no, dear. That would have been a nurse. You can see the pinafore-style uniform she is wearing, with epaulettes on the shoulders."

"Do you mind if Trinity and I take photos of this on our phones? Obviously, you will keep the original, but it would really help if we could have copies."

"Of course I don't mind. Go ahead, my dears."

Lael and I take quick snaps of both sides of the photograph.

"What sort of badge is this that the nurse has on her breast pocket?" I say, using my fingers to zoom in on it.

"My goodness, if I've asked myself that question once, I've asked it a dozen times. I always thought if I could find out which hospital that badge belonged to, I could find out what happened to the baby. I even looked it up in the library once, but I never could find a trace of it. It's one of those mysteries lost to history. We cannot realistically hope to find it…"

"Got it!" Lael and I say at almost the same time.

"What's that, dear?"

"We found the badge," Lael explains. "We did a …"

"…reverse Google Images search on our phones," I finish her sentence for her.

"And it came up as the badge of the…"

"…St Agnes of Lyons Society…"

"…which originated in France…"

"…and dedicated itself to service to the poor," I finish off.

"Well, goodness gracious me. That is an excellent lead. You must certainly pursue it. And please let me know if your research brings you any closer to finding out what happened to the baby – and to poor young Jim Grey." She shakes her head as we all stand. "What a tragedy that whole thing was. Those young lives lost, and so unnecessarily. Tell me, Miss Luhabe, are things better for young people these days?"

I think of Nosipho and Themba.

"Sometimes they are," I say. "Sometimes they are much better. It all depends on whether you are rich or poor, black or white. Awful things still happen these days, but it doesn't have to be that way."

CHAPTER 13

To: Zizi Nkomo zizinkomo@investingsolutions.com
From: Nosipho Mamusa nosiphomamusa@gmail.com
Re: Nosiphiwo Mamusa

Dear Mr Nkomo,

They told me not to write to you. They said I must leave it up to the elders to make the first contact with your family, but I know there are things they will not say to you, and I wanted to be the one to say them.

First of all, I want to make it clear that I don't want or need anything from you. My adoptive mother earns a good salary and I am a learner in Grade Ten at a private school. I get good marks and hope to study chemical engineering at university one day. My name is Nosipho and I am the biological daughter of Nosiphiwo Mamusa who lived in Daveyton sixteen years ago. She was a learner at Tom Boya Secondary School at the time. She left school when she became pregnant, although she always intended to resume her studies.

Sadly, Nosiphiwo was killed by a taxi when she was walking to the shops with her brother when I was just a few days old. Her older sister adopted me and has raised me ever since. I only recently found out that my mother is my adoptive mother. She never knew exactly who my father was, but after doing some research, she thinks it was most likely to have been you. We can do genetic testing to make sure of this, if that is what you want.

Please understand that I don't want to cause any trouble for you or your family. If you would prefer not to have me in your life, that is your choice. All I want is the chance to get to know my biological father and my family on that side. I will understand if that is not what you want. If so, I promise never to contact you again. I will, however, leave you with my details so you can change your mind at any time.

Please take some time to think about this and let me know.

Kind regards,
Nosipho Mamusa

To: Trinity Luhabe trinityluhabe@gmail.com
From: Obert Nzingane – Proprietor onzingane@nzinganeinvesti-gations.co.za
Re: St Agnes of Lyons Society

Dear Ms Luhabe,

It seems as though the St Agnes of Lyons Society does not exist anymore, or at least not in South Africa. I can find some traces of them in the south of France, but otherwise they appear to have faded away about fifteen years ago.

They were a charitable organisation that ran soup kitchens in small towns across the country in the 1940s, 1950s and 1960s. They also gave shelter to the homeless and helped them to find jobs. It seems the South African branch of the society was founded and run by Anglican nuns, known as the Order of St Agnes of Lyons.

I can't find any evidence of a hospital run by the society, or an order of nurses under their control. I did, however, find records of two maternity homes that they operated for about twenty years. One was in Caledon in the Overberg region of the Western Cape, and the other was in Vanderbijlpark, near Johannesburg. As far as I can tell, these were no ordinary maternity homes, but rather "homes for unwed mothers", as they were called in those days.

Their records were very strictly controlled back then, and even now they aren't open to someone like me. The home in Caledon was taken over by the Western Cape Department of Health, and the one in Vanderbijlpark is now owned by the Gauteng Department of Social Development. Please find attached a Google Maps pin-drop for each of these locations so you can find them easily.

Many thanks for your prompt settlement of my account, as always. I look forward to hearing whether I can be of any further service to you.

Kind regards,
Obert Nzingane
Proprietor

"I'm sure you're wondering why I've called you all here today," says Nosipho, gazing at the five of us like the chair of the board addressing a meeting.

"I wasn't, but please get on with it," Yasmin says. "My group is getting together to film a scene from *Coriolanus* for English in like ten minutes."

"And I'm supposed to be at choir," says Amira.

"I have no idea what I'm even doing here, but if you start talking about girl stuff, I'm out of here," announces Munashe.

I give him a shove in the ribs. "Listen, there are a bunch of pics on Instagram of you wearing a pregnant belly that have over a thousand likes, so you're in no position to reject 'girl stuff' at this point."

"True, but if Nos starts talking about giving birth, I might just pass out. So you will just have to deal with that."

"I'll leave you on the floor where you belong."

Nosipho is standing with her arms crossed and her foot tapping, waiting for us to stop bickering. "Are you guys quite finished?"

We sit up obediently. "Yes, sorry. Carry on."

"Okay, so here's the thing. I've decided that I can't do this anymore."

"Can't do what?" Lael asks.

"This." She gestures at her tummy. "This whole thing. The pregnancy. Giving birth. The baby. I just can't do it. So unfortunately, we are going to have to make another plan."

"Um..."

"Uh..."

We look at each other in consternation – worried glances flicking around the room like wildfire.

"The thing is," she goes on. "All that stuff you do when you're babysitting, Trinity – the bath, the nappies, those weird clothes with the press-studs. I've thought about it and I've realised I'm not up to it. I'll just make a huge mess of the whole thing, and the baby will be scarred for life. It will be much better if someone else takes over. That's why I called you all here today. We need a Plan B, and I'm open to suggestions."

"Of course, you can do it," I say soothingly, like I'm talking to a toddler who is having a meltdown. "You actually did some of it, remember? And you coped fine. You're going to be a great mom, Nos."

"An awesome mom," Amira confirms.

"A brilliant mom." Yasmin nods about fifty times.

"But what about the birth, you guys? First, I have to get through that. The thing is, I've thought about it and I really can't see it working. I mean I know the theory behind it and everything, but I just can't see it happening for me. The logistics don't make sense. So, like I say, Plan B. Who's got an idea?"

Munashe's eyes are rolling around the room. He is so out of his depth here, he must feel like he's drowning. I must admit, I can relate. It is far, far too late for any Plan B. This baby is coming whether Nosipho likes it or not. But how do we get her to see that?

I open my mouth to speak, then nearly collapse with relief when Lael gets there ahead of me.

She stands up and goes over to where Nosipho is standing, waiting for someone to deliver her Plan B. Then she puts her arms around her and pulls her into a tight hug. At first, Nosipho resists. Then she seems to melt against Lael, and tears start pouring down her cheeks.

Munashe looks longingly at the door.

"Don't. You. Dare," I mouth at him. He subsides into his seat.

Lael pats Nosipho's shoulder as she sobs, and makes soothing noises.

"It's okay, darling. It's okay. We're all here for you. All of us."

A murmur of agreement goes around the room.

"But it's not really us you need right now, is it?" Lael goes on. "None of us has been through this, so we can only imagine how scared and alone you must be feeling. You need some help from the experts."

As she says this, a light goes on in my brain. I wonder why I didn't think of this earlier.

"Prenatal classes!" I say. "I know someone who gives them. She's one of the moms I babysit for. She teaches you all about what to expect during the birth, and how to prepare for it."

"That's exactly what I was thinking," says Lael. "And also, baby-care classes. Like, literally, what to do with the baby when it's there. I bet Dr Patel's rooms have a contact for someone nearby."

Nosipho has stopped crying and is listening intently.

"I'd like that. I'd really like that. Can we find out more, do you think?"

"Of course," I say. "I'll speak to this mom I know. She's a registered nurse and midwife. And Lael will phone Dr Patel's rooms to find out about childcare classes. You leave it to us. We'll sort you out."

"Thanks, guys," Nosipho sniffs. "Thank you so much.

And you will come to the classes with me, won't you? I don't want to go on my own."

There is a nanosecond of hesitation before Lael and I say, "Yes, of course. Of course we will. Can't wait." Then Amira, who is not nearly as tactful as the rest of us, says what we are all thinking.

"What about Themba? Shouldn't he be the one to go with you?"

We hold our breath when it looks as though Nosipho is going to start crying again, but she manages to hold it together.

"Themba isn't in a great place right now, guys. He says he wants to be part of this, but every time I ask him to do something with me, he makes excuses for why he can't. It's like his feelings haven't caught up with his brain yet. I'm still hoping he will step up, but for now I can't count on him. I know that if I ask him to come to baby classes with me he will have some reason not to. So can I count on you?"

This time Lael and I don't hesitate. "Definitely!"

Despite all the drama that's going on in our lives right now, Lael and I don't fly into a panic when we get a message on Google Classroom that Ms Waise wants to see us. Instead of assuming that we've got a detention or we're in trouble, we guess that she wants to hear how we got on in Kroondal.

We decide that there's no harm in telling Ms Waise about the death of Amelia, and even showing her the photo of the baby.

She listens carefully while we tell her about our visit to Mrs Backeberg, and even seems to follow what we're saying, despite the fact that we both talk at the same time and keep forgetting details and having to go back and add them in later.

"The sad part is that Amelia is dead," says Lael.

This doesn't seem to come as a surprise to Ms Waise.

"I suspected as much. I've tried to find some reference to her on the internet, but there was nothing. For someone to disappear so completely, I guessed she must have passed away a while ago. How did she die?"

"Meningitis," I say. "The bacterial kind. It was very quick. This was about two years after the baby was born."

We carry on telling her about the funeral, and the mysterious photograph that arrived in the mail. Ms Waise's face falls when she hears that Mrs Backeberg wouldn't let us take the photograph.

"That is such a shame. I wonder what she could possibly want with it after all this time. I would have loved to see it."

Lael slaps her forehead.

"We took photos of it on our phones. Trinity?"

"Yes, I've still got it." I take out my phone. Unlike Lael, I don't delete everything after a couple of days. She has storage issues on her phone so she can only keep photos for a short while. "Look, here it is."

I call up the clearest image of the photograph I can find and hand it to Ms Waise. She stares at it for ages, using her fingers to enlarge different parts for a better look.

"Who is this holding the baby?" she asks. "It's not … it's not Amelia, is it?"

"No, it seems to be some kind of nurse or midwife," I say. "We did some research on that badge on her uniform, and it belongs to the Order of St Agnes of Lyons. They ran two maternity homes for unwed mothers in the 1960s. One was in Caledon and one was in Vanderbijlpark.

Ms Waise looks impressed.

"You girls have done an amazing job. Perhaps we really should turn this into a History project. You've done an incredible amount of research."

"It's more interesting than the Great Trek," Lael says with feeling.

"Or the Treaty of Versailles," I add.

"I'm going to ask the head of department if you can get a long essay credit for it when it's all over. The Lucites would probably have wanted Amelia to have her baby as far away from Brits as possible, right?"

We both nod. We'd had the same thought.

"But would they have gone as far as Caledon? That's in the Overberg region. It's on the other side of the country. Or would Vanderbijlpark have been far enough for them?"

"Trinity reminded me that they were farmers," says Lael.

"That's right," I say. "I have family who farm in the rural areas near Polokwane, and if there's one thing I know it's that farmers don't take holidays. I think they would have gone for the closer option."

"Well, we'll start off in Vanderbijlpark," Ms Waise decides. "And then if that's a dead end, we can phone the place in Caledon and see if it sounds promising."

Lael and I can't hide our surprise. *We*? Is Ms Waise planning on coming with us? It certainly sounds like it.

"I know you girls would like to keep going on your own." She correctly interprets our expressions. "But no government department will co-operate with minors. They might refuse to co-operate with me too, but you'll have a better chance if I'm with you."

We have to admit that this is probably true.

⚲

"It's weird how caught up Ms Waise has got in this whole thing," says Lael as we wait for Lungile to come and fetch me after school. "Don't you think it's weird? I think it's weird."

"Oh, I don't know. It is pretty interesting, you must admit – like playing detective. We're solving a fifty-year-old puzzle. And she's a History teacher, after all. This is her kind of thing."

"I suppose."

"It's weird that any of us is interested in it. This is ancient history. Who cares about the hows and the whys?"

"True. At least you saw Jim Grey, and spoke to him. It makes sense for you to be interested, but for some reason I am too."

"But we're *teenagers*!" I say in an ominous voiceover-voice. "We're only interested in texting and boys."

"And in texting boys!"

"And in clothes and boy bands."

"And experimenting with drugs.

"We are cauldrons of uncontrollable hormones!" I announce.

"Good afternoon, girls."

"Good afternoon, Dr Hussein," we say, as our headmaster walks past.

When he is out of hearing, we collapse into giggles.

"Do you think he heard us?" says Lael.

"I'm sure he heard us. We were practically yelling."

A car sweeps up to the pavement. It's Lungile, so I hop in, waving goodbye to Lael. Aaron and Caleb get in next to me – their soccer practice is cancelled.

My phone buzzes in my hand. I look at it and frown, trying to remember which app this is. The icon shows a little microphone with someone speaking into it. No, not someone. It's a ghost. A little ghost talking into a microphone. Wait, I know exactly what this is.

"Stop the car!" I yell.

Lungile and my brothers jump in their seats. Aaron gives me a pained look.

"Mara, why?"

"Stop! I need to go back. Let me out here, please, Lungile. I'll walk back. I forgot something I have to do at school this afternoon."

Lungile clicks his tongue. "Your mom said you were finishing at half-past two this afternoon, Trinity. It's half-past two. I'm supposed to take you home now."

"I know, I know! But this is really important. I forgot about it. I'll take the blame, I promise."

"And then I'll have to come back later to fetch you."

"I know. I'm sorry! Or maybe my mom can, if she's back from work."

Lungile sighs and stops the car. I leap out and start running back to school. As I run, I'm already WhatsApping Lael.

Lael meets me at the gate.

"Tennis is cancelled. There's a coaches' meeting or something."

"Oh, yes. Soccer is also cancelled. That's lucky. We can go straight upstairs."

We speed walk towards Sisulu House.

"I forgot all about that ghost-writing machine," she says. "It's been sitting there since you bought it, doing nothing. How does it even work?"

"It has a needle that responds to, like, vibrations in the atmosphere or something. It jiggles up and down electronically and creates scrawls that you can see on the screen. If you want, you can even print them out in hard copy. But nobody's got time to sit and look at a day's worth of scrawls every night, so it has a word-recognition function that looks out for anything that resembles an English word. Well, I set it for English. You can pick any language, but I figured Jim wouldn't be communicating in Russian, right?"

Lael gives me a "get to the point" look.

"Anyway. I installed the app on my phone so the ghost-writer could send me a notification any time it detected a recognisable English word. And today, for the first time in weeks, it did! In fact, it seems to have detected more than one word because it sent a bunch of notifications in a row."

"Wow! I wonder what it will say? Hopefully not something totally random."

We walk around the side of Sisulu House to get to the main entrance. As we pass the Post-Matric Annexe on the right, Lael notices me glancing in that direction.

"Do you ever think about him?" she asks.

I shrug. "Just when I wonder how I ever let myself get manipulated like that. It was like waking up from an evil spell when I finally realised what was happening."

"You were being emotionally abused," Lael says. "He was very, very clever about it. But none of it was your fault. You do realise that, right?"

"Most of the time, yes. Sometimes I still feel as though I was somehow to blame, but I'm getting over that."

I take one last look at the Post-Matric Annexe and remember Zach Morris, the golden boy from Hilton College, who lived there before he was expelled. I re-member how flattered I was when he first started paying me attention. How he made me feel special and chosen. His interest in me was like sunshine. It warmed me up.

Then he started pulling back and withholding his approval. Little criticisms became big ones, and soon I couldn't do anything right. I spent all my time trying to get back to that warm, golden place where he thought I was wonderful. I believed I was the one who had messed it up. If only I could do everything better, I would be back in that perfect place again. But instead of getting better, it got worse and worse. And then one day he shoved me and I fell backwards and hurt myself. He was about to hit me. He actually had his arm up to strike me when Jim Grey intervened and stopped him.

For that, I will always be grateful. That's why I'm so

obsessed with finding out what happened to Jim, and how he died. He looked out for me once. Now I'm looking out for him.

I only realise I've stopped walking when Lael takes my hand and gives me a gentle tug.

"Right, yes, sorry," I say. "I was thinking about last term. Let's go upstairs now and see what message Jim has left for us."

We walk up to the fourth floor, whisking past the Grade Ten dormitories so that Matron doesn't spot us and demand to know what we're up to. We pause briefly on the second floor to check that there isn't a new page of the diary visible, but it's still the same entry from when Amelia left school.

Up on the fourth floor, we have to pause and think about where our equipment is hidden. It's so long since we were up here, we've forgotten where everything is.

"I found the camcorder!" says Lael from behind some dusty old encyclopaedias.

"And here's the laser scope thingy." I hold it up in triumph.

"What's left?"

"Uh … well, obviously the ghost-writer. Or rather the Paranormal Automatic Writing Machine, to give it its proper name. And what was the other thing?"

"Found it!" says Lael. "It's the EMF-meter, whatever that might be."

"The electro-magnetic-field meter." I have to admit that this one has been a bit of a dud. It has given us exactly zero results so far. Still, we're only halfway through the year, so I'll give it more time.

"So, how does this work?"

"I have to sync my phone with the ghost-writer. It will download any words it has detected onto my phone and report on how frequently they occurred."

"And how do you sync the two devices?"

"You hold them next to each other, and you do this." I put the ghost-writer into user mode, and press sync on the app on my phone. Both devices show a blue light as they start talking to each other. It takes about thirty seconds, and then the lights turn green.

"Done! The information has been downloaded."

"Oh, man. This is so cool. What does it say? What does it say?"

I have to hold my phone over my head so Lael can't grab it out of my hand.

"Hang on! Let me look."

I open the app and click on Recent Reports. Then I click on Recognisable Words – English. Only one word comes up."

"Whisky?" says Lael, reading over my shoulder. "What does that even mean?"

"I don't know. But look – it's come up twenty-three times in the last twelve hours."

Lael looks as creeped out as I feel.

"That cannot be a coincidence."

"No," I agree. "It really can't."

"A software malfunction?"

"Could be." I scroll through the app and find a self-diagnosis function. I set it to run, and in about a minute it returns a result of "no faults detected".

"It seems to be working fine."

"What about the words that appear around 'whisky'?" asks Lael. "Do they make any kind of sense?"

We scroll through the read-outs, but all we can see are strings of gobbledegook – random letters – with the word 'whisky' appearing out of nowhere in several places.

"What does it mean?" I say.

"Whisky … whisky…" Lael muses. "It can't be a name, can it?"

"For a dog, perhaps. Not for a person."

"Or the name of a place?"

"Hmm."

We do a quick search on Google Maps for anything with the word whisky in its name, but nothing turns up. There's a Whisky Bay in Australia, but that's all.

"Could someone have been drinking whisky?" I ask. "Maybe Jim and his friends smuggled some into the boarding-house and got trashed."

"Maybe."

"Maybe someone gave Jim drugged whisky, and that's how he died. Maybe he's trying to tell us what the murder weapon was."

But even as I say it, it sounds like an episode of a TV show, not something that happened in real life fifty years ago.

"Is that it?" asks Lael. "Just that same word over and over again? Nothing else?"

I double-check all twenty-three reported incidents of a recognisable word. They all say 'whisky'.

After all that excitement, Lael and I are as clueless as ever.

231

CHAPTER 14

To: UNDISCLOSED RECIPIENTS
From: Kathy Strijdom Kathystrijdom@gmail.com
Re: Babycraft Classes

Hi Mums!!!

I am so excited to see you all tomorrow in the Rec Centre Hall for our first session in Babycraft.

I spoke to the administrator's and they have promised to leave the heater's on for us. It is chilly at this time of year and I don't want my Mums starting to shiver!!!

Please remember to bring water bottles to sip from frequently. We want you and Baby to stay Hydrated at all times. Reminder!!! There will be tea and coffee served halfway through the session. There will also be biscuits, but I'm sure my Mums don't want to poison their bodies with gluten and sugar. I will do my best to organise some Healthy Snacks for next weeks class!!!

Dad's, a big welcome to all of you as well. There is plenty that you can also learn from these classes. When its your turn to babysit the Little Ones to give Mum a break, you can do so with Confidence. So don't think of slipping off to the pub halfway through!!! LOL!!!

See you all tomorrow!
Love from Kathy xxx

To: Nosipho Mamusa nosiphomamusa@gmail.com
From: Zizi Nkomo zizinkomo@gmail.com
Re: Nosiphiwo Mamusa

Dear Nosipho,

Thanks for writing to me. As you guessed, I do have a family. My wife and I have a customary union and our families are bonded by lobola. We have two children, boys, aged three and five.

I certainly knew Nosiphiwo all those years ago, and it is possible that I am your biological father. If it is okay with you, I would very much like to confirm my paternity by means of a DNA test. It is not that I doubt your word, or that of your adoptive mother (whom I remember very well). It's just that I would like to know for sure before I get to know you better. I'm sure you feel the same way.

We can do it via an independent laboratory we both agree on. Then, if the test turns out to show a match, we can take the whole formal route of letting the elders in our families meet and establish a connection. My wife agrees that this would be the right course. If you do turn out to be my daughter, I can promise that you will be getting a very loving stepmother who is anxious to meet you. You will also have two naughty little brothers who are very mischievous and sweet.

I am excited to have a daughter, so I hope this turns out to be true.

All the best,
Zizi Nkomo

"So, what do you think of that?" Nosipho asks.

"Let me see it again." Lael takes Nos's phone and reads through the email again.

We are in the car on our way to Nos's first baby-care class. We keep our voices down so that Lungile doesn't hear every word we say. It's not that he tells on me to my parents or anything, but he is quite a gossip. Basically, my parents are the only people he *doesn't* tell our business to.

"I can't believe you wrote to him." Lael hands the phone back to Nosipho.

"I know. I can't believe I did either. I pressed 'send' before I had time to think about it. I can't believe he wrote back. And such a nice letter too. You guys don't think he's a psychopath or anything?"

"He seems like a regular dad," says Lael.

"I guess I don't know what dads are like, regular or otherwise, because I've never had one."

"Is your mom going to kill you when she finds out you wrote to him without waiting for your uncles to handle it?" I ask.

"I think she'll be mad at first, but hopefully she will realise that this was the best way to go about it. I only want to involve my uncles if he does turn out to be my biological father."

"So, are you going to take the DNA test?"

"Definitely. And as soon as possible. I want to get this sorted out before my mom gets back."

"Is she away again?" asks Lael.

"Yes, she's back in America putting the finishing touches to this business deal. Auntie Mbaks is looking after me on weekends again."

"What are you hoping for with the DNA test?' I ask. "Do you want it to be him, or not?"

Nosipho thinks for a while before answering. "I don't know. I thought I did, but it's all happened very quickly. One minute I didn't even have a dad, and now suddenly I might have a dad, a stepmother, and two little brothers. It just seems a bit quick, you know?"

Lael understands this better than I do. I already come from a big family, but she knows what's it's like to join someone else's insta-family.

"It's hard, I know. They have their own ways of being a family, and you can't really be a part of that even if they ask you to. My only advice is to take it slowly. You set the pace. Don't let things happen that you're not comfortable with yet."

We sit straighter in the car as we see the recreation centre up ahead. Nosipho is already nervous about this baby-care business, and we're nervous on her behalf.

"I don't know about this, guys. Did you see that email I got from the Babycraft lady? Why do people talk to you like that when you're pregnant? Like you've lost about fifty IQ points. Do they think pregnancy makes you stupid?" Nosipho is on a roll. "And what's this 'mums' business? This is South Africa. We call our mothers 'mom' or 'mama' or 'mma'. And since when do fathers still 'baby-sit' their own children? That's so old-fashioned. I thought it was called 'parenting' if you're a parent. uKathy needs to catch a wake-up."

By the time Lungile stops the car to let us out, Nosipho is feeling better for having got that rant off her chest, and so are we.

We're early, but other cars are pulling up now too, and pregnant ladies are getting out. To say they are older than us would be an understatement. Some of them must be forty.

"Check it out, guys – they're old enough to be our mothers, never mind the babies' mothers," Nosipho whispers.

"Older," I say, seeing as my mom is only thirty-six, and so is Thulani.

"Well, if they don't age-shame me, I won't age-shame them," says Nosipho.

All the women have got men with them. I was hoping there would be a few on their own or with other women, just to make Nos feel less conspicuous. Not all of them are pregnant, though. Some have already had their babies, and are carrying them along, tucked into car seats. I can't help wondering how much quiet time we're going to have with at least four newborn babies in the class.

When we have all settled into our chairs, a young white woman stands and spreads her arms. I assume this is Kathy.

"Welcome, Mums, welcome!" she says in a perky voice. (Yes, it's her.) "You have all enrolled here this evening to learn some basic parenting skills. We will cover the years from newborn to toddler. This course will deal with hygiene and nutrition, and also stimulation and early education. Now, some of you are still expecting your little ones, and some have brought them here with you tonight. You are all very welcome."

There is a slight wail from one of the car seats, but the dad starts rocking it, and it subsides.

"We will start off with the very first task you will be asked to do for Baby, and that will be the bath."

"Actually," I whisper to Lael, "the very first task will be breastfeeding, but whatevs."

"Sshh."

"I have here a baby bath full of lovely warm water, exactly the right temperature for a little one, and what I want from you at this stage is a volunteer. Who would like their baby to be our test subject this evening? The bonus, of course, is that you won't have to bath Baby when you get home tonight."

The four moms with tiny babies practically rush the stage. Kathy chooses a little boy more or less at random.

"Doesn't he have a lovely head of hair?" she comments as she lays the baby down on the changing table. "His hair is very advanced for his age."

The baby's mother looks down modestly, while the other moms check their own babies' heads for signs of hair advancement.

"So, once we have undressed Baby and wrapped him up snugly in a hooded towel, we hold him in the rugby-ball grip and tilt him slightly downwards. Now we scoop warm water gently onto his head to wet his hair."

Kathy is not holding the baby firmly enough against her body. He has managed to kick his towel open and is starting to feel cold. The baptism of water on his forehead isn't helping either. Some of it has run into his eyes. A slight niggling sound starts up.

"Now we grab some shampoo and squeeze a tiny amount into our hands to lather Baby's head."

As the tiny boy wriggles and kicks, Kathy clamps him under her arm so that he tips sideways. Now the water is running into his mouth, along with some shampoo. The niggling sounds get louder. His mother is hovering nearby, looking anxious. You can see she is dying to take over, but doesn't want to undermine Kathy in front of everyone.

Kathy is determined to finish the hair-washing, whether the baby likes it or not.

"Once you have massaged the scalp thoroughly to help avoid cradle cap, don't forget to rinse well." She has to raise her voice over the baby's complaints. "When the water runs clear, use the hood of the towel to dry Baby's head and keep him warm."

The baby takes a deep breath and his face turns red. I brace myself.

A blood-freezing scream splits the chilly air in the rec centre hall. There is a long pause while the baby takes another breath. The pregnant women cringe as he starts to cry in earnest – horrible, heartbreaking wails, as though he is being murdered.

His mother can't take another second of it. She bounds forward and snatches him away from Kathy. She presses him to her chest and starts trying to stuff a dummy into his mouth, but he is too far gone for that. His wailing gets louder and louder, and his mom looks even more panicky.

Lael and Nosipho nudge me from opposite sides.

"Can't you do something?"

"Trinity, I really think you should offer to help out."

I pull an agonised face. "I don't want to. It will make both Kathy and the mom look bad. I don't want to interfere."

"Well, I can't stand this noise any longer," says Nosipho, standing up. She raises her voice. "Excuse me. My friend here is really good with babies." She grabs me by the arm and forces me to stand up too.

The mom looks at me with desperate hope in her eyes.

"Can you make him be quiet? I don't know what to do. He's just been fed."

"I really don't think that an unqualified teenager is a suitable person to…" begins Kathy indignantly.

"Of course she is," says Lael. "She's a straight-up baby whisperer."

When the mom hears this, she practically throws her baby at me. I have to brace myself to catch him.

"Please make him stop," she begs.

I cuddle the baby to my chest and turn away from everyone. He doesn't need any more anxious voices or bright lights. He needs to be soothed. I use a technique I've been using ever since I first started picking up babies when I was little, but I only recently learned that it has a name. When I did my childminding course, I was told about the Five S's Method by Dr Harvey Karp. He apparently based it on the techniques of African mothers, which makes perfect sense to me.

I hold the baby firmly against me (Swaddle). I drape him over my chest and shoulder (Side or Stomach position). I make shushing noises in his ear (Shush). I jiggle him gently, but quite fast (Swing). And I give him his dummy when he has calmed down enough not to spit it straight out again (Suck).

Within a minute, he is calm and quiet, and starting to fall asleep. His mom looks at me like I'm a miracle worker. I know he will start yelling again as soon as I try to put him down, so I offer to keep holding him for a while.

"Oh, but I need to carry on demonstrating the bath," says Kathy. "I had only got as far as the hair-wash."

The mom is standing behind her, shaking her head vigorously.

"He's nearly asleep," I say. "Maybe you could carry on with one of the other babies, or even with that dummy-baby you brought along."

"But that was for the CPR demonstration."

The other three moms pull their babies a little closer. No one wants to give their kid to Kathy to demonstrate with. It will have to be the dummy. She stomps off to get it.

At last I manage to put the baby down without waking him. I return to my seat next to Lael and Nosipho, and find them holding back giggles.

"Kathy's face when you got the baby to stop crying in two seconds," Lael snort-laughs.

Nosipho high-fives me. "I've said it before and I'll say it again, I'm putting you on speed-dial when my baby comes."

As we watch, Kathy demonstrates how to wash the baby. But instead of using aqueous cream, she uses a cake of soap – as in a slab of Lux, like an adult would use in the shower. I sigh. We are going to have to find Nosipho a new baby-care class.

A week later, Lael and I get summoned to another meeting with Ms Waise straight after school.

"What are you girls doing this afternoon?"

"Djembe drumming class and then homework," I say.

"Well, there's no tennis match today because I have a bye, but I should go to practice," says Lael.

"Fine. I'll excuse you from both. We're going to the Department of Social Development in Vanderbijlpark today. I've got an appointment with someone who works there."

Lael and I are a little stunned.

"What ... like, right now...?"

"Yes, why not? It's Wednesday, so you finish early. We'll have just enough time to get there and back by late afternoon. I checked Google Maps. If we leave right now, we'll get there in one hour and fifteen minutes. All you need to do is get permission from your mom, Trinity, and from Matron, Lael – and we can be on our way."

About twenty minutes later, we are in Ms Waise's car being driven to Vanderbijlpark. We both feel like we've been run over by a steamroller. How could I have thought she wasn't serious about following up on this? She is clearly super-serious.

We grabbed toasted sandwiches and drinks from the tuckshop on our way out, so we munch in silence for a while. Getting out of Joburg in the early afternoon traffic is a nightmare, but once we are clear of the city, the road opens up and we cruise along at a good pace. It ends up taking us an hour and twenty minutes, but it is only a quarter past three by the time we arrive at the Department of Social Development.

Ms Waise pulls up in the dusty parking lot and we stare at the old government building. Could this have been where that photograph was taken? Is this where Amelia had her baby fifty years ago? In this bleak building? I know women give birth every day in much worse places, but there is something about this place that gives me the creeps. There is an air of misery that hangs over it.

Ms Waise lifts her remote to lock the car and I notice that her hand is shaking. Perhaps she feels the atmosphere here, too.

"Spooky place, isn't it?" says Lael in my ear.

"It sure is."

Ms Waise takes a deep breath. "All right, girls. Let's go in. I managed to find an administrator who used to work here back when it was a maternity home. She is very close to retirement, but she said she was willing to speak to us."

This is why grownups are useful. A government department official would not have agreed to speak to us. No way.

"Is Mrs Letwaba available?" asks Ms Waise at reception. "She is expecting us. My name is Jenny Waise from Brenthurst College, and these are two of my Grade Ten learners."

We are shown to a sort of waiting room. There are tea- and coffee-making facilities, but they don't look very tempting. The cups aren't clean, for one thing. It's all part of the depressing atmosphere that pervades this place.

A few minutes later, an older lady comes in to greet us. She looks to be about seventy. She introduces herself as Mrs Letwaba, and we all sit down around a rickety table.

"So, you are interested in the history of this place, from back when it was a maternity home in the sixties and seventies?"

"That's right." Ms Waise's voice sounds slightly odd, like she is on the verge of coughing. "Can you confirm that this was the maternity home owned and run by the Order of St Agnes of Lyons?"

"Yes, it was. They were a group of Anglican nuns, and they ran this place as a mother-and-baby home for nearly ten years."

"We've heard that it was specifically a home where unwed mothers could have their babies. Can you confirm that that's true?"

"Oh, certainly. It was kept hush-hush at the time because of the neighbours. This was a residential area back then, and the neighbours might have objected if they'd known that there were girls 'of that sort' having their babies here. But it was an open secret. Families knew that if they had a daughter who was 'in trouble', they could deliver their babies safely and discreetly here with the nuns."

Ms Waise holds out her copy of the photograph for Mrs Letwaba to look at. Her hand is shaking quite noticeably by now. Lael and I share an uneasy glance. What we are going to do if our teacher falls apart? What if she has a fit or something? How will we get home? I suppose we could always Uber.

"Do you think this baby could have been born here?"

Mrs Letwaba feels in all her pockets for her glasses. When she finally finds them, she takes the photograph over to the window and holds it up towards the light.

"It is very possible. That is certainly the uniform the nurses used to wear back then. I was a cleaner then, and I'm an administrator now, but I remember the nurses' uniforms. The only problem is, this wasn't the only maternity home the nuns used to run. There was another one in the Cape somewhere…"

"Caledon."

"Yes, that's it. So, it's really a fifty-fifty chance whether this photo was taken here or there. I can't see anything in the picture that would narrow it down. Do you have additional information for me?"

"Just that the family lived here – in the Transvaal. We thought it was more likely for them to have come here for their daughter to have her baby than to have gone all the way to Caledon. They were farmers, you see."

"I see, yes."

"What about records?" I blurt out, unable to stay quiet any longer. This visit is not going to be another dead end. I won't let it.

"What do you mean?" asks Mrs Letwaba.

"The nuns must have kept records of the babies that were born here, Mma. Do you know what happened to those? Are they still here?"

"Yes, I believe they are in our basement archives."

Ms Waise sits up. "Could we have access to them? We know the name of the mother who gave birth here, and the approximate date. Surely we could search under her surname or something?"

Mrs Letwaba shakes her head. "I'm so sorry. I'm afraid those records are not open to the public. People may only access them in very specific circumstances. You see, adoptions were done from here, as I'm sure you have realised. We cannot release any information to members of the public."

Lael looks as disappointed as I feel, but Ms Waise sits even straighter. Now her whole body is trembling.

"What circumstances?" she asks.

"I'm sorry?"

"You said people may access your records in very specific circumstances. So, I'm asking what those circumstances are?"

"Well, if you were the parent of a child that was born here, for example, or indeed if you were one of the children born here. Then we would certainly open up our records to you."

Then Ms Waise does something so shocking that Lael and I can only stare. She reaches into her handbag and pulls out an envelope. She hands it to Mrs Letwaba and says, "I have reason to believe that I was born here fifty years ago. I believe that I am the child of Amelia Lucite and Jim Grey."

Lael and I gasp so loudly that Mrs Letwaba actually jumps.

"What is it?" she says. "What's wrong?"

"You, Ms Waise?" I say. "You are Amelia's baby?"

"Why didn't you tell us?" asks Lael.

Ms Waise turns to us, tears in her eyes.

"I wasn't sure," she says. "I'm still not sure. I joined Brentwood College as a History teacher at the beginning of this year because I knew my birth was somehow connected to the school. I wanted to be able to check the records and look through old documents. Then I found out that you girls were looking into the same mystery as I was, but for different reasons."

"Wait a second…" I say, confused. "Does that mean you're not actually a History teacher?"

She laughs. "No, no. I am absolutely a History teacher – and a museum curator too. I applied for the job and got it in the normal way. But my reason for coming was to find out more about my birth parents. It was a closed adoption, you see. My adoptive parents got me from an intermediary organisation, and the records were sealed. I have documents here that I believe will prove I have the right to request access to the file on Amelia Lucite."

Mrs Letwaba is looking through the documents in the envelope now, her glasses perched on the end of her nose.

"This seems to be in order," she says. "Now, we must just hope that the girl's parents brought her here under her own name. It wasn't unheard of for people to use assumed names in those days, even though it was against the law. Please wait here while I go and see if I can find the relevant file."

As she disappears, my mind is spinning. I'm remembering how fascinated Ms Waise was to hear that I might have met Jim Grey, or at least what was left of him. How she wanted to know what he was like. I would never in a million years have guessed that it was her own father she was asking about. No wonder she seemed so interested!

"The thing I can't understand," says Lael. "How did Amelia get to the point of deciding to give her baby up for adoption? In her diary entries, she seemed so protective of her pregnancy and so excited about getting to meet her baby – her and Jim's baby. Remember how she was clinging to the hope that Jim would come around once the baby was actually there? But maybe she realised that was just a pipe dream."

Ms Waise takes a tissue out of her bag and wipes carefully around her eyes.

"Yes," she says. "What probably happened is that reality started to hit her. It couldn't have been easy being a teenage single mother in those days. She probably realised that she couldn't cope."

"Her parents could have made it easier for her," I say. I'm still angry about this. "They could have worked something out so she could have kept her baby." Then I realise what I'm saying. "Sorry, Ma'am. I'm talking about your biological grandparents here. I don't mean to be disrespectful."

"Don't worry. I've also read the diary entries. I know Amelia's parents weren't supportive. More like the exact opposite. But I suppose they were a product of their times. That was how people dealt with things in those days. For Amelia to give her baby up for adoption would have been the sensible thing to do."

I look over at Lael and can see she is remembering the same thing as me – Nosipho with her hand resting on her belly and a fierce look in her eyes, daring anyone to mess with her baby. I would like to see someone telling her that the 'sensible' thing to do would be to give it up. That person might not live to tell the tale.

The only thing that might make Nosipho consider adoption would be if she really believed she couldn't give her baby a good life. That is literally the only person she would do it for – the baby. Maybe Amelia got to that point, where she believed it would be best for her baby to be raised by someone else. Still, I'd love to see her write about it in her own words. If only we could get the diary out of that locked display case!

We all look up as Mrs Letwaba comes back into the room. She is carrying a box with some dusty paper files in it that look to be at least fifty years old. Ms Waise leans forward, visibly restraining herself from reaching out and grabbing the box.

"The good news is that the Lucites seem to have brought their daughter here under her own name. That makes everything much easier. The bad news is that some documents seem to be missing. For instance, I can't find the consent form signed by the birth mother for her baby to be put up for adoption. There are forms here that have been signed by the parents of the birth mother, but not the birth mother herself. I know she was only sixteen at the time – five years short of her majority in those days – but she should still have been required to sign."

"Does it state the name of the family that the baby was placed with?" Ms Waise asks. Her voice is shaking. Lael and I hold our breath.

"Let's see here…" Mrs Letwaba pages through one of the files. The papers are yellowed, and clouds of dust rise every time she bumps the box. "Yes, here it is. The baby – a female infant – was placed with Mr John and Mrs Letitia Waise of Farrarmere, Benoni."

Ms Waise sways in her seat. For a moment, I think she is going to faint.

"It's me!" she says. "It's really me. I thought I'd never find the truth."

"May I see your birth certificate again?" asks Mrs Letwaba.

Ms Waise hands it over and together they compare it to the documents from the Order of St Agnes of Lyons. They nod at the same time.

"I think we can regard that as definite," says Mrs Letwaba. "Congratulations, Ms Waise. Your search is over."

"Thank you. Thank you so much. May I take these documents, or…?"

"I'm afraid not. They belong to the state. But I will bring you an official request form to have these documents copied and sent to your place of residence. If you select the courier option, you will receive them within three working days."

CHAPTER 15

To: Trinity Luhabe trinityluhabe@gmail.com
From: Dean of Students – Sisulu House gcobani@sisuluhouse.
co.za
Re: The diary in the locked cabinet

Dear Ms Luhabe,

Thank you for your email of yesterday afternoon requesting the opening of the locked cabinet on the second floor of Sisulu House. We are pleased to see that you have now got to the point of asking for permission for a cabinet to be unlocked, rather than taking the key, and opening it yourself. This is progress and we celebrate it!

Unfortunately, the display cabinet forms part of Brentwood College's Heritage Collection, which means it can only be opened by certain authorised individuals. One of those individuals is the deputy headmistress Mrs Govender, who is on long leave this term.

I understand that this situation is "urgent" because you believe that "the diary may be haunted", and it is "against your religion" to stay in a building that might contain a haunted diary. However, first of all, you don't stay in Sisulu House any more – you are now living at home. And secondly, I think that if the diary were really haunted, a priest or an exorcist would be more helpful in dealing with it than a schoolgirl.

So, while we remain sympathetic to your request, we are not in a position to grant it at the moment, as the only key-holder to the cabinet is currently on sabbatical in New Delhi.

Kind regards,
Grace Gcobani
Dean of Students
Sisulu House
Brentwood College

To: Trinity Luhabe trinityluhabe@gmail.com
From: President of the Paranormal Association of South Africa
admin@paranormalSA.com
Re: Ghost of Sisulu House

Dear Ms Luhabe,

Thank you for your letter of last week asking for information about the word "whisky" as a paranormal phenomenon. While we remain greatly fascinated to hear that our modern and fully digital Paranormal Automatic Writing Machine™ has repeatedly thrown up the word "whisky" in recent weeks, we are at a loss to explain it.

We conducted some research and found that "whisky" does not have any particular significance in paranormal circles. Do you know anything about who your Otherworldly Visitor was before he crossed over to the Other Side? Perhaps whisky had a special importance in his life. We must also consider the possibility that Whisky could be a nickname for someone important to him, or even the name of a pet – a dog or a cat, maybe.

Perhaps you would be interested in purchasing our full-colour coffee-table book entitled Translating the Meaning of Messages Sent from Beyond. This indispensable guide will help you in understanding all kinds of messages that have been sent by the Dearly Departed. You might not even realise that you have been sent a Message from Beyond, until you read this book and learn how to interpret the signs.

Translating the Meaning of Messages Sent from Beyond retails for R899.00, but we are offering it for our repeat customers for a special one-day-only price of R779.99. But you must act now. Place your order right now, and we will throw in an Ectoplasm Detection Kit for FREE! That's right – the Ectoplasm Detection Kit normally sells for R49.99. This is your chance to get it ABSOLUTELY FREE. Just add a few drops of the Ectoplasm Detection Kit to water and it will quickly change colour to tell you whether there is any ectoplasm in the water. Red is negative and purple is positive. We look forward to receiving your order today so you still have time to take advantage of this incredible offer!

Kind regards
Eufemia Batton
Paranormal Association of South Africa

I am sitting in History waiting for the lesson to start when Lael comes puffing into the classroom with her bag half-on and half-off her back. She looks as though she has run all the way from Sisulu House, which she probably has – she always struggles to get going after breakfast.

"Now that Ms Lieberman has consented to join us, we can get started on the Dawes Plan," says Ms Waise. "Now, who can tell me what kind of state the Weimar Republic was in by 1925?"

Sophie Agincourt puts up her hand. Because of course she does.

Lael flops down next to me and pulls her History book out of her bag. I can see she is dying to tell me something.

"What?" I whisper.

"You'll never guess."

I sigh. "I know I won't, which is why I said 'what?' Don't be mysterious, dude."

"Guess what's happened? Just take a guess."

My glare convinces her to move things along.

"Okay, I'll give you a clue. It's something on the second floor of Sisulu House."

"Ooh! You don't mean…?"

"Yes, I do. The page has finally turned! There's a new…"

"Ms Lieberman! Ms Luhabe!"

We look up guiltily as Ms Waise switches on her scary-teacher voice.

"If your conversation is more important than our discussion about Gustav Stresemann, perhaps you would care to share it with the whole class?"

Don't you hate it when teachers do this? I really hate it when they do this.

"Oh, no, Ms Waise," says Lael. "Definitely not."

I shake my head emphatically.

"No, come on. Tell us what you were talking about. It was obviously of vital importance."

"We would really rather not," I say. "We promise to stop talking now."

"Either you tell us what you were talking about, or you write out a timeline for the demilitarisation of the Ruhr."

This is why no one talks in Ms Waise's class. Like, ever. Except Lael, who is a dumb-ass.

"Ma'am, Lael was just telling me about the historical display on the second floor of Sisulu House," I say. "She noticed that one of the items, a diary, has changed since last night. There seems to be a new page showing today. She thought I would be interested to hear that. Isn't that right, Lael?"

To say that Ms Waise is struck by this would be an understatement. She looks like someone has just hit her over the head with a sack of wet sand. She has to swallow twice before she can speak.

"Really? A new page? Is this true, Ms Lieberman?"

"Yes, Ma'am."

"Uh … that sounds really interesting. I would love to see it. Unfortunately, I'm teaching all the way up to first break. I don't suppose you took a photo of it?"

"Sorry, Ma'am. I didn't have a chance."

"Okay, well … I guess I'll see it at break, then."

With great difficulty, she pulls her attention back to Weimar Germany and the Dawes Plan. Lael looks as though she is still bursting to say something, but manages to restrain herself until History is over. Next, we have a free because our English teacher is absent. We're being supervised by one of the Bio teachers, and are supposed to use the period to catch up on homework or do some studying. A small amount of talking is usually tolerated in these lessons, so Lael and I take full advantage.

"You didn't really miss your chance to take a photo of the diary, did you?" I ask.

"Of course not. It only takes half a second. And the next time we go and look at the cabinet, the page might be gone. I couldn't take that risk."

"I knew it! But, shame, why didn't you tell Ms Waise?"

Lael pulls a sad face. "I know! I feel bad about that. But I wanted us to see it first. After all, our agenda is different to hers. She's trying to track down her parents. We are trying to find out how Jim died. I wanted us to have a chance to study the diary entry first without any other input. As soon we've had a proper look at it, I'll send it to her phone."

"Send it to me first so we can read it at the same time."

A moment later, my phone vibrates and we both settle down to read.

DEAR DIARY | DECEMBER 1968

I don't know how to write the things that have happened in the last few weeks. I don't know how to put them into words. Perhaps I should just start by going back to when I was last happy.

It was a few weeks ago, Diary. My time was getting closer and I was so excited about meeting my baby at last. I had been feeling him (or her!) kick and roll and move around for months. It was unbelievable that I would soon get to hold this little person in my arms. And yes, Diary, I will admit that in

255

the back of my mind was the thought that when Jim got to see his little bundle of joy, his heart would soften towards both of us.

I chose a name for a boy and a name for a girl. Jack, if it was a boy, in honour of my father and my brother, and Margaret for a girl in honour of Jim's mother. I was going to call her Meg or Meggie for short. Oh, Diary, why does no one warn you how hard those last few weeks are? The time seems to crawl past. You are so hot and uncomfortable, and you can't sleep, even though you know how important it is to rest now because the baby is likely to be wakeful at night for the first few weeks after birth.

I was also worrying about the fact that my parents were making no preparations for the baby. No nursery had been prepared or anything. And I couldn't ask them about it because even talking about the baby sent them into such a rage. So I took a wooden drawer out of an old chest of drawers that was standing in the garage, and I lined it with some dolls' blankets that I still had in my room, and I made a lovely little nest for the baby. My mother must have seen it in my room, but she said nothing.

Then the day came that I started having pains. My parents put me in the back seat of the car and drove me a long way to Vanderbijlpark. I tried to be quiet, but sometimes I made a noise when the pains were really bad. They took me to a nice, clean nursing home run by nuns. When we arrived, I honestly thought the baby was about to come, but it turned out to be hours before that happened. I remember thinking at the time that this couldn't possibly be right. That all women couldn't possibly have to go through this every time they gave birth. That something must be wrong.

In the end, I was just locked into my own little world of

pain and pushing. Nothing mattered except getting the baby out of me. My mouth was dry with fear that I was hurting it. At last, I felt things starting to move. I managed to push the head out. Then the sisters made me take a breath, and I pushed the whole baby out. I heard a tiny cry, and my heart just flooded with love. Someone said, "It's a girl."

I had a daughter! My own baby girl! Oh, Diary. I couldn't wait to hold her, to have her in my arms at last.

"Give her to me," I said. "Please let me hold her."

But one of the sisters turned to me and frowned. She said it wasn't encouraged for the birth mother to hold the baby or even to see her after the birth. She would be taken straight to the nursery to be cleaned up and fed. I said that I was ready to feed her. My breasts had been leaking for months now. Why would they give her a bottle when I was ready to feed her?

They told me that babies who were being adopted were never breast-fed, and that her new family was coming to collect her later that day. I explained that there must be some mistake. They had the wrong person. My baby was not being given up for adoption. I was going to raise her myself, and her name was going to be Margaret. They asked me if I was Amelia Lucite, and I said I was. They said my parents had signed all the necessary paperwork for my baby to be adopted.

I started screaming, dear Diary, I couldn't help it. I said nobody was going to take my baby away from me, and that this was being done without my consent. I said I wanted to cancel the adoption and that I was going to look after her myself, even if we had to beg on the streets. I said no one could take my baby away without my agreement, and that I wouldn't sign their stupid papers. But then came the worst. They told me that my signature was not needed. I was a minor child, and my parents had made the decision on my behalf.

I tried to get out of bed. I wanted to snatch my baby from the arms of the sister who was holding her, but they restrained me. I kicked and screamed and fought. They took my baby girl out of the room, and in that one instant, dear Diary, I saw her. She had a tiny red face with dark eyes and a lovely head of dark hair. She was the most beautiful thing I have ever seen in my life.

I screamed and cried and tried to get to her, but they just held me back as the nurse took her out of the room. Then one of the sisters came and sat on my bed and explained to me very patiently that I was being selfish in wanting to raise her myself. She explained how many advantages she would have growing up with a mother and father who were married and could afford to give her the best start in life. She could go to the best schools, and have the chance to meet a decent man to marry one day. Did I really want to deny her all that?

And I don't, dear Diary! Of course I don't. Of course I want her to have the best possible start in life, but as her mother I feel so strongly that she would have the best start with me. No one could ever love her or care about her more than I would. Am I wrong to feel that way?

And so I went home again. My breasts were aching with milk, but that has gone now. My arms were aching to hold her, and I don't think that feeling will ever go.

My parents refuse to discuss her with me. It is as though she never existed. In three months, I am to go to a secretarial college to try to get some qualifications so that I can get a job. Apparently, I will never return to school. My only hope, dear Diary, is that when I go out into the world on my own I can find a lawyer who will help me to track down my baby girl. Even if I can't have her back, I can at least find out that she is safe somewhere.

I never understood before what it meant to have a broken heart, but when my baby was taken out of the room that day, and I caught that fleeting glimpse of her, I felt my heart snap in two.

Love,
Amelia

A loud sniff makes me look up. Lael has tears running down her cheeks.

"Dude," I say. "Don't tell me you're crying."

"I'm not crying. You're crying."

I touch my face and realise she's right. I've been crying for ages and I didn't even realise it. I take a pack of tissues out my bag and we both wipe our eyes and blow our noses.

"That is the saddest thing I've ever read," Lael says after a while.

"Right? That part where she sees her baby for just a second before it gets taken out of sight."

"And the part where her arms are still aching to hold her baby!"

"I know!" I hiccup. "It's sooooo sad…"

We both start crying again and have to wipe our eyes and blow our noses all over again.

"The worst part for me," says Lael, "is picturing Nosipho in that same situation. Imagine if she had just given birth and someone took her baby away from her forever, and there was nothing she could do."

"Stop! I'm going to cry again."

"Her parents must have been monsters. How could they have watched her go through all that?"

"I don't know," I said. "They probably thought they were doing the right thing for Amelia and for the baby. In those days, I don't think they realised how this could cause lifelong trauma."

"Exactly. I mean, look at Ms Waise. She's a grown woman of fifty, and she still made a career decision to take a job at Brentwood just to find out more about her birth parents. And it sounds as though her adoptive parents were perfectly nice. She just needed to know more about her origins. It's obviously a feeling that never goes away."

"Like Nosipho too. What was the first thing she did when she found out about her biological father? She tried to contact him, even after the family warned her not to, and told her to leave it up to them."

I look up and see the Bio teacher glaring at me. She holds a finger up to her lips.

We pretend to work for a while. Then I whisper as quietly as I can. "What about Ms Waise? Are you going to send this to her now?"

"I'd better, hey? I just hope it doesn't upset her too much. If it made us cry, what is it going to do to her? That's her in the diary. She's that baby who was snatched away from her mother."

It is such a weird thought I can hardly get my head around it.

"I think she came here looking for answers, and this diary entry will give them to her. She has probably been wondering all this time why her biological parents put her up for adoption. If I were adopted, that is what I would wonder. Like, was it to give me a better life, or because they couldn't cope or couldn't look after me? And at the back of my mind I would worry that there was something wrong with me: that I wasn't good enough. Like, maybe they just didn't want me, you know?"

Lael nods. "I know. But I think that hardly ever happens. Like, that is literally never the reason."

"When Ms Waise sees the diary, she'll see how much her mother loved her and wanted to keep her."

"Exactly, yes! I'm sending it to her right now." And she does.

"You know what else I noticed?" Lael says once the diary entry has been sent off. "We're nearly at the end of the diary. It looks like there were only a couple of pages to go to the end of the book. One more entry about the same length as this one, and it will be finished."

I can't help feeling a bit panicky.

"The end?" I say. "Really? Already? But we haven't found out how Jim died yet, and that was the whole point of our investigation."

"I know. And we're running out of time. It's nearly June exams."

I give her a strange look. June exams are still two weeks away. That is heaps of time. Heaps! That is like a century of time.

"Please tell me you've started studying, Trinity."

"Of course I have." I roll my eyes. "I have totally planned to start studying any day now. I've drawn up a schedule for myself, which everyone knows is the hard part."

"Um … no. I think you'll find that the hard part is actually doing the studying."

"Pessimist."

"Slacker."

"Getting back to Jim," I say. "The only thing we have to go on is the word 'whisky', which might or might not be important. And one more diary entry. I don't think it will be enough."

"I know," says Lael.

"I'm starting to doubt whether Amelia even knew what happened to Jim. He was still at school while she was living on her parents' farm and going to secretarial college. They probably lost touch."

It is starting to look as though we may never know why Jim died, and I find that really hard to accept.

☥

"Okay, this is better." Nosipho looks around the hall. "This is much better."

Lael and I look around too, and we have to agree. For one thing, Nosipho and I are not the only black girls in the room. For another, we are not the youngest people by about twenty years. And for a third thing, the lady at the front of the hall looks like someone's mom – i.e., a person who has actually given birth – not a perky twenty-something who doesn't know one end of a baby from another. Three good things right there.

We are at the Teen Mothers' Support Association in Bramley. We phoned Dr Patel's rooms and explained that Kathy's group wasn't working for us. They were very apologetic. Apparently, they keep flyers for various baby-care classes in their rooms, and just recommend the one closest to you. They don't necessarily know anything about the class itself.

But this is one that Dr Patel recommended herself the last time Nosipho went for a check-up. They specialise in teaching baby care to teenage moms. There is a board outside the hall that says "JUDGEMENT-FREE ZONE". Some girls are here with their mothers, some with their boyfriends, and some – like Nosipho – are here with their friends. All the girls are still pregnant, so there aren't any actual babies around, which makes everything less stressful.

"Wow!" Nosipho looks at some of the girls going past. "Look at that. I'm not going to get that big, am I?"

Some of the girls are months ahead of Nos in their pregnancies. Some of them look like they're about to pop at any moment. The only thing we know for sure is that Nosipho is going to get *way* bigger than she is now. But right now, she needs to live in denial.

"Nah!" says Lael.

"Of course not!" I agree. "Look at you – your tummy is tiny."

"You're right," says Nosipho, relieved. "Although … I read a thing on the internet the other day about how most of the baby's growth occurs in the last trimester of the pregnancy."

"Fake news!" says Lael.

"Absolutely," I add.

She sighs. "Nice try, guys. I guess I'd better face it – I'm also going to look like that in a few months. Anyway, let's go and sit down."

Half an hour later, all I can think is that this is more like it. There are enough bath and changing stations so that each girl has a chance to practise bathing, changing, and dressing a baby. And the baby-dummies are incredibly realistic. In fact, they are almost creepily real. When I hold one in my hands, it feels like it's alive, with its floppy neck and soft skull. I kind of expect it to sit up and start talking to me. Like Chucky.

Best of all, is that you can choose whether to bath a black, brown or white baby, and a boy or a girl baby, if you know what you're having. Nosipho heads straight for a little black girl baby.

"You guys, I come from a family of women," she says. "There hasn't been a boy born in my family for a generation. The last one was my Uncle Linda, and even he has twin daughters. This kid is definitely going to be a girl. I can feel it in my bones."

"Okay, you're already a mom if you're talking about feeling things in your bones," laughs Lael.

There is a very nice lesson on breastfeeding after the bathing section. It is very non-judgey. They make it clear that breast is best for the baby, but not always for the mom, and not to feel guilty if you don't get it right. They promise to cover bottle-feeding and nap times at next week's class.

At the end, Lael and I are in great spirits, practicing swaddling the baby, and choosing cute outfits for her from the onesies on offer. It takes us a while to notice that Nosipho has gone a bit quiet.

"Hey, what's up?" I say when I see her watching some of the other girls.

"Ag, nothing, I guess."

I notice that Nosipho is looking at the ones who came to class with the fathers of their children. And I must say, it does look as if they're having a really special time, bonding with their pretend babies.

I put my hand lightly on her shoulder. Nosipho doesn't always like to be touched when she's upset, so we all try to be sensitive to that.

"I know it's hard," I say, feeling inadequate.

She moves away from my hand. "How do you know? How can you know how I feel?"

"Okay, I don't know, but I can imagine."

She paces in a tight circle.

"Sorry," she says. "I'm taking it out on you and it's not your fault. You guys gave up your evening to come here with me. I'm grateful, really I am."

"You don't have to be grateful," says Lael. "We also wish that Themba could have been here tonight. But there's still lots of time. Maybe he'll still come around."

Like Jim did?

The question flits through my brain. Because that's the thing. Sometimes boys don't come around. In fact, most of the time they don't. Sometimes they don't ever face up to their responsibilities. Sometimes they just don't care – or else they shut off that part of their heart that would let them care.

"Yes," Nosipho says sadly. "Perhaps he will."

Ms Waise calls us into her classroom the next day after school. This is the first time we've seen her since Lael forwarded her the most recent diary entry. I expect her to look different somehow, but of course she looks exactly the same.

"Hi, girls. Thanks for coming. I found out something new about Jim Grey. I know you two are particularly interested in what happened to him, so I thought I'd share it."

"Yes, please," we say at once.

"Okay, so when my documents arrived from Vanderbijlpark, I found out some things. For instance, they included a copy of the death certificates for both of my birth parents – Jim Grey and Amelia Lucite. I am their only living descendant, so I am entitled to all their documents. Amelia died of bacterial meningitis, just as Mrs Backeberg said, but you must see Jim's death certificate."

She opens her desk drawer to take out a copy, while Lael and I almost fizz with excitement. At last! After all this time! The goal we have been aiming towards this whole term is about to be achieved. Death certificates always include the cause of death, don't they? This will tell us how Jim died. We'll find out the truth.

Lael and I almost pounce on it when Ms Waise hands over the piece of paper.

"Date of birth … blah, blah … place of birth … Male Caucasian," says Lael. "Wait, here we are … place of death, Johannesburg. Cause of death … misadventure."

"Misadventure?" I say, looking up. "What does that mean?"

"Well, that's where it gets interesting," says Ms Waise. "Misadventure usually means an accident of some kind – something that you accidentally do to yourself."

"So if you got into a fight with someone and that person killed you, that wouldn't be misadventure?"

"No, that would be murder or culpable homicide. Why, what are you thinking of?"

"It seems as though the media suspected Amelia's brother Jack for a while, but he had an alibi. There was a theory that he had gone to confront Jim for getting his sister pregnant."

"Really? But they decided he couldn't have done it?"

"That's what we found out. What would be an example of misadventure?"

"Like hiking in the Drakensberg and falling off a cliff. Or taking part in a pie-eating competition and dying of overeating. It's when you voluntarily assume a legal risk, and then die from it."

"He was sitting in the common room of Sisulu House," says Lael. "It's hard to imagine how he could have got into trouble like that. But obviously he did, because that's where they found him."

"But that's not all," says Ms Waise. "There is also a toxicology report that was done at the time of his death. It is a very faded copy, as though it was made on a photocopy machine that was running out of ink. There are things I can't read, but have a look here. What word do you see written there?"

She turns the page towards us and we both have a close look. Ms Waise is right – this copy is so faded you can hardly see a thing. Plus, in the old days, people used to write in cursive with fountain pens, which makes no sense to me. I mean, if you wanted people to be able to read what you were writing, why would you even do that?

Lael and I practically have our noses pressed against the paper, trying to make out what Ms Waise is pointing to. Then we raise our heads at the same moment.

"Whisky!" we say.

"That's right," says Ms Waise. "I'm glad you agree. It looks like 'whisky' to me too. I wonder if they found a whisky bottle next to him? The report mentions his blood alcohol level. I just don't see how…"

But Lael and I are not listening. We're dancing around the classroom, going, "Whisky! Whisky! It really says whisky."

Ms Waise looks at us like we've lost the plot. "Um … girls?"

"Sorry, Ms Waise," I say. "Sorry. It's just that…"

"It's a bit hard to explain…" says Lael.

Ms Waise folds her arms and gives us the teacher-eye. "Try."

I take a breath. "Okay, well, it all started at the beginning of this term when we decided to set up some … equipment in Sisulu House."

"You decided!" says Lael, throwing me under the bus without hesitation.

"*We* decided!" I glare at her.

"Okay, we."

"What kind of equipment?" asks Ms Waise.

"The kind that is supposed to detect … um … unusual visitors, if you know what I mean? Like Jim, last term."

"You mean … ghost-hunting equipment? Like in *Ghostbusters*?"

"Yes, but the reboot, because we're girls."

"Goodness." Ms Waise sits down at her desk. "And what did this equipment do?"

"Well, not much, to be honest. Except for this one thing that is like a ghost-writer or something."

"Paranormal Automatic Writing Machine," says Lael. "It picks up vibrations from, like, the ether, and transcribes them into letters and words."

"It's gobbledegook most of the time, but a couple of

weeks ago, it kept throwing up the same word over and over. We've been wondering what it means ever since."

"Whisky!" Lael yelps. "The word was whisky!"

"Really?" Ms Waise stares at us. "Of course, it might be a coincidence…"

"I think it means something," I say. "I think it's important."

"Why would a sixteen-year-old boy have been drinking whisky? He was underage."

Lael and I manage to keep a straight face.

"Because that's what boys do," Lael says. "They do dumb stuff just because it's there to be done. Girls do it too. We're teenagers and sometimes our life choices are super dodgy. It's like – I don't know – we always believe we're going to have a second chance."

"I just wish I knew exactly what happened that night," says Ms Waise.

I close my eyes and try to insert myself into that time more than fifty years ago. It's night-time. It is dark in Sisulu House. All the girls have gone home for the holidays. Wait, I mean boys. It was a boys' hostel in those days. All the boys have gone home for the holidays. There are cleaners who come in once a day in the mornings, but apart from that, the place is deserted.

I'm not supposed to be there. I am out of bounds and could get into big trouble if I'm caught, but I don't care because…

Okay, I'm not sure why not.

I have a bottle of whisky with me. I'm planning to drown my sorrows. I got it from … my father's liquor cabinet? Maybe. I know I'm safe from being disturbed because this place is a ghost town at night during the school holidays. So, I sit down in one of the armchairs and I start to drink.

"Trinity?" says Lael. "Earth to Trinity. Have you fallen asleep?"

My eyes snap open. "Sorry. I was just trying to visualise what might have happened that night. Could he have drunk so much whisky that he died? Is that even possible?"

"I've been researching that," says Ms Waise. "It's surprisingly hard to do. Your body forces you to throw up before the alcohol reaches toxic levels. Or you fall asleep, which puts a stop to the drinking."

"What about people who fall asleep and choke to death?" asks Lael. "That's a thing, isn't it?"

"It is, but why wasn't it mentioned in the press? That's what I've been wondering. Why was it made into a big mystery?"

None of us can imagine what it was like living in that time when babies were legally snatched from their mothers, and teenage boys died without a whisper of a reason reaching the press. And that was in the white community. We all know that much worse things were happening to black people, and that those perpetrators were never held responsible.

A knock at the door makes us all look up.

"Hello, Nosipho."

"Hi, Ms Waise. Sorry to disturb you. I was just looking for Trinity and Lael."

"Not to worry. You're not disturbing us. How are you feeling? You look gorgeous."

Nosipho rubs a hand over her little bump. "I feel okay,

thanks, Ma'am. I have much more energy these days, and I can concentrate better."

"That's good. They say the second trimester is easier. Your Vietnam essay was very good, by the way. You'll see when I hand them back tomorrow."

Nosipho's smile is a mile wide. She is all about the marks, that girl.

"Thank goodness! I thought I might not have understood the question properly." She turns to us. "I just came to tell you guys – you know that old diary you've been obsessed with all term?"

"Yes?" we say eagerly.

"There's a new page open. You might want to go and check it out."

♀

The first thing we notice as we crowd around the display case is that this is the last entry in the diary. There are no more pages after this.

"This is it," says Lael. "Our last chance. If this doesn't tell us what we want to know, I don't know what will."

"It was written a few months after the last entry," says Ms Waise. "About eighteen months before she died, the poor girl."

"It's quite long," I say. "And the handwriting is tiny."

We each take a picture with our phones and then retire to the Sisulu House common room to read it. I sit down in the chair that Jim always used to sit in. I'd come into the common room, and there he'd be, checking out the girls in the quad through the window. Probably making inappropriate comments about them, too.

I wonder if this was the chair he died in. It certainly looks ancient enough.

Then I open the photo and I start to read.

DEAR DIARY | MARCH 1969

I hardly know what to make of what just happened. My mother tells me not to worry - that it's all nonsense - but I'm not sure. But let me tell you from the beginning.

I have been going to the Sandra Pullmann Secretarial College in Brits during the day, and doing my homework at night. It hasn't been easy, although I haven't complained to my parents. I know they have been through a lot and that they don't deserve a moaning, ungrateful daughter to add to their problems.

I did a bad thing and I deserve all the punishment I have got for it. If I hadn't been bad, my baby wouldn't have been taken away from me and I wouldn't have had to leave school. It is all my fault and I must face the consequences.

I know I am lucky to have this second chance in life and that I must work hard and not mess it up. I am lucky that my baby is being brought up by a wonderful, kind family who will be good to her - much better than I could ever have been.

It is just my ungrateful nature that makes me cry sometimes and feel so much pain. My mother says so, and of course she is right. It is time for me to pull myself together and start behaving better. I think I am managing during the day, but at night I don't have as much control. I often wake up crying. I don't always remember what I'm dreaming about, but there is usually a baby crying in the distance and I can't seem to get to her.

272

I fear I am rambling, dear Diary. Probably because I don't want to write about what happened. But I must and I will, because it is important.

Two days ago, I was taking my lunch break after my morning classes at Sandra Pullmann. We get an hour for lunch. I normally make my sandwiches the night before and take them into college in a brown bag. I go outside to eat them on a bench in a little park close to the college. Sometimes, one of the girls comes with me, and sometimes I am on my own.

Officially the college knows nothing of what happened to me, but sometimes I wonder if they suspect. Most of the girls are eighteen, you see, Diary, and I am just sixteen. They know I dropped out of high school and they probably suspect that I might have got into Trouble. Still, nobody has said anything, which is a relief.

Two days ago, I was sitting on my favourite bench in the park eating my sandwiches when someone came to sit next to me. Oh, Diary! You will never guess who it was! I thought my heart would leap out of my chest in a single bound.

It was Jim!

I remembered that school holidays were starting, and of course he lives near here. How I managed to keep calm, I will never know. I wanted to scream and cry, and hug him, and...

Well, of course I did none of those things. There were people all around us, after all - including people from the college who would certainly report me if they saw me fraternising with a boy during college hours.

I asked him how he was and he said he was well. He said I looked pretty - prettier than he remembered. Oh, Diary! Wasn't that lovely of him? Jim Grey called me pretty. He hadn't spoken so kindly to me in such a long time.

He asked me what I was doing and I told him all about my college course, and how I was going to be a qualified secretary when it was finished, so I could get a good job and save my parents the expense of looking after me.

I kept glancing at him, dear Diary, at his dear face. It seemed to me that he did not look well. He was pale and his hair was unkempt. He who had always taken such pride in his own appearance. His manner seemed subdued to me too - almost depressed.

There was a long pause between us, Diary, and I knew he was steeling himself to ask me about the baby. I was sure he would be pleased to hear that she had been placed in a good family.

"So ... um ... what did you have in the end?" he asked. "Was it a boy, or ... or a girl?"

"It was a little girl," I said.

"A girl..."

Diary, I wish I could describe the look that came over his face at that moment. It was as though he were struggling with himself, as though he longed to give way to the tenderness within, but didn't know how.

"A little girl," he repeated. "A daughter."

I couldn't help smiling, although the words were melancholy to me.

"Yes," I said. "You are the father of a daughter."

"We still won't pay anything," he said quickly. "Don't think you can go bleeding my father dry. He's wise to those tricks. But I might want to see her, you know. If that happens, you must make the necessary arrangements."

I told him then, Diary, as gently as I could, what had happened to her, what had happened to my darling little Meggie.

There was a long silence and his face was unreadable.

274

"Good," he said at last. "That's good. I'm glad."

But, Diary, he did not look glad at all. He looked shocked. Whatever he had been expecting me to say, this was not it. He sank into an attitude of deep thought.

Several times he turned towards me as if to say something, but no words came. He did not know how to express what he was feeling. I noticed that the back of his neck was dirty, Diary, and that a sour smell rose when he moved. He had not been taking care of himself.

I tried to be cheerful and talked about how the baby was with a loving family, just as my parents had reminded me, but it didn't seem to help. He became increasingly withdrawn.

My lunch hour was running out, but then he began talking so recklessly, I couldn't leave him. Diary, it shocked me to my core, but he said things that made me believe he had been thinking about self-harm. It was as though he could no longer see the point of his existence.

I would have taken all this as the ravings of an exhausted mind, but the more I looked at him, the more I could see how he had changed - how thin he had become, and how he was neglecting himself. This wasn't the same boy I had left behind at Brentwood College all those months ago.

He started talking about how he would do it, if he were to end his own life. He said he would take Valium pills from his mother, and whisky from his father, and consume them together. He said that would "do the trick".

Oh, Diary. I started sobbing at this point. I couldn't help it. And I'm glad I did because it seemed to recall him to himself. He stopped ranting about killing himself, and put an arm around me instead. He said I wasn't to pay any attention to him because he was just talking nonsense, and of course he would never do anything to hurt himself.

Then he stood up abruptly and walked away, without even saying goodbye. It took me many minutes to compose myself sufficiently to return to college. I was late for my shorthand class.

Diary, I have been filled with dread ever since. I told my mother, and she said that people who talk about killing themselves never actually do it, and that he was just looking for attention. I want to believe her, Diary, I really do, but I can't help feeling terrified.

If anything were to happen to Jim, I don't think I would survive it.

Love,
Amelia

I stay sitting in the chair in the common room.

Ms Waise and Lael have left. Ms Waise is a bit of a wreck, to be honest. She came in here knowing that her birth parents were dead, but now she knows why, and it's not easy. She is going to spend the night with a friend, and make an appointment to see her therapist tomorrow.

It makes me feel better knowing she is not alone.

Lael and I were also tearful, but we held it together out of respect for Ms Waise. This is her tragedy, not ours. Lael had to go to dinner in the dining hall. None of us realised it was already six o'clock. I try to imagine Jim – in the grip of despair and suffering from depression, possibly for months already – coming in here with whisky and Valium he had taken from his parents.

I imagine him sipping the whisky and taking the pills

all alone in the common room. He would have known he had all the time in the world. Everyone had gone home for the holidays, and no one was due in until the next morning.

Did he think about the daughter he would never see? Did he regret the choices he had made? Did he think about what Amelia had been through? Or was he not thinking clearly about any of that – caught in the sticky web of depression as he was?

There have been times when I've felt close to him here, in this common room, in this chair, but today I don't. Today, I feel the urge to go upstairs to the fourth floor, where I used to see him last term. The stairs creak under my feet as I climb the four flights of stairs.

This place is genuinely creepy at night. I first noticed that back in January when I spent a night here alone before the other learners arrived for the term.

I pass by the display case with Amelia's diary in it, and wonder for the millionth time who has been turning those pages for us. As soon as I get up to the room on the fourth floor, my nerves settle and I feel calm again. I glance around at all our ghost-hunting equipment and know that we'll be dismantling it soon. Tomorrow, probably.

I sit on one of the old-fashioned desks and swing my legs.

"I know what happened," I say, in a conversational tone. "I know what killed you, and it wasn't just whisky and Valium. Oh, I know that's the official cause, but I'm talking about what really happened."

I take a deep breath.

"They killed you, didn't they? The ones who taught

you that there is only one way to be a man. The ones who told you that it's the girl's fault when she gets pregnant, and that it's your job to pretend you had nothing to do with it. And then when it was too late, 'they' weren't there to hold you at night while you thought about what you'd lost – about what you'd never get back. These days we call it 'toxic masculinity'. It hurts boys nearly as much as it hurts girls. It hurt you so badly that you died."

I look around the room, at the dust motes floating in a beam of light.

"She's fine, you know, your daughter. She has turned into a woman you would be proud of. I think she had a happy childhood, although the questions about her birth parents never stopped haunting her. I hope she finds some closure now. Maybe she'll reconnect with members of your family. Or Amelia's family. I think she would like that."

I can't just leave it at that, but I don't know what I'm looking for here – a response? An acknowledgement? Maybe I'll recognise it when it happens.

"She doesn't blame you, or resent you, Jim. She's a historian. She knows what it was like in those days. You were kids – you and Amelia – the same age as me and my friends."

And then I remember the thing Ms Waise told us just before she went home this evening.

"Your daughter is going to change her name, Jim. She's going to court to have her middle name officially changed to Meg – the name Amelia chose for her. Your mother's name."

The beam of light grows stronger, as though someone

changed the bulb. Then it is gone, and I can't see where it came from. All the hairs on my arms stand up. A sense of peace comes over me, and I know that he has left this place forever.

EPILOGUE

Lael's Uber arrives at the same time as Lungile pulls into the parking lot. She hops out carrying a small wrapped gift.

I don't hop out so much as squeeze my way out of the car, trying not to pop balloons while I'm at it.

"Did you rob a gift shop on the way over here?" she asks.

"Ha," I say. "No. Help me with this teddy, please."

Lael staggers under the weight of the teddy bear I pass to her. "Babe, this thing is bigger than I am. It's going to give the baby nightmares."

"Nonsense, she'll love it. Or he will." We still don't know what Nosipho had. All we got was a WhatsApp from her mom saying that the baby was here and we could come and visit. I still can't believe how long it took. She went into labour, like, ten hours ago.

"Now hold these." I pass her a huge bunch of pink 'It's a Girl!' balloons.

"And these." I pass her a huge bunch of blue 'It's a Boy!' balloons.

"I see you're hedging your bets."

"Exactly. It's definitely one or the other."

"What if the baby doesn't identify as either a girl or a boy?"

"Then we'll buy it a bunch of rainbow pride balloons when it's older. We'll be the cool aunts that it can tell stuff like that to."

We giggle and do a little dance of glee. It is impossible

to describe how excited we are about this birth. Lungile promises to come back when I message him and drives off. Lael and I walk into the Morningside Fem-Clinic, bubbling over.

"Where do we go now?" I say, looking up at the board. "Dr Brown's rooms?"

"No, the maternity ward. Look, it's on the second floor."

We take the lift up to the second floor and sign in through tight security. Apparently stealing babies is a problem, so all the clinics are being careful. The nurse at the nurses' station tells us that Nosipho is in Private Room 2, so that's where we go.

The door is standing ajar. Lael knocks softly and walks in, with me one step behind her. What we see inside makes us both stop in our tracks.

Themba is standing next to Nosipho's bed. He is holding a wrapped bundle in his arms and looking down at it with a rapt expression in his eyes. Nosipho's mom and aunt are sitting on the other side of the bed looking as if they are too scared to breathe in case they interrupt.

I wondered why it was so quiet in here.

Then Nosipho spots us and the spell is lifted. The room explodes into noisy congratulations and laughing and crying. None of us can get near the baby because Themba is not giving that kid up yet.

"When did he get here?" I whisper to Nosipho.

"A few hours ago," she says. "I was still in labour and he just pitched up here with his mother. I think she shamed him into it. You know his mom and my mom are friends?"

"Sure."

"His mom definitely wants to be involved. I'm so happy about that. I want my baby to know Themba's side of the family. Themba is a bit doubtful about the whole thing, but you can see how fascinated he is. Now that he's not fighting it any more, they seem to be bonding."

"That's incredible! I'm so happy for you."

"I know. Look, we're not back together or anything. A boyfriend is the last thing I need right now. But my baby is going to have a father and grandparents, and that makes me happy."

Big, fat tears start leaking down her cheeks, making me feel panicky.

"What did you have?" I ask quickly. All I can see is a white blanket with a white beanie and a little brown cheek underneath it.

"It's a boy. We're going to call him Itumeleng because it means Joy and we both have uncles by that name. Don't say anything, because we have to announce it in the traditional way first. I can't believe I was growing a boy inside me all this time. I was so sure it was a girl. But the moment they put him in my arms, I just thought, "It's you. I know you, and you're mine.""

I hug her, and look at Themba, just waiting for my chance to have a turn with little Itumeleng.

Themba is looking down at his son with exactly that expression on his face: *It's you. I know you, and you're mine.*

Printed in the United States
By Bookmasters